Coming Home

Coming Home

by
Katharine O'Flynn

The publisher gratefully acknowledges the financial assistance of the Canada Council for the Arts and the Ontario Arts Council.

Canada Council for the Arts
Conseil des Arts du Canada

ONTARIO ARTS COUNCIL
CONSEIL DES ARTS DE L'ONTARIO
an Ontario government agency
un organisme du gouvernement de l'Ontario

Library and Arhives Canada Cataloguing in Publication

O'Flynn Katharine, 1940-, author
Coming home / by Katharine O'Flynn.

ISBN 978-1-927079-42-3 (paperback)

I. Title.

PS8629.F59C64 2016 C813'.6 C2016-904202-2

Editor: Bernadette Rule
Front cover photo courtesy Creston & District Museum & Archives, Creston BC.
Design and Typography: Julie McNeill, McNeill Design Arts

Published in 2016 by
Seraphim Editions
4456 Park Street
Niagara Falls, ON
Canada L2E 2P6

Printed and bound in Canada

To Libby and John

Acknowledgements

I would first like to offer my sincere thanks to editor Bernadette Rule, publisher Maureen Whyte and designer Julie McNeill for their very kind help and encouragement in bringing this book to completion. Their commitment to and enthusiasm for the project kept me going. Thank you.

Thanks also to the staff of Creston Museum for their help in providing access to their excellent archival collection.

I would also like to express my thanks to the late Huw Evans for information about the Evans family in Australia. And finally, of course, thanks and fond remembrance to Olwen, my mother, who even in old age never forgot Creston and loved to talk about her childhood there.

The following chapters first appeared in slightly different form in these publications:
For King and Country in *Engraved, Canadian Stories of World War One*, 2014
Love Calls me by my Name (under the title Leaving Saskatchewan) in *CommuterLit Selections Arrivals and Departures,* 2014
Leaving the Empire in *Canadian Stories*, Vol. 16, No. 92, 2013

Grace Paley once said that any story told twice becomes fiction. The stories of *Coming Home* have been told at least twice, and probably several times more. In my re-telling of these family stories, I have changed some names, occasionally altered the sequence of events, and imagined people's thoughts and conversations and the settings for these, but, as far as I know, the events and the characters of the stories are true.

Table of Contents

Chapter 1	Westward the Star of Empire Takes its Way	11
Chapter 2	Rosebank	37
Chapter 3	Ruth's Songs	61
Chapter 4	For King and Country	72
Chapter 5	Fear of Falling	84
Chapter 6	A Love of Trees	97
Chapter 7	The Return	106
Chapter 8	Orphan	115
Chapter 9	A Hero's Home	125
Chapter 10	The Black Sheep	134
Chapter 11	Coming Home	147
Chapter 12	Saving the Grand Piano	160
Chapter 13	New Shoes	175
Chapter 14	Love Calls Me by My Name	189
Chapter 15	We Have Done Very Well	201
Chapter 16	Leaving the Empire	220
Chapter 17	The Hero on the Wall	231
	Afterword	247

Chapter 1

Westward the Star of Empire Takes its Way

My Gran, Mildred Young, had one blue eye and one brown. This was not a matter of subtle shading; one eye was distinctly pale Viking blue and the other a deep, dark Celtic brown. This anomaly gave her a strange, somewhat disturbing appearance like a Picasso portrait. She herself was not at all embarrassed by the peculiarity. Indeed, she considered it a distinction. "To have eyes of different colours is a sign of great beauty," she claimed.

Even as her hair turned grey and her blue eye and her brown dimmed, she continued to think of herself as an exceptionally attractive woman and felt it was only right that she should adorn herself in a manner appropriate to such beauty. She could not limit herself to only one piece of jewellery at a time. Rows of colourful brooches flashed across her ample bosom like military medals, and ropes of artificial pearls and glass beads clattered among them. She favoured garments of silk and velvet in rich colours: peacock blue, crimson, or purple. And she would never dream of leaving the house without topping off the ensemble with a magnificent hat, laden with artificial flowers or fruit, ribbons, veiling and feathers. As she was not tall – barely five feet – and stoutly built around a narrow waist in a pouter pigeon sort of shape, it required confidence to carry off the look. Gran believed in her beauty.

"How nice you look, Gran!" always brought a regal smile in acknowledgement of the obvious.

"But how I wish you could have seen me when I was young," she might say then with a sigh, "when my complexion was unblemished, and my hair was golden and hung to my waist. Then it was that my beauty caught admiring attention on all sides."

She liked to tell the story of how as a young girl, she had once hurried through the streets of London, late, late at night. "My sister Lucy was ill with fever; my father was away; my mother could not leave Lucy's side. I was the only one who could go to fetch the doctor, so I went. I ran through the dark and dangerous streets of London, a beautiful and defenseless girl with long blond hair rippling loose. I was only sixteen years of age, and all alone in the midnight city. The wonder was I wasn't captured for the white slave trade or kidnapped, or worse. How I ran with my golden hair streaming behind me! I fetched the doctor." She loved that image of her beauty shining through a dark and dangerous landscape, and so did all who heard her story.

But my story of Mildred begins later in her life, in 1907, when she was forty-seven and proprietor of a boarding house for professional gentlemen in the Hammersmith district of London. In her years of youth and beauty she had never imagined that her life would bring her to earning her own living, but so it had turned out.

She had been born into a family of writers, not the great writers of the Victorian era, but competent essayists and writers of popular sketches. She had had no formal education but she had acquired the arts and graces considered appropriate for young ladies of the time. She could paint pretty scenes in watercolours, though in truth she preferred to sketch dresses and hats. She excelled in needlework both plain and fancy. She learned to carry herself with dignity, to sit with a ramrod straight back, to converse politely in society. Because her family was not so very well off, she also learned to keep a sharp eye on the servants and the tradespeople's bills, and when necessary, she could pitch in and help with household chores. Proud of her family's connection with the literary world, she was well read, attended the theatre and opera regularly, and spoke like a lady in a Jane Austen novel.

At seventeen, she married James Young, a clerk in the Office of Public Works, charged with monitoring the expenses of the royal household. He also held the post of external examiner in mathematics for Cambridge University. Mildred and James had five children. Whether or not theirs was a happy marriage is not known. One suspects it was not, for James had a reputation as a martinet with a fierce temper. Examination candidates, though grown men, were said to quake before him and his children were terrified of him.

At the early age of forty, James died of a heart attack, a victim perhaps of his own choleric temperament. He collapsed in a railway carriage on the way to an examination and was dead on arrival in Cambridge. (One likes to imagine the astonished relief of the examination candidate on hearing the sad news!)

Mildred was left in the classic sad story situation of the penniless widow with growing children to care for cast suddenly adrift in the harsh world. Fortunately, she was not the kind of woman to sink down spinelessly into genteel poverty. Instead, she turned the family home into a boarding house for single gentlemen: clerks in government offices, most of them. She learned to make substantial and tasty meals with cheap cuts of meat, lots of potatoes, and large, sweet, filling puddings. She became a careful shopper, finding the best prices among the local greengrocers and fishmongers. She supervised her two servant girls strictly and she stood for no nonsense from her gentlemen boarders. She managed well.

Mildred's children grew to adulthood. Her two sons found employment, her eldest daughter a suitable husband. Now there were only the two youngest daughters, Sarah and Charlotte, at home. Mildred had more rooms to let. The boarding house business was going well.

At that time a new boarder moved in, Tom Evans, a young Welshman working as a clerk in the post office. Mildred liked him at once for he was an aspiring poet, a literary scholar, and a professed admirer of the works of her no longer illustrious grandfather and father. Tom was handsome in a romantic, gypsy-like way, with wild, thick black hair and a swarthy complexion, and he had the Welsh gift for poetry and song and lively talk. Evenings, when he wasn't out singing or poeticizing with his Welsh friends or drinking with the Bohemians at the Café Royale, he would get up entertainments in Mildred's parlour: play readings, musical programmes, hymn sings, recitations. These cultural evenings brought Mildred to relive the happy days of her childhood when literary lions gathered for talk and readings in her grandfather's parlour.

All the residents of the house enjoyed the performances and were eager to participate. Mildred recited Tennyson, Tom read from the work of the new poets Stephens, Middleton or Davies, and the girls gave comic performances of Belloc's newly published *Cautionary Tales for Children*. Some evenings there were play readings: Mildred was Lady Macbeth, the girls were giggling witches and Tom was Macbeth. Mildred was Lady Bracknell and Sarah was Gwendolyn Fairfax. Some evenings Tom pounded out hymns on the cottage piano and everyone sang; or Sarah played while Tom and Charlotte sang a duet; Sarah and Tom sat side by side at the piano and played a duet and Charlotte danced. Once in a while the company might persuade Tom to read from his own work. His poems were in Welsh so none but the Welsh cousin who shared his room could understand a word, but Mildred said it sounded very nice anyway and Sarah and Charlotte agreed. "That is because Welsh is the language of Heaven itself," the cousin told them with a serious satisfaction.

One evening, after Tom had been living in the boarding house for a few months, he sat beside Mildred on the settee. They had just finished a reading of selections from *A Midsummer Night's Dream*. "May I have a word with you, in private?" Tom asked.

"Certainly." Mildred's heart began to beat quickly. He would ask then. She had thought he might, though she was, to be sure, more than ten years older than he, but still, you might say, in the prime of her beauty. She touched her hair, its rippling gold fading perhaps just a little. She willed the others to drink up their tea quickly and go. The boarders went off, one by one. There were only Sarah and Charlotte and Mildred and Tom left.

"Run along to bed now, girls; it's late. Tom and I have a business matter to discuss," Mildred said. Since the arts entertainments had begun, all the occupants of the house were on first name terms, a familiarity Mildred had never before allowed her boarders.

Charlotte wanted to linger to pester Tom with questions about a reading list he was preparing for her, but Sarah, the dear girl, dragged her off.

"Now?" Mildred turned towards Tom.

"Sarah," Tom said without any introduction. "I love her. Have I your permission to court her?"

The tea cup in Mildred's hand trembled in its saucer. She set it down on the small table beside her. "Sarah?" she said. And again, "Sarah." Through her mind rushed a stream of images: Sarah sitting close to Tom on the piano bench, their hands crossing and recrossing each other playfully along the keyboard; Sarah playing an adoring Juliet to Tom's Romeo; Sarah brushing against Tom as she reached to take his tea cup or pass him another slice of cake. Mildred should have paid closer attention, read the message in these signs. "Sarah is very young," she managed to say.

The stream of images went on: Sarah trying to pronounce the words of some Welsh poem and Tom's hands moulding her cheeks to the desirable shape for the double 'll' sound; Sarah beside Tom when they all went walking on Hampstead Heath one fine afternoon – Sarah, who was no longer a child, but a nineteen-year-old beauty with ash blond hair and pale blue eyes. "She is too young."

Tom was twenty-five, Mildred knew. That made him, when reckoned more carefully than she'd been inclined to do, twenty years younger than she was, not ten. In his view she would be an old lady, a game old girl reciting poems from the last century, a mother of grown children, and far too old for him. She saw it now with perfect, painful clarity. What could she have been thinking of? Well, she hadn't thought; that was the problem. She had only felt and let her foolish feelings run riot over her common sense. Now it was quite clear: Sarah was the obvious magnet for Tom's affection. Charlotte was too young. She, Mildred, was too old. Tom had chosen wisely and well.

"Sarah is nineteen," Tom was saying, as if Mildred didn't know. "Old enough, surely. So beautiful." He blushed, and added, "In character, as well as in her person. I love her dearly and thanks to the promotion I have had, I am now in a position to support a wife."

Mildred took a deep breath. "And Sarah? Have you made your feelings known to her? Do you have reason to think that she reciprocates your affection?"

"I believe I can safely say she would be willing to be courted," Tom said with a knowing smile. "With your permission, Mildred."

"Then I grant you my permission," Mildred said with a self–control that cost her dearly.

She should have seen how it was. She should never have allowed herself those fanciful dreams of running her hands through Tom's thick black hair, of drowning in his deep dark eyes. She could only be thankful that those dreams had remained unspoken and, she was fairly certain, unsuspected by Tom or anyone else.

She might have wept a little in the privacy of her own bedroom that night, but by next morning she showed no signs of any disappointment she might have suffered. She had never spoken of the feelings she had cherished, she never would, nor would she allow herself even to think of them ever again. She would rejoice in her Sarah's happiness, and Tom's.

Fearing that Charlotte might also find Tom's choice disappointing, Mildred woke her youngest with a cup of tea and the bad news. As she had suspected it might, the revelation threw Charlotte into a torrent of bewilderment, anger, jealousy, disappointment. "I thought he loved me too," she wept. "He does love me too."

"He does, indeed, but not in the way he loves Sarah," Mildred said. "Some day, when you are older, you too will experience the feelings those two have for each other. It is quite different from the affection you feel for him and he for you." It was hard on the poor girl. "Try to be happy for your sister," she urged. "It is her time now. Your turn will come when you find your own love."

"I have found my love," Charlotte wailed. "And he has chosen Sarah!"

"I think not, not yet, my dear," Mildred said, but Charlotte would not be comforted. Though the sisters had always been close, Charlotte now avoided Sarah as much as she could. She would no longer join in the musical evenings or the readings. She pretended to suffer from headaches and spent a lot of time in her room.

Mildred behaved correctly. She sewed wedding clothes and hemmed sheets and pillowcases and smiled at the happy couple whispering together on the sofa, stealing kisses when they thought she wasn't looking. She was happy for Sarah, although sometimes a look from Tom, or the way he laid a hand on her arm as he made a point in his impassioned talk of poetry, made her want to be as sulky and cross as Charlotte. She did not yield to the impulse. Self-discipline was one of the great Victorian virtues she was imbued with.

Mildred encouraged the young lovers to marry as soon as they liked. Both she and Charlotte would be much better off without Tom's presence in the house tempting their thoughts to stray where they should not go. Sarah and Tom married early in 1907.

And then Mildred announced her plan to emigrate to Canada.

She discussed with no one the reasons for the sudden departure. In truth, it wasn't just the marriage of Sarah and Tom that had brought her to the decision. Years ago her parents, her brother Percy, and younger sister Mae had gone to Canada. She had envied them the adventure. But she was a wife and mother by then, and travel to distant lands was out of the question for her. In her family's letters she had read accounts of vast forests where deer and bear and wolves still roamed, of lakes as wide as seas, towering mountains, vast plains, busy new towns and cities, and a railroad that crossed the whole huge country. She had longed to go to Canada and see this new world for herself. And now she was free. Now she could go. In the streets of London she saw posters and red wagons advertising the new Dominion with pictures of bright maple leaves and fields of wheat. The slogan on the posters, "Westward the Star of Empire takes its way", appealed to her. She made her way to the Canadian Emigration Offices on Charing Cross Road and booked passage for herself and Charlotte to Canada.

"Why?" her astonished family asked. With her business running smoothly and only one child left in her care, Mildred could sit back and enjoy her later years in comfort and security, they thought. Why ever would she want to strike out for a new country now?

She wanted to go because now with her children, all but one, married, independent and established in their own households, she could follow an old dream of her own and at the same time escape the pangs of a more recent dream that had failed. She didn't care to discuss all this with her children. "I think it best," she said.

"Why Canada?" Sarah asked.

"It is a land of cold winters and deep forests. I fear you will miss the cultural amenities of our London," Tom said.

That is not what she would miss. "I have always wanted to go to Canada. We have family connections there." Though her parents had returned to England, her brother and sister had remained in Canada and still sent reports of life on the frontier there, and another brother, blind from birth, was completing his education at a special school in Brantford. She would visit them and see the country for herself.

"But the rest of your family, your children, and a grandchild now as well, are here in England," her son Took pointed out.

"Charlotte will travel with me."

"I don't want to go to Canada," Charlotte protested at once. Charlotte was the delicate flower of the family, beautiful as Mildred herself had been, with the same golden hair, though both her eyes were blue, a dreamy grey-blue the colour of an early summer dusk. Charlotte had been singled out by a rich aunt to receive a convent education in Belgium. She could speak French, and sing prettily and dance and paint charming watercolours and Tom had recently awakened her interest in the theatre arts, in which she showed considerable talent. She did not wish to waste these talents on lumberjacks and cowboys and red Indians in some remote colony.

Mildred did not care to argue with her children. "I am sure you will like Canada very much. And so shall I. We leave in a fortnight."

Charlotte continued to protest. She had hardly spent any time in London at all. She did not want to be separated again from her dear brothers and sisters. She did not want to leave her friends here. Tom was getting up a play and she was to have the starring role in it.

Charlotte was too young to know what was good for her. "There is a great deal to be done and time is short," Mildred told her. She had bought the tickets and given notice to her boarders and recommended other boarding houses and residential hotels to them. She had written letters to the Canadians of the family, advising them of her impending visits. Now she had to divide up her furniture among her married children. She had to run up smart travelling costumes with matching hats and a couple of light summer dresses as well for wear in the Canadian summer, which was said to be very warm. Charlotte could help with the sewing. She took some slight interest in this, which Mildred took to be a good sign.

All was settled: the leasehold sold, the lodgers gone, the furniture disposed of, the tickets in hand.

Tom accompanied the ladies to Euston Station to see them on to the boat train. He embraced first Charlotte, who wept and clung to his coat shamelessly, and then Mildred, who herself had to fight back tears as she received a first and last chaste kiss from the lips of her handsome, beguiling, and all too dangerous son-in-law.

Mildred would not allow herself to pine for what was past. On board ship she dressed in her most elegant new costumes. She enjoyed the delicious and ample dinners served in the dining saloon. She joined whist parties and gambled small sums of money and occasionally won. Charlotte, despite continued lamentations at her hard fate as an exile from all she held dear, did sometimes appear to find a few moments of pleasure in the evening dances and entertainments and occasionally she condescended to promenade the desk with some suitable young man.

But on the train journey that followed the sea crossing, Charlotte's complaints grew more bitter, with, Mildred had to admit, some justification. Hour after hour for a day and a night and another day the ladies sat in a swaying drafty coach, passing by woods and fields and very few towns, waiting to arrive at their first destination, Brantford Ontario and its School for the Blind. There were no entertainments to pass the time on the train as there had been on the boat. Charlotte was bored and cross, and even Mildred found the journey wearying.

At last they reached Brantford and the school, and found Bob waiting for them in a reception room. Tall and thin with a mop of bright red hair, he looked more like a growing boy than a man in his thirties. "Caaaaan it reaaally be you, Miiiiildred?" he greeted his sister and reached to touch her face to make sure. His voice was a screeching, high-pitched drone.

"It is I, and here is Charlotte with me."

"Chaaaarloooootte!" Bob searched the young woman's face with his fingers. "Beauuuuutiful, like her moooother."

Poor Bob, Mildred thought. How would he ever know such a thing? But it was gallant of him to say so. "You look well yourself, not a day older than when you left England," she told him.

"Aaaaand you as weellll," Bob assured her.

Mildred was pleased to see how Bob had profited from his stay at Brantford. He was able to show his visitors around the school and grounds. He walked confidently through rooms and corridors, avoiding furniture and obstacles, opened and closed doors, pointed out trees he was especially fond of on the lawn, and introduced the ladies to teachers and pupils they met on their tour.

In a private interview with Mildred, the director praised Bob's skills: he had learned braille quickly and had become an avid reader. He had achieved a high level of independence in getting about and in looking after himself. Unfortunately he was not so apt a pupil in learning the trades taught at the school: chair caning, hammock weaving and piano tuning. He was clumsy with his hands and had no ear for tonal distinctions. There had been some hope that he might become a teacher of braille, but his manner of speech would be a torment to pupils in the classroom, the director feared. Unfortunately, there was no other work available for Bob. He must resign himself to living on his family's charity.

It would be hard for Bob to know himself excluded from useful employment despite all that he had learned, Mildred knew, but it could not be helped. Apparently he could not learn to speak with normal pace and intonation. Mildred's other brother in Canada, the Reverend Percival Young, had offered to take Bob into his home in Edmonton. Perhaps there he would find some useful tasks he could perform and some pleasures he could enjoy. Mildred and Charlotte would accompany Bob on the journey to Edmonton, and would look about with a view to settling in that city.

"Diiiiistances in Caaanaada are considerable," Bob informed the ladies when they boarded the westbound train. They were appalled to learn that they would be on this train for two days and two nights. Bob didn't seem to mind. He ate his way contentedly through large meals in the dining car, or sat looking out the window at endless dark forests and snow-covered plains he could not see, while Mildred and Charlotte found the scenery dull and the coach drafty and dirty and wondered again and again if the next station mightn't be Edmonton.

Eventually they arrived, in the middle of a snow storm. "Snow! In April! Mildred exclaimed. "Dear me!" She took an instant dislike to Edmonton. The northern frontier had sounded exciting in letters and stories, but in actual experience Mildred found it cold and bleak and uncomfortable. She soon knew she could never live here. She was sorry to leave Bob in such a place, but there was nothing else for it. He seemed to have settled in easily. In two weeks, Mildred and Charlotte were ready to move on. "Westward the Star of Empire takes its way."

This time the journey was one of only a few hours, and more south than west to Pincher Creek in southern Alberta where Mildred's sister Mae lived. Mae had, since her emigration to Canada, married a Swedish settler by the name of Helmer. It was a delight for Mildred to see her dear sister again, but she hardly knew what to make of her taciturn brother-in-law. She couldn't help but think he was angry at the presence of two extra females in his household, although Mae assured her that Helmer was always rather silent, and a little shy because his English was not quite fluent. Mildred and Charlotte could stay as long as they wished. Mae was very glad of their company, and so was Helmer, even if he didn't say so.

But they did not wish to stay long. Pincher Creek was even worse than Edmonton in Mildred's estimation. Here the snow had yielded to a sticky, cold mud. The houses were small and mean and far apart and hardly anyone in town spoke English. People were mostly all as silent as Mae's husband. Even Mae herself seemed to have lost the knack of lively conversation. The talkative and gay young woman Mildred remembered from earlier years had become a stout matron, slow of speech and seldom brought to laughter. Perhaps living in this hard new country made people harder, sterner, shaped them like the landscape itself. Mildred confided this theory to Charlotte as the two women prepared for bed in the cold, cramped bedroom they shared.

"No surprise there," Charlotte agreed at once. "You'd be feeling quite grim too if you had to face a lifetime in this country. When are we going home?"

"We are not going home," Mildred answered. "We have emigrated."

Charlotte brushed her hair with short, angry strokes. "We should never have come," she said. "Never. We were quite happy enough at home in England."

They were not quite happy in England, Mildred knew. In any case, she would neither argue nor put up with defeatism. "We shall stay here with Mae for at least a week or two," she said. "Mae is my sister and we have much to talk about.

She suggested a distraction that might amuse Charlotte. "Why don't you try some sketching of the scenery?"

"Paint scenes of brown mud? I don't think!" Charlotte flung herself into the bed and pulled the blankets over her head. She hadn't wanted to come to Canada; she didn't like the country, and she was not going to hide her displeasure at having been made to come. But Charlotte was young, she would adapt and come to love this strange new country, Mildred told herself as she unpinned her long, thick hair that had once been her crowning glory. Now it flashed with silver amid the gold in the pale glow of the oil lamp on the dresser. Yes, Charlotte would soon feel at home in Canada, but would Mildred herself? Change and adaptation do not come as easily to the old. For the first time, doubts about the wisdom of the venture crept into Mildred's mind. Thus far she had been almost as disappointed in Canada as Charlotte was, though she would never admit that aloud. This country was too large, too raw, too close to the emptiness of the sky. One could be lonely here, as she guessed Mae was lonely among the silent Swedes and the vast fields and the endless railway. Her parents had not loved the country enough to remain long. Percy had stayed, but he had his vocation to spread the gospel that kept him here, and Mae had her silent, but kind, husband. What was there here for a middle-aged widow and a pretty, talented, eighteen-year-old girl who had hopes and dreams of love and a beautiful and happy life?

Mildred did not allow herself to think such discouraging thoughts for long. Perhaps, she told herself, their next place of call would have more appeal. They were to move on to Creston in southeastern British Columbia. There they were to stay with Mae's daughter from her first marriage, Olive. Olive had married an English army officer after the Boer War and emigrated with him to this small town in the Kootenay

Mountains, close to the American border, and she seemed to be very happy there.

If they found nothing to hold them in Creston, Mildred didn't quite know what she'd do. Move on to Victoria at the very outside edge of Canada? Return to England and set up another boarding house? In truth, she feared she hardly had enough money left for either of those schemes. She was disappointed and a little frightened as well. But she was not going to admit it. "I am sure we will both like Creston very much." Mildred climbed into the cold bed and blew out the oil lamp.

For the next week Mildred and Mae talked and talked about a past that didn't much interest Charlotte, who stared out the window and sighed. When Helmer wasn't at work, he sat silent in a corner smoking his pipe, and slowly reading a newspaper, pointing to each word. He was doing this to improve his English, Mae explained. On Saturday evening everyone got dressed up and neighbours arrived by foot and in wagons to meet the visitors from England. It was a subdued gathering. Hardly anyone knew enough English for a conversation and those who did hardly knew what to say. They ate cake and drank coffee. One red-faced young man engaged Charlotte in a brief conversation about the weather and then blurted out a marriage proposal. "No thank you," Charlotte answered politely and turned away. So did the young man. He hadn't really expected an acceptance. Charlotte didn't even know his name. She almost felt sorry for him. He probably didn't like being stuck in this forlorn place either.

Sunday morning they attended a church service in a hall above the general store in town. At least they heard English spoken there.

And then at last it was time to move on to Creston.

Helmer helped the ladies into the coach and stowed their bags on the luggage rack. As Mildred hardly felt on kissing terms with this brother-in-law, she shook his hand in farewell, but Charlotte offered her cheek for a kiss, either out of her naturally affectionate nature, or out of joy at the departure. Then Helmer hurried out to stand beside his wife on the platform. Mildred waved vigorously. "Do wave to

Mae," she urged Charlotte. "She'll miss you, you know. She says you remind her of her Olive."

Mildred watched the two silent figures growing smaller on the bare platform. Only when they and the station had disappeared did she turn away. It was too sad to think that her sister lived in such a place with such a man, however kind he was inside his silence.

Charlotte removed her hat and gloves and settled back in her seat. "Another train journey," she sighed.

"This one won't be so very long," Mildred answered.

"That's what you said when we left Saint John. That's what you said when we left Brantford. This country goes on and on. Forests and fields. Forest and fields. It never ends. We shall fetch up in China eventually, I expect."

"Nonsense. I've spoken to the conductor. We arrive tomorrow morning, he says." In the distance they could see a range of mountains on the skyline.

"Creston is situated in those mountains," Mildred said. "I think we shall like it very well there."

"Hmmm," was all that Charlotte replied to that. But when the train puffed its way in among the mountains, she sat up and looked at the scenery with some interest. As they were carried deeper into the mountains, her admiration for the scenery increased. She and Mildred marvelled at the snow-covered peaks, the steepness of the wooded valleys, and the wild torrents of cascading streams as the train wound its hair-raising way over high trestle bridges, puffed up grades and ground down them, clung to ledges that dropped away into chasms far below. It was magnificent. "I do wish I had my sketchbook to hand."

It was the first positive thing she'd said about Canada so far, and Mildred was pleased to hear it. "We'll unpack your painting things the minute we arrive," she said. "I expect we shall enjoy this visit very much. Olive writes that Creston is a delightful place. I believe you will find Olive a most congenial companion as well. She is a cheerful soul and close to your own age. Mae says you are very much alike in manner."

"I suppose Aunt Mae said Pincher Creek was delightful too," Charlotte said, reverting to her poor opinion of Canada again. Yet only a moment later she was admiring the intense blue of the sky against the bright green of new-leafing trees.

In due time the conductor called out, "Creston! Creston is the next station stop." Mildred and Charlotte adjusted their hats and straightened their wrinkled and soot-smudged travelling costumes. The conductor pulled their ticket stubs from the clip above the window and swung down their cases from the luggage rack. "This way out, ladies!"

On the station platform a tall man with a great deal of blond whiskers about his face strode towards the travellers and swept them up in hearty hug. "You must be Aunt Mildred. And Cousin Charlotte. How do you do? Welcome. Welcome." This was Olive's husband whose name was Robert George Lester William Sinclair Smith. People in Creston, Mildred soon learned, called him Alphabetical. He let go of Mildred and waved to the conductor. "Hello Rodney. How's tricks?" Without waiting for an answer, he turned back to the ladies. "How was the journey? Terrible? But you've stood up to it well, I see. Olive is looking forward mightily to your visit. It's because of her condition she isn't here at the station, don't you know? That'll be your box?" He gestured towards a leather trunk being unloaded from the baggage car. "Hi there, Ed," he called to a young man in a smart checked suit and a brown bowler. "Give a hand here."

Ed and Alphabetical heaved the trunk into a high-wheeled wagon that stood beside the station, then Alphabetical linked his hands to form a step. "Up you go, ladies." When they were settled, he pulled himself up and shook the reins over the team of well-matched blacks. "Walk on, lads!"

They drove along a muddy thoroughfare, lined with wooden storefronts, picking their way through tree stumps, throngs of people afoot and on horseback, and the occasional pig or cow. At least there wasn't any snow on the ground.

"We'll have those stumps out by next winter," Alphabetical said. "And sidewalks put in. You wait and see. This is a go-ahead kind of place." He certainly was not afflicted with the silence of this country, Mildred had noticed straight away. He pointed out the sights, asked questions about the journey and didn't wait for answers. Mildred and Charlotte had only to sit and gaze around them.

Creston was built on the lowest slope of Goat Mountain, set between ranges of mountains that rose to the east and to the west, purple-blue masses in the hazy blue-white sky. Below, the Kootenay River wound its way through a widening valley where grass rippled like a green sea.

"Beautiful!" Mildred said. "The mountains. The valley. So very beautiful."

"Yes, yes, the scenery is grand," Alphabetical agreed. "And just wait 'til we get this town going. Creston is going to be the centre of a vast fruit-growing region. We've got the soil for it. We've got the railway. We're working on the roads. We're seeing about getting telephone lines. We'll upgrade the hotels." He frowned as a couple of drunken men lurched out of the open door of a shabby wooden shack bearing a sign saying "Hotel and Bar" over its door. "We've got new businesses coming in. New settlers. New fruit ranches. We're a go-ahead place here, growing every season. It's a grand place, Creston."

"Indeed," Mildred murmured politely.

Olive, hugely pregnant, was waiting at the open front door of a white-washed frame house to welcome her visitors. "Here you are. Come in. Come in. How lovely to see you! I'll wet the tea while you wash up. Let me show you your room."

She bounded up a steep narrow staircase while Mildred tried to protest, "We'll find our own way. You must rest. In your condition…"

"Nonsense. I don't know why women make such a fuss of confinements. I've never felt better. Bring up that trunk, Bob," Olive shouted down to her husband.

Mildred was hoping for a bit of a rest, but Olive said, as she left them, "Hurry along now. I want to hear all about home before the party starts. I've told people to come at two."

"There is no need for a reception. You must not tire yourself," Mildred called after her. "In your condition…"

"Oh, baby will wait a day or two more, I expect," Olive shouted back. "Why miss a chance for a party?" Olive, it seemed, was as much of a go-getter as her husband.

Mildred had barely time to brush off her skirt and dab cold water on her face and hands before Olive was calling up, "Tea's ready! Do come. I'm dying to hear all your news."

The ladies enjoyed a cup of tea and thick roast beef sandwiches and Mildred was just starting in on an account of their journey when there was a rap on the door and without waiting for an answer to the knock, the first of the visitors walked in. "Mind you enjoy yourselves, you two!" Olive advised Mildred and Charlotte in a stage whisper as they hurried from the kitchen to the front room to greet the visitor. "You'll have your choice of beaux. Men outnumber women about ten to one here. The bachelors are all dying to look you both over."

Charlotte giggled and wondered if she would receive another sudden proposal such as she had had at Pincher Creek. Mildred tutted at the silliness of the very idea.

Olive introduced the first arrival, an eager young man by the name of Andy Talbot. He immediately took up a position beside Charlotte and started a conversation, but before long a half dozen more men were crowding in on him. Older men bowed politely to Mildred and asked her how she did, and how she was liking Creston so far. There were a few couples as well. Mildred shook hands with Mr. and Mrs. Mallandaine and remembered she'd seen him at the station. She met the Rogers and the Frenches and then she began to forget names. The new postmaster, and the pastors of the Anglican and the Methodist Churches were there, and the shy schoolteacher who had not long ago arrived from Spokane Washington, and a courtly gentleman from Tennessee who was "considering prospects," and the bank manager who was so excited when he had a chance to talk with the beautiful Charlotte that he spilled his tea and retired in confusion. Mildred answered questions about the state of "the old country" and nodded at invitations. "Come out and see our orchard." "Let me drive you down to the flats." "Do you play cards? You must come round for a game one evening soon." "We must get up a picnic to the falls." She guessed Charlotte was receiving as many invitations, probably more, and no doubt more sincerely intended. Some of the young men were close to elbowing each other aside in their eagerness to secure positions close to the young lady, or to urge tea or lemonade and cake upon her.

"Well, Mrs. Young, what do you think of our little town so far?" The question was delivered by an older man. Fred Little was his name, Mildred remembered. He sat in the most comfortable of the overstuffed chairs and Mildred had noticed that he was treated with great deference by all. Now the hubbub of general conversation quietened and everyone listened as Mildred answered politely that she found the town was most scenically situated and seemed to be a centre of great activity. She could not bring herself to say "a get up and go sort of place".

Little seemed satisfied with her answer as a launch for his story of the town's founding, a story he'd most certainly told before, and enjoyed telling again. "I staked the first claim in this township," he began, "back in 1892 that was. I looked at this valley, saw the good soil and knew at once what a great place this could be. The railroad was a-building then, and I knew it was through this valley it would have to come. I could see a town here – houses, schools, stores, churches and people. I could see wheat growing on the flatlands and orchards on the benchlands. I could see market gardens, dairy farms. All we needed was that railroad to bring in supplies and settlers, and to ship out the fruit and grain we'd grow and the lumber we'd cut and the ore we'd dig out of these mountains.

"Well, in '98 the CPR survey team came through, just as I knew it must do, and I welcomed those boys with open arms, by golly, I did. Ed here can tell you all about that."

He waved to Ed Mallandaine who took up the story seamlessly. "Yes I brought the survey team in. Fred told me his idea and I could see he was right. I liked the potential. I liked it so much that when I'd done the survey, I bought land and stayed on."

"And here we are in the best town in the best province in the best country in the world," the patriarch Little cut in. "Isn't that so?" As a Londoner Mildred took a sceptical view of that assessment, but she nodded and said, "Indeed!" as if she agreed.

At five the guests began taking their leave. "So nice to have met you. Do come and see us soon," they said in farewell. They shook hands and the young men held Charlotte's as long as they dared.

On the following morning, having satisfied herself that Olive was unlikely to give birth within the next few hours, Mildred set off with Charlotte to explore the "best town in the best province in the best country".

Though the streets were muddy, and the buildings of unpainted wood seemed to be set here and there at haphazard among stump grounds and piles of lumber, still Creston was beautiful. It was May. Through the settlement and the surrounding benchlands apple trees were coming into full bloom. Masses of palest pink petals glowed like bridal bouquets. Their sweet scent mingled with the raw, tangy smell of fresh cut pine and fir, the gunpowder smell of stumping powder, and the smoke of burning slash on land being cleared. Farther off the mountains ranged like battlemented walls to east and west, guarding the valley and the lush green plain below. The air seemed filled with the tension of new agricultural development mixing with the old west of forest, Indians, trappers and prospectors. On Canyon Street a bearded old-timer loaded up his packhorse with a grubstake getting ready to head up out into the wilderness. Lumberjacks and miners caroused their pay away in one of the many noisy bars. A Siwash brave, with buckskin leggins and a store-bought shirt, his long black braids hanging down his back, engaged in horse trading on the corner by a hotel while his wife offered hand-made rush baskets for sale. Two ladies in long silk dresses, carrying dainty parasols, studied the window display at the general store. Mildred didn't recognize them from the party of the evening before. Were they ladies, she had to wonder, or those dance hall girls she'd heard about? A Chinese laundry man, his eyes downcast, scurried by with a heavy bundle of sheets from one of the hotels. Andy Talbot, the first visitor at the previous evening's gathering, dashed out of the livery stable and, uninvited, took up the post of guide and escort. The gentleman from Tennessee emerged from Hatfield's barber shop and pool hall, smoking a cigar, his soft leather riding boots polished to a perfect shine. He bowed and wished the ladies a pleasant morning and attached himself to the tour. At the blacksmith's a Mr. Compton joined them and then a Mr. Murdoch. Had the town been a large one they would soon have formed a parade, Mildred reflected. From this public spectacle Mrs. Rogers saved them by calling from her neatly fenced front garden to "come in, all of you and have a cup of coffee." Mr. Murdoch, Mr. Compton and the gentleman from Tennessee whose name no one seemed to know, regretfully cried off, having business to attend to. But Andy Talbot stayed with the ladies and before they finished their coffee Mildred and Charlotte had agreed to a drive out to Alice Siding to see the Talbot orchard on Friday afternoon and, at Mrs. Rogers' urging, to attend a whist party at the Mercantile Hall that same evening. "And a fortnight hence, there'll be the blossom ball," Andy said. "Everyone comes to that."

"I shall look forward to it," Charlotte answered with her prettiest smile.

After their coffee, nothing would do but that Mr. Talbot accompany the ladies back to the Sinclair Smith residence, choosing a most indirect way, Mildred noted, that involved walking down the hill and back up again when surely they could have simply followed Canyon

Street straight along. Charlotte seemed not to notice the detour. Along their way, they met other acquaintances from the evening before, who enquired after their health and urged them to drop in for a visit any time.

"Well, what do you think of Creston now?" Mr. Talbot wound up the tour at the Sinclair Smith door.

"I think it the prettiest town, in the prettiest province in all of Canada," Mildred answered with a slight smile. "And the inhabitants are very friendly." Mr. Talbot seemed pleased with her answer and bade the ladies farewell.

In the front room Olive was resting in the big armchair. Mildred saw the signs and at once took charge. She first helped Olive up to bed, then sent Charlotte to run back to Speers store for arrowroot and Bovril, tied on an apron, built up the kitchen fire and set to work making custards, beef tea, and arrowroot broth, as well as a more substantial dinner for Alphabetical himself when he should return from his business concerns in town.

Early the next morning Doc Henderson was sent for, and by that evening Olive was delivered of a fine healthy boy. The doctor said it was about the quickest and easiest first confinement he'd ever attended.

"My wife knows how to go about these things," the proud new father boasted. "She's a go-getter."

Nevertheless, Mildred insisted Olive take at the very least ten days' bed rest, and Olive was content to lie back against the pillows and admire her son, while Mildred ran the household.

Charlotte was excited about the new baby, but not so excited that she forgot the drive Mr. Andy Talbot had promised her and Mildred, and she reminded Mildred of the engagement on Friday morning while she cleared up the breakfast things. "We'll have to postpone it. I can't possibly leave Olive alone," was Mildred's response.

"It's only for an hour or two. Olive will be all right. She's fine. She says she is. And baby sleeps all the time anyway."

But Mildred was a conscientious nurse, and she was in charge. "Next week, perhaps," she told Charlotte, who was already dressed for the outing in primrose yellow muslin with pale blue trim, hidden now under one of Olive's large aprons.

Charlotte said they couldn't let Mr. Talbot down at such short notice. "He'll be on his way here by now. Or," she suggested with an innocent air, "perhaps he and I could go without you."

"Unchaperoned! Never!"

Charlotte sulked and must have told Olive about her disappointment because, when Mildred brought up her lunch tray, Olive said young ladies in Creston were not so closely chaperoned as in London. "There's no need for it, really. Everybody here knows what everybody else is up to. If Andy should so much as lay a finger on Charlotte – which he would never do; he's a good fellow – he'd be run out of town in ten minutes and never dare show his face again. Charlotte will be perfectly safe with him."

"That may very well be, but there is indiscreet talk as well as indiscreet action. Your vigilant citizens can hardly monitor conversation, I believe." Mildred took baby Sonny from Olive's arms and rocked him gently.

Olive reached for the lunch tray. "Andy's a gentleman. You can trust to that. But if it will make you feel better, I daresay Mrs. Hunt would enjoy a run out to Alice Siding. Tell Charlotte to run over and ask her.

"Now, don't you think I could go ahead with a bit of cherry pie or something a little more substantial than custard for dessert?"

"You need the milk in it," Mildred said, but she allowed Charlotte to go off in Mr. Talbot's buggy with Mrs. Hunt as chaperone.

Over the next two weeks Mildred ran the Sinclair Smith household with the efficiency she'd learned in her Hammersmith boarding house. She saw to the laundry and cooked substantial meals. She soon realized that it was best to provide extra at each meal as Alphabetical was likely to bring home a new settler or a prospective businessman. Often the two kingpins of the town, Fred Little and Mr. Mallandaine would drop by to discuss some new business plan and stay for dinner or tea.

The cleaning up Mildred left to Charlotte who did it in a slap-dash sort of way, but no one complained. Cleaning had never been Mildred's forte; she found she couldn't take the same interest in it as she took in cooking or sewing. It didn't matter. Olive was so besotted with the baby and its care that she didn't notice the odd dust bunny or stained tea cup, and Alphabetical, like most men, paid no attention to the state of the household as long as meals were served regularly and his wife and child and guests were happy.

Charlotte practised dance steps as she swept or mopped, sang as she washed dishes and always found time to go out walking or for a carriage drive or a sketching party with the young people of town, properly chaperoned if the party consisted of only one young man and herself. As Mildred had predicted, Charlotte and Olive became good friends. Charlotte doted over the new baby almost as much as Olive herself. Olive teased endlessly about the conquests Charlotte was making among the young bachelors in town, and Charlotte blushed and protested and giggled and got Olive to tell her all the gossip about each of them. Not once since they'd arrived in Creston had Charlotte asked when they would be going home to England. Mildred noted all this and was pleased.

By the time of the blossom ball, Olive was ready to step out into Creston society again. She consulted with Mildred about a dress to wear. She held a blue silk gown in front of herself at the bedroom mirror. "Do you think you could let this out enough so that I could fit into it?"

"Surely you're not thinking of going to that dance!" Mildred said, but she took the gown Olive was holding and began to examine the seams.

"Everybody goes to the blossom ball. I couldn't miss it."

Mildred thought it inadvisable, but she could see that Olive was as bent on going as Charlotte was. "I suppose I could get you three good inches at the waist." She sat by the window and set to work picking out stitches. "My velvet opera cloak would go very well with this. You must wear it."

"You'll wear it yourself surely," Olive said.

"I shall not. I shall be right here watching over little Sonny," Mildred said.

"Nonsense. Everybody goes to the Blossom Ball. We'll take Sonny in the picnic basket."

"An infant barely two weeks old ...You can't..." Mildred began, then stopped herself. People did things differently here. As a visitor, it was not her place to give orders. Sonny would be comfortable enough in the picnic basket, she supposed. And if she went too, she could keep a sharp eye on him. "Very well," she said.

Mildred anticipated a decorous and dull evening during which she would sit on the sidelines, sipping fruit punch and watching Sonny in his basket. Nevertheless she took care to dress suitably for the occasion in her best yellow satin with the black lace overskirt. She wore her amethyst necklace on a modest décolletage and pinned three of her favourite brooches to the bodice. She borrowed a black lace shawl from Olive in exchange for the fur-trimmed opera cloak which she insisted the young woman wear because of her still delicate condition.

She and Olive had barely found a safe, warm place in the hall for Sonny and his basket when, to her surprise, Fred Little approached, bowed and asked her for the honour of a dance. She discovered that although she might be an old woman in some men's eyes, she was not at all too old to enjoy the glide and whirl of a waltz. Alphabetical claimed her for the next dance, and then Mr. Speers. Even that brash young man Andy Talbot asked her to dance. He held her firmly and led with such mastery that she felt herself able to swirl ever more quickly and gracefully. For a moment she remembered her son-in-law Tom and wondered what it would have been like to dance with him. But he was Welsh and the music he loved was too sad for dancing.

When the dance was over, Andy saw her back to her place and swept Charlotte away into a lively polka.

Sonny slept peacefully in his picnic basket..

Olive was dancing too many dances and too vigorously in Mildred's opinion, but then she herself was being asked to dance far more often than any middle-aged woman had a right to expect, and she was enjoying it too.

Charlotte of course danced every dance. Mildred watched her laughing with her new friends, flirting with the bachelors, graciously allowing herself to be trotted around the floor by some of the old-timers, helping to serve the sandwiches and cakes, speaking to people whose names and likes and dislikes she seemed to be familiar with already. In only a few short weeks she had found her place in this small town society, and appeared to be happy in it. She was on the way to forgetting her English past, and looking forward to the future, like a true go-ahead Crestonite. It was a quick transformation. Only the other day, there had come a letter from Tom, and Charlotte had glanced through it quickly before dashing off to help decorate the hall for tonight's dance. Mildred read the letter more slowly and more carefully, but she too was happier now. She'd had some few moments of doubt since leaving England, but now she knew she had done the right thing. She and Charlotte would do very well in Creston, she was sure.

Chapter 2

Blossoms fell and spring turned to summer. The weather was hot and fine. Olive's home was a hub of activity. Visitors came and went, some to discuss business with Alphabetical, some to admire the baby and gossip with Olive, some to chat with the ladies from England. Mildred served tea and scones at all hours of the day. Evenings there were often card parties or musical soirees in different homes or entertainments in the hall above the Mercantile.

The strawberry crop ripened. Mildred made strawberry shortcake and strawberry trifle and strawberry jam. Then the raspberries came in, and the apricots. Mildred had never tasted such sweet, fine fruit as grew in Creston. When she told that to Fred Little, he quoted her all through the town.

Telephone lines were run along Canyon Street. An office was set up in the Sinclair Smith front room and Olive was the operator. There were six subscribers. "Central here," Olive would answer in a business-like voice when the ring sounded. "I will connect you, sir." Then she would return to the kitchen to tell Mildred and Alphabetical, "That was Fred Little calling Ed Mallandaine. They'll be talking about this new Board of Trade they want to set up."

The Board of Trade was set up, and Mallandaine was its first president.

A Knights of Pythias lodge was organized and Mallandaine was its first Grand Master.

The new Goat Mountain Waterworks was established to pipe fresh water from the river into town. Mallandaine was the president of that project.

Mallandaine was a man who'd always had a knack for being in on any important doings. If you look at the famous photograph of the driving of the last spike at Craigellachie on the Canadian Pacific Railway, you will see a very young man in a round felt hat standing right behind Donald Smith, watching the proceedings. That's Ed Mallandaine, in on the action even then.

Fred Little had founded Creston. Ed Mallandaine was getting it running. He was making it into a go-ahead kind of place. Alphabetical, who thought of himself as ex-army officer more than business man, confined himself to helping in an advisory capacity for every go-ahead project.

When the harvest for the early apples and plums started, Charlotte appeared at the breakfast table one morning in her plainest cotton dress. She was going to work as a picker at the Mason's ranch that day, she said.

"A daughter of mine, working as a farm labourer! I think not!" Mildred set her cup down decisively and tea washed over into the saucer.

"Oh, everyone works at the harvest," Olive said, as if Charlotte's doing so was nothing unusual. "I'd go picking myself if I weren't needed here for the telephone."

"For wages?" Mildred was appalled. "Like a factory girl?"

"Of course for wages. You couldn't expect a person to work all day in the hot sun for your profit and not her own, now could you?" Olive asked the question of Sonny who sat on her lap and gazed at Mildred incredulously.

"Women as well as men?" Mildred couldn't quite take it in. She poured the slopped tea back into the cup.

"You worked at the boarding house to make money," Charlotte reminded her.

"Not for daily wages," Mildred said.

"But for money all the same. Have some more tea, Ma. That will be cold." Charlotte gestured with the teapot and Mildred passed her cup.

To Mildred it seemed obvious that arranging rooms and preparing meals for a dining room full of guests and being handed a discreet envelope at the beginning of each month was a far more respectable way of obtaining money than laboring in a field, keeping a tally of bags or baskets and lining up for a pay packet at the end of a day or a week, however pickers might be paid. She remembered rowdy bands of hop pickers filling the trains out of London to Kent: gypsies and vagabonds and poor folk getting up to who knew what in the hop fields. She turned to Alphabetical who, as an ex-army man, was more conscious of social distinctions than was his wife. "What kind of people are these fruit pickers?"

"Townspeople. The same people you meet on Canyon Street, in the Mercantile, at the whist parties, at church." Alphabetical was no more concerned than Olive about the idea of Charlotte's working as a field labourer. "Everyone works at the harvest. You need have no fears."

"You need have no fears." Mildred remembered that slogan from the posters advertising emigration that she had read back in London. "You need have no fears." Canada was a safe country. Things were done differently here, that was all. Here women could work for wages in the fields alongside men. Mildred drank her tea and Charlotte went off to work in the new and flourishing orchards wearing a gingham dress, a plain white pinafore, a broad-brimmed straw hat and no gloves because, Olive said and Alphabetical confirmed, "You can't pick with gloves on."

The girl would ruin her beautiful soft hands.

Mildred herself donned hat and gloves and sometimes carried a parasol as well whenever she ventured out in the summer sun. This she did most days, now that Olive was up and about. Mildred's favourite walk took her down the Fourth Street hill to the place where she could see the flat valley of the Kootenay widening towards the south, protected by the mountain ranges to east and west. She liked the sense of shelter the mountains gave. They stood in magnificent wilderness, but it was wilderness bounded, keeping the benchlands and the valley safe. Here in Creston one "need have no fears".

Mildred liked the way this scene was always stirring, always changing according to the weather and the time of day. On still days the mountains were no more than hazy, pale mauve shapes in the distance. On brisker days they seemed to draw nearer, sharp-etched against an intense blue sky. On the valley floor the grass rippled green or blue or purple, sometimes even black, according to sunlight and cloud.

After enjoying the view for a while, Mildred would turn around at the pretty little cottage with the For Sale sign on the porch and make her way up to Canyon Street. There she was likely to encounter townspeople who would greet her and stop to chat. She knew their names now, and the names of their babies and children and even their pet dogs and cats. Her advice was sought on matters as diverse as fashions in London, remedies for teething and stomach aches, transcontinental travel and millinery fashions.

Mildred liked the Creston people. She admired their generous pioneering spirit. They pitched in wherever they saw help was needed, welcoming newcomers with advice and know-how and the loan of tools or implements to tide them over 'til they got themselves established. The women didn't consider it beneath them to undertake menial jobs like scrubbing floors, washing clothes, digging gardens or picking fruit for some needed cash money. The men were able to turn their hands to any kind of work: they could run a business, administer an organization, read the lesson in church. They knew how to go about clearing land, planting and tending orchards, building roads and houses, breaking a horse, hunting bear, draining swamps, connecting telephones. These were people who got things done.

They liked a good time too. They were never too busy to organize a party, games, a picnic, a drive. They would travel miles through any kind of weather to attend a dance and stay at it with gusto 'til the small hours of the morning. The best dancer of them all was Andy Talbot, and as the summer turned to autumn, Mildred could see he was dancing his way into Charlotte's heart.

It was time to find out more about this young man. Mildred chose a morning when she and Olive were at work in the kitchen peeling and slicing apples for drying. "I can't help but notice that Charlotte seems quite smitten with Andy Talbot," she began. "Who is he? What kind of family does he come from?"

"His family are in Ireland," Olive said. "Andy's a good worker, an honest friend, a churchgoer, and great fun. He's as good a man as any in Creston."

Andy was a pleasant young man but he had not, thus far, struck Mildred as a likely choice for Charlotte, who expected and was expected by all the family to "marry well". "What does he do for a living?" she asked.

"He's taken up land near Alice Siding, wants to go in for fruit ranching. He's already planted apples and plums, and he's putting up a tidy little house on the property, doing the work himself. He clerks at the Mercantile sometimes."

"What is he then? A carpenter? Or an agriculturist? A shop clerk?"

"He's a rancher," Olive answered. "Like most newcomers here. This town's prosperity will be built and sustained by fruit growing. We have the soil and the climate and the railroad. Some see a future for the dairy industry as well. But fruit ranching is a sure thing." She sounded as though she was quoting her husband.

"I see," Mildred said. Andy Talbot was one of those jacks-of-all-trades who were building this pioneering community. Such men were admirable. But however capable he was, Andy was hardly gentleman enough for Charlotte, who was surely destined to wed a man of distinction: a great musician or writer, a Member of Parliament, a barrister, a bishop or even a baronet. And now here she was, apparently infatuated with a penniless backwoodsman who grew apples and clerked in a shop. This was, Mildred had to admit, her fault. It was she who had brought Charlotte to a place where there were no barristers, bishops or baronets to woo and win her.

They should not have stayed here so long. They should have moved on west to Victoria. Victoria, Mildred had heard, was a cultivated little city with a pleasant location on the sea. Living in Victoria, some said, was almost exactly like living in England. There were Members of Parliament in Victoria, and very rich lumber barons and ship owners. And surely also writers, musicians, and men of culture and refinement. Instead they had lingered in Creston, beguiled by its beauty and by the welcome of its people. Mildred had thought too much of their present comfort and pleasure, and not enough about Charlotte's future. But perhaps it was not yet too late to rectify the matter.

She mentioned the idea at dinner one day and shocked the entire Sinclair Smith household. "You're surely not thinking of leaving Creston!" Olive wailed and her astonished cry woke Sonny and set him to howling. Alphabetical's fork was paralysed half way to his plate. "Victoria? Nonsense! You don't know anyone there. You wouldn't like it at all. Creston is the place for you. You're comfortable here, aren't you? You'd say if you weren't. You stay here. Creston is where you want to be."

"It's where I want to be," Charlotte said with such certainty that Mildred felt unable to argue the point further.

Besides, Alphabetical was right. Mildred knew no one in Victoria. She had no idea how she'd go about finding a place to stay there nor what they'd live on if she did find accommodation. Her financial resources were dwindling. It seemed that she and Charlotte were settled in Creston for better or worse. For herself, Mildred was glad of it. She didn't really want to go to Victoria, however charming it might be. She liked Creston. She only wished Charlotte had set her cap for that bank manager, or the schoolteacher, one of the pastors or the nameless gentleman from Tennessee instead of for that dancing Irishman with the winning smile. She liked Andy well enough; he was personable and pleasant, and a popular man in town. But there was no telling what kind of a family he came from. With an accent like his, it could hardly be a good one. She wished he would at least call himself by his real name. She loathed that vulgar diminutive 'y' some people chose to attach to half a name.

Over the next days Mildred watched Andy Talbot more closely. He worked hard on his own property and just as hard and just as cheerfully when he was clerking or carpentering for others for wages. He it was who organized a benefit concert for a new family whose cabin had been destroyed by a brush fire. He'd also got up a committee to see to setting up rules to prevent and contain forest fires which too often threatened the homes and orchards of the town. He was friendly with the native Siwash and spoke on their behalf when there was a dispute about their rights to graze their horses on the flats. He was usually the last to leave a party, one of the few gentlemen who volunteered to help the ladies clean up, although Mildred suspected that was a ruse to give him more time to flirt with Charlotte, who herself had become quite community-minded in offering her help at church and social events. Mildred reflected further. Society was organized differently in this country. Andy was a carpenter and a fruit rancher now, but things moved quickly here. Who knew but what some day he might become a Member of Parliament or mayor of the town or a great landowner? What was certain was that he made Charlotte happy, and Mildred could not help but rejoice in that. The two were the very image of joy when they moved together on the dance floor.

And when one late August evening Charlotte and Andy walked hand in hand up to the porch where Mildred and the Sinclair Smiths were enjoying a soft cooling breeze and said that they would like to marry, when she saw Charlotte looking more beautiful than ever, bronzed from her work in the sunny orchards and radiant with happiness, when she saw the happy hope in Andy's eyes, when she saw Olive and Alphabetical already beaming with delight, what could she say but, "God bless you both. I hope you will be very happy." This was a marriage Mildred never would have imagined for Charlotte, yet she grew more certain as the days went by that it would be a happy one.

The young people wanted to marry soon. Mildred set to work. There was the wedding gown to sew and a bit of a trousseau as well. Charlotte should have a wedding gown fit for a princess. Mildred made the gown, and then she made a pale blue travelling costume for the honeymoon trip to Spokane, and a hat to match. She made two afternoon dresses with matching hats. She made three extra hats because she loved making hats best. She sewed nightgowns and petticoats and hemmed sheets and towels.

In the evenings when the light started to fail she and Olive baked. They made cheese straws and pie dough and shortbread and lemon curd. As the wedding day drew close, they made pies and dainty cakes and cooked a ham. Since the new church was not yet completed, the wedding and the reception were to be held in the Sinclair Smith drawing room. Olive and Mildred filled the windows with banks of flowers and Olive warned all telephone subscribers not to dare to make a call that afternoon.

Charlotte was a dream of a bride in ivory satin with an overdress of white lace. The mother of the bride was resplendent in lilac silk with beaded jet fringe, the outfit topped off with a huge sort of turban in lilac tulle adorned with purple ostrich plumes.

The guests admired the finery. "Did you order your hat from New York?" Mrs. Mallandaine asked.

"No," Mildred said with quiet pride, "I sewed it up myself."

"Too clever of you!" Mrs. Rogers said. "So chic!"

"Thank you." Mildred bowed in acknowledgement of the compliments, and the purple plumes of her hat nodded.

Charlotte had found her life's place in Creston. It was time for Mildred to settle her own life. She had had a letter from Sarah and Tom in England. They were expecting their first child in the New Year. "Will you come home in time to be with me for the confinement?" Sarah wrote. She had never really believed in her mother's departure as emigration.

"No," Mildred wrote back. "I have grown to like Creston very much. I shall make my home here." She felt a little cruel to write that, but even if she had wanted to go back, which she didn't, she couldn't go. She couldn't afford the journey.

Nor could she stay on indefinitely with Olive and Alphabetical even though they were kind enough to say that she was a member of the family now. She mustn't think of leaving, they told her just as they'd said when she mentioned Victoria. They'd never manage without her. But Mildred knew her help was not needed now as it had been in the month or two after Sonny's birth. Olive could manage her household very well without her, and the young family would appreciate having their home to themselves. Mildred needed to find a place of her own.

Money was the problem. Mildred had thought she possessed great riches when she left England, but the expenses of the journey and then the wedding had whittled the fortune down to exactly forty-three dollars and twenty-seven cents. She needed money. The only way she could think of to earn it was by running a boarding house as she had done in Hammersmith. "Do you know of any houses to let?" she asked her advisors, Olive and Alphabetical.

"This isn't London. People here generally don't take a lease on a house; they just buy it," Olive answered.

Mildred could never afford to buy a house. "Or rooms, then?" Perhaps she could work out something with sub-tenants.

"The only rooms to let would be at the hotels, and you certainly don't want to stay there!" Alphabetical said.

Mildred thought of that pretty little cottage on Fourth Street that she passed on her daily walk through town, the one with the For Sale sign in front of it. She did admire that house. She'd noticed lately that the lot around it was becoming more and more overgrown. It needed work done on it soon. Perhaps the owners would be willing to rent it, at least for the time being.

She mentioned the idea. Alphabetical thought. "That little place on Fourth? About half way up the hill? I'll ask about it for you tomorrow."

But in fact he asked about it that very evening over a game of whist with the Mallandaines in the front room.

"Ah yes, that little cottage. Nice enough and on a good lot. If you like it, why not buy it?" Mr. Mallandaine arranged his cards with a satisfied look.

It was all very well for him to talk. He was the richest man in town. Mildred coughed delicately. "My financial situation at this time, I fear, precludes the purchase of property."

"Have you got five dollars cash?" Mallandaine asked in his forthright Canadian manner.

"Certainly I have that much," Mildred said with a sniff, and took the trick.

"Offer five dollars as a down payment. Pay the rest off as you are able." Mr. Mallandaine re-arranged his cards.

Mildred was confused. Surely five dollars was too little. "Do you think…? The amount seems so small?" she stammered.

"No harm in offering." Mallandaine shrugged. "It's the Langs own it and they probably want rid of it. See what they say." He snapped down a winning card, and another. It was irritating the way he almost always won.

"I'll run you over there first thing in the morning if you like," Alphabetical offered and swept up the cards for the next deal.

And so it was that almost before she knew what was happening, Mildred bought a house in Creston for five dollars down and a mortgage of two hundred and ten dollars.

"I shall call my house Rosebank," she announced when the deal was done and she was enjoying a celebratory cup of tea with Olive after the signing.

"Rosebank. I don't remember seeing any roses on that property," Olive said.

"No, but there will be," Mildred promised.

Rosebank was small. Mildred paced the rooms and thought about how she would place furniture, if she had furniture. But no matter how she arranged things, there was really only one rentable room, perhaps two if she herself slept in the enclosed porch. Rosebank was too small for a boarding house. Moreover she soon learned that single gentlemen in Creston preferred to stay in a hotel room with a bar on the premises and single ladies stayed with their families, not in boarding houses. Mildred's boarding house idea was a failure before she even moved in.

Still she could not regret her purchase. Her mind churned with plans for the house and even more so with ideas for the garden. She would plant fruit trees on the south facing slope and set out a kitchen garden on the west side of the house and leave a few shade trees in the east corner to form a spinney. There'd be two wide herbaceous borders leading to the front door and climbing roses growing along the fence and over an arbour at the gate and, most important, there'd be a formal rose garden with tea roses of every shade of pink and red. Rosebank would be a beautiful place.

To realize this dream, she needed an income. Since she couldn't run a profitable boarding house, she would have to find a job. If Charlotte could work for wages, so could she. Unfortunately it was too late for fruit picking or packing now, for the harvest season was over, but Alphabetical might know of something, or Mallandaine or Fred Little. She'd ask.

Fred Little knew of something. A cook was wanted out at the Elsie Holme mine. He told Mildred about the position at afternoon tea in Olive's kitchen. "About thirty men to feed, I believe. Pay's good." He buttered a scone and added a dollop of cream and then strawberry jam.

"Oh but Aunt Mildred, you'd be the only woman on the place. You really couldn't…" Olive for once showed some hesitation about the proprieties.

Mildred had no qualms. "I cooked for gentlemen lodgers in Hammersmith."

"Those miners out at the Elsie Holme are a far cry from civil service gentlemen in Hammersmith," Olive said.

"I needn't associate with them, only cook for them," Mildred argued. At the mention of the good pay, she had warmed to the idea of working at the mine. Cooking would be an easy job. There was nothing to it. Men were easily pleased with any kind of food as long as there were plenty of potatoes.

"Shame to waste your fine cuisine on a bunch of rough fellows like that," Alphabetical said and helped himself to another fresh-baked scone.

"The pay is good," Little repeated. "And they like to keep their workers well-fed and in good health. They're not a cheese-paring outfit. I've enjoyed a dinner or two out there myself. Good wholesome food is what they require, and a cook who won't stand for any nonsense in the eating hall. I expect you could handle the job."

"I believe I could," Mildred said. "I think cooking at the mine would suit me very well, if they would have me,"

"I'll speak to the boss up there," Little promised.

"That would be very kind," Mildred said.

The next day Fred called in on his way home from dinner at the hotel. "Well, Mrs. Young, are you still thinking of taking up that cooking job at the Elsie Home?" He accepted the cup of tea she handed him.

Mildred loved the way people here spoke of employment as something the applicant chose to take on, almost as if only to oblige the employer. It was quite different back home. She remembered from the time when her sons were looking for employment as government clerks how nervous they'd been when they were granted an interview, how honoured they felt when they were at last successful.

"Yes, I thought it appropriate to try for the situation," Mildred answered, trying to sound as though she'd be doing the mine owners a favour by consenting to consider the job.

"Well, that's settled then. I've spoken to Hugh about it." Fred set down his cup, slapped his knees, and stood up.

"But will Mr. Philips not want to interview me?"

"No. He'll take my word on you. When did you say you can start? Next week?"

Why not? "Yes," Mildred said.

Rosebank was hers, but for a time her home would be somewhere on a rail line out in the wilderness. Mildred handed over the keys of Rosebank to Alphabetical who promised to keep an eye on the place in her absence.

Fred Little was to drive Mildred to the station. He arrived in his buggy with a large brown and white spotted dog sitting in the luggage trunk. "This is Tinker," he said.

"Hello Tinker." Mildred patted the dog and his tail thumped loud against the wooden floor.

"Good. He likes you. I thought he would," Fred said. "I got him off a prospector fellow I know raises good dogs.

"He's yours now. Keep him by you all the time up at the mine there. Keep him in the kitchen with you in the day and keep him in your room at night. He'll see you come to no harm."

Mildred lived in a lean-to at the back of the cookhouse, a log building with a huge black range and two long oilcloth-covered tables. She cooked bacon and eggs, steak, beans and flapjacks for breakfast; pot roast and Yorkshire pudding or stews for dinner with berry pies or suet pudding for dessert. Suppers were thick soup with ham and cabbage, or scalloped potatoes with cheese and sausages, or fried potatoes with salt pork. Sometimes there was fresh trout one of the men had caught, or roast venison or bear stew. In the spring there were berries from the ranches of the valley and fresh lettuces and celery and radishes. With all the meals there were gallons of tea stewing in giant blue granite pots on the back of the stove. The miners thought Mildred was a fine cook.

They were polite to her, as she was to them, and they kept their distance. The faithful Tinker stayed at her side, day and night. She never had any trouble at the mine.

And at the end of a year she had saved enough money to buy a few sticks of furniture and move into Rosebank. Now Mildred was ready to create the house and garden she'd dreamed of. But once again she had no money. She would have to find another job and this time she wanted work that would enable her to live in her own home while she earned a livelihood. She made enquiries.

Fred Little helped her out once more. He asked if he might eat his dinners with her instead of at the hotel. Such an arrangement would be convenient for him, as he lived directly across the road from Rosebank. He'd pay the same rate as he was paying at the hotel and as an added bonus he would give Mildred one of the prized Jersey cows he'd had shipped in from Ontario so that she could have fresh cream daily. To that proposal Mildred agreed at once. It was not exactly a boarding house business but something on the way towards it. Perhaps in time she would find other gentlemen requiring dinners but not rooms.

But Olive came up with a better idea. "Why don't you set up a hat making shop, Auntie? You make wonderful hats, and Creston could do with a good milliner."

That was true. The Mercantile carried only a few dowdy, old-fashioned hats that no woman would buy unless she was desperate. And women were desperate for hats, for no lady ever went anywhere, even to the post office, without a hat. And more and more women were coming to Creston; there'd been new families claiming lands all through the summer and many more scheduled to arrive in the spring.

Yes, a millinery establishment might do very well indeed, Mildred reflected. And she loved making hats! She began planning with enthusiasm. She could run the business from Rosebank. The enclosed side porch would be perfect for a showroom. She hired Andy in his role as carpenter to build shelves for the merchandise. She sent away to Montreal for buckram shapes, felts, velvets, straw, ribbons, feathers, flowers. As her clientele would be all female, she might as well carry waists and corsets too. And perhaps things for babies and small children. A fancy goods shop. But the millinery would be the main attraction.

When all was ready, she placed an ad in *The Creston Review*. "Full Line of Millinery," it said. "Showing all the Very Latest Fashions in Ladies' Hats, Trimmings, Flowers, Ribbons."

Customers came. Soon all the ladies in town wanted to have one of Mildred's original hats. Large hats were in vogue in those pre-war years and no one was ashamed of extravagance. More was more, and Mildred loved it, giving free rein to her delight in ribbons and bows, feathers and flowers, and swathing veils. Her hats were much more elegant than any you could get at the Mercantile. Of course, you paid a little more, but you got an original; you wouldn't meet yourself going into church or taking tea after the musical program in the concert hall. And Mildred had a knack for knowing exactly what little extra touches would make the hat perfect for a new dress or costume. Also, it was much more agreeable to look at corsets and undergarments in the discreet and all female ambiance of Mildred's shop than to have to pick out such things with a male clerk hovering near. The business thrived.

One morning not long after the opening of Mrs. Young's Millinery, Charlotte sat at Mildred's kitchen table. She picked up her tea cup and put it down. She rearranged it in its saucer. She retied the bow at the neck of her maternity smock, then made sure her hair was correctly fastened back. Mildred continued to sew artificial pansies on to a wide ribbon. "Who is the hat for?" Charlotte asked. She'd asked the same question a few minutes before.

"Mrs. French," Mildred answered again. Then, because this kind of nervousness was most unusual in Charlotte, she had to ask, "Whatever is wrong, dear girl? Is everything going as it should?" She nodded towards Charlotte's growing girth.

"Yes, yes. Everything's fine. I'm fine."

"And Andy?"

"Andy's fine. He's working at the store this morning."

"Yes. You mentioned that before." Mildred continued sewing and waited.

At last Charlotte managed to say, "It's about you, Ma. People are talking about you and Fred Little. They say he's over here every day."

"He is. He's arranged to take his noon dinner here as a paying guest. I've told you that. The arrangement works well for both of us."

"Just the two of you?"

"Just the two of us, most days," Mildred confirmed. She smiled, remembering how, not so long ago, she had been concerned about chaperoning Charlotte. Now Charlotte seemed to want to chaperone her. "I think we are old enough to behave ourselves."

"Fred was seen last week carrying a bouquet of roses to your door, hot-house roses he must have ordered from Nelson."

Creston people didn't miss much that went on in their little town. "Yes, he was kind enough to give me flowers."

"Well, for heaven's sake, what does it all mean? What's going on? Tell me!"

Mildred set down the flowery ribbon. Charlotte might as well know. If people were talking it would be better to set out the truth sooner rather than later. "Fred asked me to marry him. I refused. Of course." Mildred spoke with the weary self-assurance of a beautiful, single woman who is quite used to receiving marriage proposals that she has no choice but to refuse.

Charlotte was silent for a few moments. Then, "Why do you say 'of course'? You like Mr. Little, don't you? He has a nice house. He's rich. You could have a good life with him."

"I have a good life now." Mildred liked owning her own home, she liked the hats she made, and she liked earning her own livelihood. She liked Fred, but she preferred independence. She had put romance behind her when she came to this country. "I have no wish to marry again," she said. "You might mention that if you hear any more gossip on the subject. And please, say nothing about the roses. I wouldn't like Fred to feel embarrassed."

Charlotte couldn't argue against the certainty in her mother's tone. Whether she squelched the rumour, or whether it simply died away for lack of further evidence, the idea of a romantic liaison between Mildred and Fred Little was soon forgotten in the town.

Mildred's hat shop continued to prosper. Each spring and fall Creston ladies were invited to come to Rosebank to take tea and look over millinery styles for the coming season. These teas were grand events. Ladies arrived dressed as if for a reception at Buckingham Palace. Mildred herself was attired in her best silk ornamented with an impressive array of brooches and necklaces. Sitting ramrod straight at a lace-covered table she poured tea from her silver tea service, a relic from her past when as Mrs. James Young she had served tea in her Hammersmith home, never dreaming that one day she would be a working woman pouring tea for potential customers in her own shop.

She directed a banal conversation about the weather 'til she judged the time was ripe. Then she led the ladies into the side porch where the new hats were displayed on tables and shelves. Some relaxation of decorum was now allowed. Ladies might express their delight in excited little cries, and try on the hats.

Any woman crass enough to mention the word "price" was frozen with disapproving silence. Shows were social events, not sales. The purchase of a hat was a matter to be settled privately.

The business thrived and so too did the garden. Mildred cleared out brush and undergrowth. She planted an apple tree and a cherry tree and an apricot, as well as raspberry canes and currants. She got Andy to renovate an old shed on the property to house the Jersey cow and a flock of chickens, then to build an arbour over the gate for the climbing roses. She dug up ground for herbaceous borders. She studied seed catalogues and drew up plans. Each season the garden grew more and more beautiful. Flowers bloomed according to the season: peonies, iris, day lilies, bachelor buttons, delphiniums, foxgloves, daisies, dahlias, asters – just like the English country gardens pictured in the copies of *Country Life* that her daughters sometimes sent out from England.

This was a working garden too. Vegetables grew aplenty. Fruit trees and canes flourished. The chickens provided eggs and the occasional roast. Tinker kept away marauding deer and foxes.

But the real pride of the garden were the roses: roses of every shade of pink and red, yellow and white, climbing roses, shrub roses and tea roses, hybrids, damasks, and floribundas, blooming all summer long and filling the air with their sweet, nostalgic scent. Mildred tended them almost as if they were children.

Rosebank had become the home that Mildred had dreamed of. "The best home in the best town in the best province in Canada," she boasted, and Fred Little concurred.

Late in 1912 I arrived at Rosebank with my mother, Sarah, and my younger brother, and I met Mildred, my Gran, and began my life in Creston. I was five years old; my brother David was three. How Gran felt about sharing her tiny house with the three of us, I don't know. It made something of a crowd in the cottage intended for one.

But it was only a temporary arrangement. In the spring, when our father arrived, we would move to a place of our own. Perhaps we'd go in for fruit ranching, like Uncle Andy and Aunt Charlotte. Or perhaps our father, who worked in an office in London, would prefer to work in the post office or the bank. Something suitable would be found.

Meanwhile Creston was fun. We loved Gran and Tinker and the Jersey cow. We loved Fred Little who came to dinner every day. We called him Gramps.

Gramps was proud of being Creston's first pioneer. At the dinner table he told stories about the old days in Creston. "When I settled here," he said "there were no roads, only paths through the forest. There was no railway, no stores, no post office. The nearest place where we could get supplies and mail was Port Hill, down at the border. We'd have to tramp down there and tramp back with fifty pound packs on our backs on a rough trail and cross the Goat River on a bridge we made out of downed trees. It was not an easy trip. And what we could get at Port Hill was nothing fit for a cook like your Gran. Our bill of fare, it was always the same: bacon and beans and mush, mush, mush six days of the week. On the Sabbath for a change we had beans and bacon, left out the mush and went hard on the bacon. Summer or winter, that was what we had. You youngsters don't know how good you have it with all the fancy things you can buy uptown nowadays, and your Gran, the best cook in Creston, fixing it for you." He winked at Gran to show his appreciation of the meal he'd done justice to.

He was a pioneer, he said, because he saw not just what was there now but what could be there in the future. "I can see the way the wind is going to blow," he told us. "I have an eye for the future."

Shortly after our arrival, his eye for the future saw the automobile as the coming boon for mankind. He went to Cranbrook and bought one, a beautiful maroon red machine with "Pioneer" printed in gold letters on the wind shield. He was the first car owner in Creston. He didn't drive himself, said he was too old to get the hang of it, but on fine days he'd get Mr. Bevan to take him out for a spin and sometimes he'd take me and Dave and Mum along. Gran refused to enter that 'noisy and dangerous machine'. Pretty soon Mr. Mallandaine bought a car too, and others in town, but Gramps was the first, the Pioneer who saw the way the wind blew into the future.

Once in a while Gramps would go through a spell when "he was not himself" as Gran described it. She would lock the house door then and though Gramps would pound on it and shout, she would not open it. "I am not at home," she would call out the kitchen window, which struck Dave and me as very funny, but neither Gran nor Mum laughed.

By the next day, Gramps would have quieted down. Gran would leave a pot of stew or soup on his doorstep and after that he'd be back at the dinner table, only maybe looking a little pale and not talking so much as usual.

In December the first snow fell. It was beautiful snow, soft and white, not at all like the grey slush we'd called snow in London. In the darker afternoon light it turned blue, then purple, striped with black shadows of the trees in the yard and down the hill. Down the hill! Sledding was our greatest joy in Creston winters. Everyone went sledding, adults and children alike. Well, not Gran; but Mum was a great sledder and an expert steerer. "Lean!" she would shout at just the right moment, and we'd lean and whiz past a tree or a fence. Fourth Street was the best of the sledding hills. We'd start at the station and slide down, way past Rosebank, waving to Gran as we passed.

Gran was not our only family in Creston. The town was full of our cousins and aunts and uncles. There was Uncle Robert, who most people called Alphabetical. He was easy to talk to because he answered all his own questions. He and Aunt Olive lived in a big new house and knew everyone in town. Their boy Sonny was a little older than I and didn't much like playing with girls, though he did sometimes if our mothers told him to. Out at their ranch at Alice Siding lived Aunt Charlotte and Uncle Andy and their three kids. The oldest, half a year younger than me, had the strange name of Noonie. Then there was Andrew and Charles was the baby, but soon he wouldn't be, for a new baby was on its way, Aunt Charlotte told us. Visits to their house at Alice Siding were always fun. The house was small and cramped, but there was room for a large trunk of dress up clothes: costumes from plays Aunt or Uncle had been in, an old top hat, a real cowboy belt with holsters, a wedding veil that was more holes than lace, and fancy bits of trimmings from Gran's hats. Mum and Aunt Charlotte and Uncle Andy would often join in the dress-up games and sometimes even Gran. We'd play out a fairy tale or the grown-ups would teach us a minuet with lots of bowing and curtseying and stately strutting. Later Mum and Gran and Aunt Charlotte would get to talking out on the verandah and Andy would lead us kids away to set up some kind of practical joke, like sticking the ladies' tea cups to their saucers or rigging up a pail of water to dump on the head of the first person who opened the door of the outdoor biffy. Gran was not amused, and Mum and Aunt Charlotte would say they weren't either, but they'd laugh all the same. Andy would let us drive his team of horses on the sleigh. He let us climb trees our mothers considered too high, and let us sled down hills they thought were too steep. "They'll come to no harm; they know what they're capable of," he'd say when the mothers scolded him. We were never afraid with Andy there. He'd see that we came to no harm.

In town Mum was making new friends through Aunt Olive and Uncle Robert. She became a member of the group that called themselves the Ish Kibbidle Club and usually met in Aunt Olive's house, so that she could keep an ear out for any telephone calls coming through. They played cards and had play readings and musical evenings. Gramps teased them about their highfalutin' tastes and called them the "codfish aristocracy".

With the aunts and uncles and sometimes with Gran too, Mum went to concerts at the Mercantile hall, to lectures, box socials, masquerade balls. Uncle Andy was often the emcee for these events, and generally the life of the party as well. He squired all three of "his" ladies – Aunt Charlotte, Mum and Gran – and always declared them the undisputed belles of the ball, though we knew he really meant Aunt Charlotte.

There was always something doing in Creston. We were all happy to be there. But sometimes on a quiet afternoon as I sat inside watching Gran sew on one of her hats, while Dave slept and Mum read a book from the lending library, I would think of my father alone in London and not having any of the fun we were having. I wished he was here too. I knew we were not a proper family without him, not like Aunt Charlotte and Uncle Andy and their kids, or Aunt Olive and Uncle Robert and Sonny. "When is Daddy coming?" I would ask Gran then.

"When he can get away."

"But when?"

"You'll have to ask your mother."

I ran over to Mum's chair. "When is Daddy coming?"

"In the spring, most likely." Mum would turn back to her book to show she wasn't going to answer any more questions on that subject. Then I would stand at the window watching the shadows on the snow and sing softly one of the songs my father and I used to sing together.

Winter ended in a rush. Ice broke up in the river and the water rose and frothed with coffee-coloured foam, flooded the flats, and then ebbed back to its banks, leaving the earth green with new grass. The tamarack by the side porch turned pale, feathery green and in the orchards the tree limbs sprouted green and then blossomed pink and white and beautiful.

Now there were new games to play, and new events to observe: Gran's spring show of hats; the church garden party, which was to be held that year at Rosebank; a travelling show come to town; the Sunday school picnic.

Once school was out we made new friends among the town kids. Creston was small and we were allowed to roam all over the place as long as we promised that the older kids would look after the younger and that we'd all stay off the railway tracks. On Canyon Street we lay on our backs on the ground under the new wooden sidewalks and looked up through the cracks and made naughty comments about the ladies' underwear we saw, or imagined we saw. We sat on Rosebank's front steps and talked with the Siwash when they stopped for the 'muck-a-muck' Gran gave them: tea with lots of condensed milk and sugar and raisin buns or thick slices of bread and butter and jam. We made forts and teepees in the spinney, made dolls out of faded hollyhock blossoms, pestered Gramps with questions about life in the pioneer times, hunted for bear in vacant lots. There was always lots to do.

At harvest time Mum and the aunts worked in the orchards, picking and packing, and Gran made hats and hats and hats because women had to have good hats for all of the goings on around town, and everyday hats for wearing when they went uptown. We kids had little jobs to do around the place to help out; we picked raspberries and currants for Gran, fed the chickens and collected eggs, fetched the paper and the mail when the trains came in.

There was so much going on that I didn't think about my father much anymore. By autumn, when he had still not arrived, I came to realize his non-arrival was a taboo subject, though I didn't know why. He was never mentioned any more, not by Mum or Gran or any of the aunts and uncles. My brother didn't talk about him because he couldn't remember him at all, and my memories of him were faint, though I remembered the songs he and I used to sing. I didn't miss him, not really. We had Uncle Andy and Alphabetical and Gramps to tell us new stories and teach us new songs.

I started school, then the next autumn Dave did. We liked living with Gran. She knew just about everyone in town. She knew all the Anglicans because she was a pillar of Christ Church, especially in the matter of organizing refreshments for ladies' teas and the Sunday School picnic and the annual Garden Party. Through Aunt Olive and Alphabetical she knew the smart set of the Ish Kibbidle Club. She attended every whist drive in town and was known as a high roller who played for stakes as high as twenty-five cents when she was on a winning streak. She knew all the shopkeepers. Being known as a good cook, she was sometimes call on to help out in the kitchen of the hotel when they were short staffed. Because she bought ginger and licorice roots from the Chinaman at the laundry and gathered medicinal roots and weeds like the Siwash woman, she gained a reputation as a healer, though when she was asked for medical advice, her answer was almost invariably, "Take a small glass of port mixed in a pot of clear tea, rest, and if you don't feel better in two days, go and see Doc Henderson." Because of the friendly Tinker, she knew all the town's children and they and Tinker all knew enough to keep their distance from her flowers, especially her prized roses. Most of the kids and adults too called her Gran just as we did. But she was really our Gran and we were proud of her.

When I think now of Gran and Rosebank in those days, it seems in my memory to be always summer. The garden is blooming with roses of every colour and the house is full of marvellous hats, and warm sunshine, and love.

Chapter 3

Ruth's Songs

I loved my Creston aunts and uncles and cousins. We had good times together. But I had had other aunts and uncles in England. Some of them were not as much fun as the Talbot gang, as Mum called them, but some were, especially the ones who talked the way my father talked. I thought about them sometimes. I remembered Uncle Will who found sweets for me in the strangest places and Uncle Llew who also gave me sweets but I had to say a Bible verse first, and Aunt Megan whom Mum used to imitate behind her back. My favourite was Aunt Ruth. She was my aunt, but she wasn't even a grown up; she was just a big girl exactly ten years older than me. She'd come to live in our house right after I was born to help Mum look after me. As I grew, she and I became good friends. She told me about her terrible life before she came to live with us. She'd lived in Wales in an orphanage full of children who had no families to look after them. They had to behave very, very well, those children or they'd get a beating and only bread and water for their dinner. I was glad she'd come to live with us, and so was she. We had good times together, Ruth and I. She played games with me, and showed me how easy it was to remember Bible verses if you sang them to yourself instead of saying them. And she taught me many songs, so that we could always find a tune to suit a Bible verse.

But when we left our house in England, she disappeared. She'd put me to bed one night, and the next morning Mum woke me up and told me were going to Canada. My father took us to the station and settled us into the train, but Ruth wasn't there. Then he got out and stood on the platform, and only when the train started up did I realize that he wasn't coming with us. Mum and David and I were going to Canada, but not my father and not Ruth. Why, I wanted to know.

I couldn't ask my father because he was out on the platform waving and getting left behind, and I couldn't ask Mum because she had covered her face with her scarf and she was crying behind it. So I cried too, and David, who was too young to know what was happening, cried because I was crying and then he fell asleep.

After a while Mum stopped crying. She mopped my face with her handkerchief and said we'd have a nice cup of tea. When the train stopped, she opened the door and a man brought us milky tea in heavy white mugs, and big iced buns. I was so excited about this picnic that I forgot to ask about my father and Aunt Ruth.

When I asked about them later, Mum's answers were short. She sounded as if she was angry. "Daddy is coming to Canada later," she said. "Auntie Ruth can't come. You will meet your Aunt Charlotte and Aunt Olive in Creston. And your cousins too." I would have preferred my father and Aunt Ruth but I knew I wasn't going to get them any time soon.

In fact, I never saw my father again. And it was more than fifty years later and I was an old woman before I tracked down my dear Aunt Ruth. Not that I'd tried to keep in touch through the intervening years. She'd dropped out of my life when I was a child and as a child I simply accepted that that was the way it had to be. It was 1968 when I at last revisited England and thought of looking up Ruth. I was able to get her address from an aunt in Australia. Ruth was living in a small village in the Midlands, I discovered, and would love to see me.

Her husband answered the door to my knock and ushered me in like a butler. "Please step this way, madam." The cottage was dark and low-ceilinged. I stood at the threshold of a room and saw in the dimness a figure seated by the window. All I could distinguish was a mass of white hair and a flash of dark eyes. It was Aunt Ruth and she was waiting for her dramatic moment. She rose. "*Croeso, Olwen fach*! Welcome, my little Olwen!" In a strong, rich contralto she began to sing a Welsh song:

Huna blentyn,yn fy mynwes
Sleep my baby, sleep in peace,

Somewhere in the storehouse of my memory, a door creaked open, and the words of her song came to me. I began to sing with her.

Huna blentyn, nid oes yma
Ddim i roddi iti fraw;
Harm nor hurt will never touch you

She danced towards me and I towards her. And there we were: two crazy old women, laughing and crying, dancing and singing an old Welsh lullaby of our childhood, long ago.

After that, we settled in to talk. We talked through the three days of my visit. I told her my life and she told me hers. We drank tea and we talked. Every so often Ruth would call out to her husband, "Make us some more tea, will you? There's a love." She'd roll us a couple of cigarettes and we'd light up and go at the talking again.

"I loved living with you in London," she told me. "It was so good to be free of the orphanage, to be in a real family with my big brother Tom and in the great city of London."

"Why were you in an orphanage anyway?" I interrupted to ask.

Ruth shrugged. "There were ten children. Our mother died. Our Dad couldn't manage. None of the relatives wanted to take me in. That's just the way it was in those days."

She went on with her story. "You were an easy baby to look after. God knows, I'd had lots of practice with the babies in the orphanage. They were training us girls at the orphanage to be domestic servants, you see, nurse-maids or scullery girls. I knew more about how to keep a house and care for a baby than your own mother did, though I say it who shouldn't. I was very fond of you.

"I didn't have to work very hard. I was happy in your house, especially when your father was home. We'd have singing then, and dancing. He showed me how to play the piano, and I practised whenever I could. 'You've got a gift for music,' he told me. Your mother said so too.

"Some evenings Tom would read us his poems or plays. Your mother wasn't so happy then, because she couldn't understand. I don't know why she didn't learn Welsh. She just didn't.

"And many evenings your father wouldn't be home at all. I could see your mother was lonely for him, and then she'd get angry. 'Your place is here at home,' she scolded him when she had him there to listen to her. 'Not always gallivanting off with your Welsh friends.'

"When I was older, Tom occasionally took me to a concert or play if it was in Welsh and your mother didn't want to go. They were wonderful, those theatre evenings. Tom and I would come home late, talking about the play we'd seen, acting out scenes from it. Or if it was a concert we'd been to, the music would still be playing in our heads and we'd have to try it out on the piano, as soon as we got in. Your mother would come down in her nightgown, with her long golden hair in a braid down her back, saying 'Sh! You'll wake the baby.' But Tom could usually jolly her out of her anger and we'd have a midnight concert, the three of us.

"Oh yes. Those were happy days."

"And then your mother decided to go to Canada. I wanted to go with you, but there wasn't enough money. My job as nursemaid was at an end."

Ruth was fifteen. It was time for her to find a proper situation in domestic service. She hated the idea of going into service and opposed it with all her will. "I didn't want to slink in and out of the servants' entrance of some great house; I didn't want to bow and bob and say 'yes, ma'am' and 'no ma'm.' Oh no. Not me.

"What I wanted was to sing and dance. I had ambitions for a music hall career. I had, as your parents had pointed out, a gift for music. And I was, though I say it who shouldn't, quite a beauty. An exotic, foreign sort of beauty, you know: black curly hair, coal-black eyes, an olive complexion."

Her husband set down a tray with fresh tea on the table. "She was beautiful all right," he whispered to me. "Still is, for a girl of her age." Ruth smiled and tossed the dregs from our last cups of tea over her shoulder and poured fresh. Her house looked immaculate, yet I noticed that she tossed tea leaves and scattered cigarette ash wherever she went. I supposed it was her loving husband who cleaned up after her, unobtrusively.

"Your father tried to help me, but nothing came of it. We couldn't find gigs that paid enough for me to live on, and I didn't have the luxury of waiting for a breakthrough to stardom; I had to earn my own living."

In the end, Ruth got a job at a London hospital as a sort of nurse's aide, serving and scrubbing and fetching and looking after people. But at least she wasn't a servant. Not quite.

And she was noticed. With her personality and looks and her habit of singing and dancing through the corridors when matron wasn't around, she could hardly not be noticed. The young doctors were impressed, and soon she was being invited to smart parties where people were having fun, despite the wartime austerity.

"For one of those parties I dressed up as a gypsy. I had a Spanish guitar. My brother Will had won it in a card game and gave it to me. I'd often listened to the gypsies playing in the markets and at fairs, and it was easy to pick up their tunes. So I had my guitar, and I wore all three of my skirts, one over the other, and a paisley shawl and a kerchief over my head and went barefoot. Everyone said I looked the real thing. I sang and danced and played the guitar. I sang in Welsh and said it was gypsy language and no one knew the difference.

"After that, every party I went to, they'd always beg me, 'Bring your guitar, Gypsy-Ruth. Sing for us, and dance.'

"And I did. I sang 'Counting the Goats' and I counted them white and black, blue and orange and pink, pink, pink, and they thought I was singing of wild loves.

"I sang the sad words of Myfawny's love:
Forget now all the words of promise
You made to one who loved you well.
Give me your hand, my sweet beloved,
But one last time to say farewell.

"'Those gypsy songs are real heart-stirrers,' people said."

After the war, Ruth became engaged to one of the young doctors. "He came from up north, around Carlisle. He was very upper class, very rich, but not a snob, not a looking-down-your-nose sort of gentleman at all, I thought. His name was Alan. He took me to parties and to the cinema and to the music halls, or we'd drive out to the country in his car and have a picnic and almost make love but not quite, because I was a good girl, and I knew from my days at the orphanage what happened to girls who didn't wait for marriage, and what happened to their poor little babies too.

"He gave me a ring: a diamond as big as an acorn with little rubies all around it. I was happy as a princess.

"Then one day at the hospital I was carrying a tray of empty cocoa mugs down to the wash-up, when I heard Alan and his mates talking in the stairwell just below. As I got closer, I realized they were talking about me, so I crept over to the stair rail to listen, thinking how I'd tease Alan later about what I'd heard him say about me.

"'You're not seriously going to marry that little chit, are you?' one of the doctors asked.

"'We-e-ellll,' Alan answered in one long drawn-out, indecisive word, and everyone laughed, and my heart's blood froze.

" 'She's a pretty little thing,' one of them said, 'but, do you know, I wouldn't be a bit surprised if she really was a gypsy. Imagine marrying into the travelling people!'

" 'Oh, he's just having a joke,' someone else said. 'I bet he hasn't taken her home to meet the family, have you, you devil?'

"Alan didn't answer and it came to me for the first time how odd that was, since we were engaged and all. I'd introduced him to my brothers.

" 'Just as I thought,' the other fellow jeered. 'Your intentions are not honorable, sir. And thank God for that. You'd ruin your career if you married a little tart like our singing gypsy.'

" 'I suppose. But, oh, I do love that sweet little body of hers,' Alan said and drew pictures of me in the air and the men all laughed again.

"I dropped the tray of cocoa mugs down the stairs so they'd be sure to know I was coming. I walked down towards those men as though I was the Queen of England and they were a gang of convicts I'd just ordered to be executed. I was in a rage, but a calm white rage, not the least bit inclined to cry or shout. That came later.

" 'I believe you dropped this,' I said to Alan and threw the ring he'd given me at his feet and it pinged on further down the stairs. I walked slowly after it.

"When I glanced at it at the bottom of the stairs, I saw that the stone had fallen out. If it was a half decent ring that would never have happened. I think he must have bought the damned thing at Woolworth's."

Alan ran after her and apologized and offered excuses, said he was only joking with the fellows. But Ruth would not forgive him. "You're a cad. A sly, low, lying cad," I told him to his face. "Whatever high class family you come from, however much money you make at your gentleman's job, you don't deserve me," I told him. "I told him straight. And I'm glad I did, though my heart was breaking. What a fool I was, ever to have believed his promises.

"I wasn't as kind as Myfawny's lover. I wouldn't 'take his hand but one last time to say farewell'. I was through with him."

A month later Ruth married Fred Anstruther, a porter in the hospital. Fred was a humble man who had worshipped the ground Ruth walked on from the day he had first held open a ward door for her. He was overwhelmed with happiness at the one marvellous stroke of good fortune in his existence that had made the beautiful Ruth his wife. For the rest of his life he loved her with unquestioning, unswerving devotion, like a pet dog.

Ruth wouldn't work at the hospital any longer. "The General wasn't big enough for me and Alan. 'We shall go to Australia,' I told Fred.

" 'But we don't have the fare, Ruthie dear,' Fred said.

" 'We'll get it,' I told him."

Ruth took her gypsy act to the street, and it was just as much a hit with people in queues in front of the cinemas or theatres, or with the vendors and shoppers in the markets as it had been with the bright young things at the posh parties. Only now, the act had a concluding flourish: Fred passed the hat.

They got to Australia.

There Fred got a job in a hospital in Sidney. "I could probably have found work there too, but I wanted to look around for something different. I was so tired of scrubbing and carrying.

"And then" – Ruth's voice implied a fanfare of trumpets – "and then I met Roland. It was love at first sight. Love that thrilled right through me." Ruth's face lit with remembered joy as she told me about it. "This was a love that pounded through the blood in my veins, throbbed right into my fingertips. This was a love that made me think the feelings I'd had for Alan were nothing but flirtatious silliness.

"This was a love whose force there could be no holding back. I loved the sound of his name and the way he walked and the clothes he wore. The smell of him. His voice. The way his jaw tightened when he was serious, and the way he laughed. I wanted the times with him to go on forever and yet I was almost sick with the force of the joy and excitement of them."

She paused for a moment in her account, and her expression darkened. "But I didn't hope for anything either. Anything beyond one more hour with him. After Alan, I never let myself have hope of lasting love."

Roland was, as he told her straight off in the first days of their relationship, a married man with no intentions of leaving his wife. When Ruth became pregnant with his child, he gave her the money to go back to England with Fred. She went. "I didn't see what else I could do. Since I couldn't have Roland, I didn't care where I went or what I did. It was best to go home, away from the hope of the chance of meeting Roland in the street or in a store or at the cinema.

"But I didn't regret the months I'd had with him. Never."

Back in England there were more hard times and more singing on street corners, for now she and Fred had little Rhys to support as well, and Ruth was determined that Rhys would be well-fed, well-dressed, and well-educated. She wanted the best of everything for him. All the passion of her heart turned to love for her son.

One day she saw an advertisement in the newspaper: 'Wanted for widower with infant son: butler/housekeeper couple for small estate in Midlands countryside. Would accept couple with child. References required.'

"I'd seen my brother Will cook up references. It was easy enough. I wrote one in the name of a parson's wife and gave the address of my sister in Cooma, Australia. Odds were the widower would never take the time to write to Australia and then wait for an answer.

"Fred was scared, of course. 'But, Ruthie dear, I don't know how to be a butler,' he said.

"'Fred,' I told him, 'you were born to be a butler. Here, take this tray, and we'll practise.'

"He was a natural. He bowed and bobbed and said 'yes, sir,' and 'no, sir' with perfect humility.

"We got the job. After all my years of trying to avoid domestic service, there I was in the end, a servant, and happy to be one. I suppose you could say it was my fate catching up with me.

"This particular situation had one great advantage. I'd seen the possibilities of it in the advertisement. I told the master I could mind his son as well as my little Rhys while I did my work. 'My son could be a companion for your lovely little boy,' I said. I knew that's what the man wanted. Why else would he have said he'd take a couple with a child? 'And you would be spared the expense of a nanny,' I pointed out to him.

"We were good servants, Fred and I. And Rhys grew up with the son of the house, enjoying all the advantages the gentleman's son had: acres of park to play in, and farmland to roam through, a tennis court, an ornamental lake where the boys learned to swim and boat. They had a private tutor for their education. The master thought his son was delicate, and didn't want him to go away to prep school like most of his class do, so we were very lucky there. Rhys learned all the things a gentleman learns: how to ride, how to write in Latin and do algebra sums. He could swim and dance and play cricket and tennis, and his manners were perfect.

"It lasted 'til the master's son went to Eton. Then Rhys was able to get a place at the grammar school in Coventry, and got his A-levels. He couldn't have had a better education. But," she sighed, "it's his heart that's got him into trouble since he's been a grown man, and who am I to blame him for that? The village girls were all in love with him before he even finished grammar school, and older women too, who should have known better. He loved them all, but he'd never settle on one. He went off and joined the navy. I don't see him often now. I miss him. All those lovely girlfriends, and he still hasn't married and settled down. But he may yet. Don't you think so?"

"Sure," I said to please her. "Lots of men don't marry until they're in their late forties and even their fifties."

Ruth concluded her story. "Fred and I worked on at the great house. We were used to it. We liked the master and suited him well. Before he died, he gave us this cottage to live in. He was good to us. So you see, I was fated to live a life in service, and it turned out to be not so bad."

She stood up. "Come along now. I must go to the church to look over the music for tomorrow. I'm the organist now.

"Fred," she called as we left, "you can clear up the tea cups and peel some potatoes for our dinner. There's a love." We walked along the village street, past the half-timbered pub and the one store and post office to where the grey stone church with its squat tower stood looking out over the rolling farmland beyond. We walked through the lych gate flanked by dark yew trees and along the gravel path through an overgrown graveyard. At the church door Ruth paused to take a last drag on her cigarette before butting it out, and then we passed from the bright blue day into the dim amber light of the church and the smell of cold stone, mildewed hymn books, furniture polish, candle wax and dying flowers. It's the smell of Anglican churches everywhere and it hushes you into religious readiness as soon as you catch a whiff of it.

Ruth sat at the organ bench and began to push buttons. "When did you learn to play the organ?" I asked.

"Oh, I don't know about learning. I just knew I could do it. You can play any instrument, I think, if you listen to it a while and let the sound of it into your heart."

Ruth played some hymns and some Bach and Mendelssohn while I sat in the front pew and listened. Then she turned and smiled and launched into the lullaby she'd greeted me with, and once again the tears came, and the shadow of old, old memories of a home and a family and a language I'd been born into and lost in a new world.

Chapter 4

For King and Country

On August 4, 1914, King George V declared war on Germany. In our remote corner of his empire, in Creston, British Columbia, we didn't hear about the declaration until the next day. Then the whole town went wild. People rushed up to Canyon Street to find out what others knew and to share their excitement. When the train came in from Nelson with yesterday's papers, everyone hurried to the station to see what had been reported so far. Nothing much, except that Britain was at war, and so, of course, was Canada.

The news was not unexpected; the politicians had been talking about readiness for the past month. And certainly the news was not unwelcome. Most of Creston's citizens were British born or of British descent, and their loyalty to the British cause was unquestioning. "Canada is loyal to the very core" the editorial in *The Creston Review* declared.

Everywhere people were eager to show their support for the war. The Dominion government sent a million bags of flour to Britain in a gesture of "practical patriotism" and the government of British Columbia followed that up with a carload of tinned salmon.

In Creston, young men dashed around trying to find out where the deuce a fellow went to enlist. The ladies stormed the Mercantile and plundered it of all soldierly brown and green yarns and material available. My mother carried off two yards of beige cotton, and began cutting out and hemming military handkerchiefs for the volunteers. Gran cornered a dozen skeins of brown wool and started knitting.

The Review preached: "It behooves all young men of Creston to join and assist those who have been put in charge and help bear their share in the dissemination of loyalty to our glorious Empire."

Half a dozen men from Creston enlisted straightaway, including our uncle, Alphabetical Smith, who was a soldier already, having served in the Boer War. Others soon followed. These men were feted as conquering heroes before they even got their uniforms.

It came as no surprise to us to learn that Mr. Mallandaine also was already in the army, had been since the North West Rebellion, in some sort of reserve force. Now quite naturally he was ready in place for the important business of organizing recruitment and getting Creston on a wartime footing. We were to call him Captain Mallandaine.

The rector at Christ Church preached on Sunday and on many following Sundays about the glory of war, the wickedness of the Hun, and the righteousness of the British cause. He told us that even those of us who were not going into battle ourselves could help win the war by showing support for our soldiers in every way we could. We took his message to heart.

Gran was knitting socks for the gallant boys, setting herself a goal of a pair a week. She and Mum taught me how to knit too. Young as I was they agreed that I too could do my bit. As soon as I could make a four-inch square, with the rows even and no dropped stitches, I was entrusted with the knitting of a scarf in brown four-ply.

I worried that the war would be over by the time I got it finished.

The volunteers worried that the war would be over before they'd got themselves kitted up and trained and transported to England, and from there to France.

Patriotism swept through the country and through our little town. Union Jacks blossomed everywhere. Advertising got on the bandwagon. There were flags or military insignia or information about the armed services in ads and on packages of just about everything, so the consumer could feel patriotic by drinking Frye's cocoa or using a Gillette safety razor or putting True Blue blueing in the white wash.

Gran bought red white and blue ribbon and tried, in vain, to include the colours in the new autumn models for her hat shop. In the end, aesthetics triumphed over patriotism in the millinery sphere. "If the war is still on in the spring," she reflected, "I could do the red, white and blue in boater styles, but it simply can't be done with felts. I won't have my ladies looking like the chorus in the pantomime."

"The war will be long over by next spring," everyone assured her. "But never mind, you can use the ribbon to decorate the Odd Fellows Hall for the farewell party."

The only two people I knew who were not wildly keen on the war were Uncle Andy, and Dorothy Bacon.

Uncle Andy said the war was nonsense, a fool's game. This upset Mum, but Gran told her to pay no attention to him. "It's the Irish in him," she explained. "He says what he says to lead you into an argument. I'm sure he doesn't really believe it. I would advise you to ignore him."

Dorothy Bacon, who came two afternoons a week to Gran's house and shop, Rosebank, to do the plain sewing for the autumn show, didn't like the war because it would take her fiancé Bill Mason away from her. "I wouldn't mind so much if it was only to Vancouver or Calgary he was going," she told us, "but England is so far away, and France farther. I'll miss him fearful bad."

"Away is away, whether it's two hundred miles or two thousand," Mum said. "You must be very proud that your future husband will be a hero. And don't worry; the war will be over and he'll be back before you know it."

"I suppose," Dorothy said, but there was still doubt in her voice and she got weepy when she tried to teach me songs like "Let me Call you Sweetheart" and "Love's Old Sweet Song" as she sat sewing ribbons.

Among the volunteers, Archie Murdoch was our special friend. During the weeks of preparation for departure he often came round to Rosebank for afternoon tea. Mum and Gran were making him handkerchiefs and socks and gloves. "I'll be the best equipped soldier in the front lines," he said as he tried things on.

Often when he visited he brought his wonderful dog Bobby with him. Bobby was a border collie-spaniel mix, a clever and patient dog, capable of performing a dozen tricks. While the adults had their tea, my brother David and I would get Bobby to do a special show of "Roll over and play dead German," or "Chase the wicked Germans away" for their entertainment.

One afternoon when Mr. Murdoch arrived at Rosebank's gate with Bobby trotting at his heels as usual, he called out, "Olwen! David! Could you keep Bobby from destroying Gran's borders while I talk to your mother for a few minutes?"

Sure we could.

Presently, Mum and Mr. Murdoch walked out to the garden. "Mr. Murdoch has a request for you children," Mum said in a very serious way.

A request? For us? I was puzzled. We were children. Adults told us what to do; they didn't make requests of us.

"What it is, children," Archie said, "is I was wondering if you would look after Bobby for me while I'm away at the war? Your Mother says she thinks you could manage it."

Would we? You bet we would! Gran's old dog Tinker wouldn't be so enthusiastic about the idea as we were, but he would tolerate the newcomer with the calm patience he was known for. Mr. Murdoch shook hands with David and me, as if we'd concluded a serious business arrangement.

I felt immensely grown up and patriotic and happy. Looking after Bobby would be much more fun as war work than knitting that interminable scarf. There was no hope of its being finished in time to present to Mr. Murdoch.

A few days later, the volunteers were ready to leave. Everyone, absolutely everyone, even Uncle Andy, went to the station to see our boys off. David and me and lots of other kids had Union Jacks to wave. The brass band played and there was a holiday mood in the air.

Captain Mallandaine gave a speech and got everyone to stand at attention for "God Save the King" and our soldiers stood self-consciously the straightest and the tallest and the most solemn men there. Then Gramps Little led hoorahs for our gallant boys and the holiday mood returned.

"Give the Kaiser what for!" people shouted. No one had scruples about expressing aggressive hatred of the foe.

The only people who cried at the station that afternoon were Mr. Hastings, the widower, saying goodbye to his only son. Poor old man, it was embarrassing for him, but still, he shouldn't have come to the station if he couldn't keep control over himself, was the general opinion. And Dorothy Bacon clung weeping to her fiancé Bill 'til the very last minute, "making an exhibition of herself," as Gran remarked.

At last the train puffed out of the station with the soldiers leaning out the windows and we ran along the platform as far as we could, waving our flags and shouting wildly until the train was out of sight.

"Those boys will have the war knocked into a cocked hat by Christmas," Mum said with satisfaction as we walked back Fourth Street towards Rosebank.

Through the next months, news came back from our boys. They were at Sam Hughes' great army camp at Valcartier in Quebec, training. They hoped to be sent overseas soon. Alphabetical Smith wrote that there were ten thousand more men than were needed for Canada's first contingent to the war. He feared that married men might be sent home. But in fact he was one of the first of the Creston men to get to France, having been attached to the Strathcona Horse Regiment.

David and I put out a bowl of water for Bobby every morning. We fed him twice a day on leftovers and bones and scraps the butcher gave us. "It's for Archie Murdoch's dog. We're keeping him while Archie's away at the war," Mum explained so the butcher would be sure to give him a good bone, and she'd get something extra for old Tinker too.

"Your master will be home soon," I told Bobby, stroking his thick black and white fur or rubbing under his chin which made him close his eyes in ecstasy. "Just as soon as he gives the Kaiser what for."

My scarf progressed one sweaty row at a time.

In September, the Masons received news that their boy Bill was ill in hospital in Quebec. While they were deciding whether they should travel all that way to see him, a telegram came. He had died of pneumonia.

"And he didn't even get to the war," people exclaimed over and over, knowing what a disappointment that must be to the Masons and to Dorothy, his intended. "Perhaps she had a premonition," my mother speculated. "Remember the way she carried on at the station the day the boys left?"

She was taking the news of his death hard, her family said. "Stayed in her room howling, for hours," they reported.

Gran and Mum and I paid a sympathy call. Dorothy was up in her room and wouldn't come down. "Why don't you go up to her?" Mrs. Bacon asked me. "She's fond of you. Maybe you could cheer her up a bit."

I liked Dorothy, even if she was a bit soppy. She had started to teach me how to crochet, and she was going to teach me how to do lace making. I hoped all this howling wasn't going to put an end to her afternoons with us at Rosebank. I went upstairs.

I found Dorothy sitting on her bed, with piles of clothes and linens around her. She wasn't howling, but she was sniffling. "Is there anything I could do to help?" I asked. Mum had told me to say that.

"Yes. Go to the Mercantile and get me a roll of white tissue paper." Dorothy gave me a dime. "And come straight back."

I ran to the Mercantile and back with the tissue paper. By then Dorothy had a large trunk ready in the middle of the floor. "Everything has to be wrapped in tissue," she told me. "To save it nice."

I cut the tissue into squares and she wrapped each item and packed it neatly into the trunk. There were fine lawn nightgowns with lace work on the collars, and linen sheets with drawn work hems, embroidered pillow cases, appliqued luncheon cloths and napkins, tea towels with smiling tea pots embroidered on them, and hand towels with wide crocheted borders.

"Bill died for King and Country just as much as if he'd been killed in battle," I said. That's what my Mum had said to Bill's mother.

"No, he didn't," Dorothy said. "He died of pneumonia because of sleeping in a damp tent. It was a stupid, stupid waste. He shouldn't have gone at all." And then she began to sob out loud.

I wasn't being much of a comfort about Bill, so I tried another subject. "Where are you sending all these things?" I asked. "To the Belgian refugees?" This didn't seem like the kind of stuff that went into packages for the soldiers.

"I'm not sending them nowhere," Dorothy said. "I'm just keeping them nice."

And she did. She would keep them nice all her life long.

She showed up for work at Gran's again the next week, and she finished teaching me how to crochet, but we never got started on the lace making. There was no more singing, and of course she didn't talk about Bill any more. She didn't talk much at all now, so it was no fun anymore sitting with her while she worked.

Meanwhile our Creston boys had progressed from Valcartier to England. Archie Murdoch wrote from Salisbury Plain. They were closer to the war, but not in it yet. Worse luck. It was cold and wet, and war would be a treat, compared with the endless marching through the mud they were doing just now. He hoped Bobby was well.

In February he wrote again. All the other Creston boys had gone off to France. Only he'd been kept on at Salisbury to do some stupid office job. "Just my rotten luck," he wrote. "How's Bobby?"

On the home front, patriotic fundraising was in full swing. There were teas and dances and concerts for the benefit of the Patriotic Fund. We schoolchildren were recruited to stage a patriotic pageant and sing "Rule Britannia" and "Oh Canada". Of course we'd sing "God Save the King" at the end as well. Every show and concert always finished with "The King". I longed to be chosen as Britannia for the pageant, or failing that, at least Canada. Two pretty blond girls got those roles. I got to be "our native friend". Gran gave me her plaid shawl to wear and several strings of beads and a pair of moccasins from her shop. Mum braided my black hair and tied a ribbon around my head and said the Siwash would greet me as a long-lost cousin. I wondered why a real native child wasn't given the role, but Mum shushed me up and said that wouldn't do at all.

In March the Hastings boy was killed in action. The news sobered all of Creston. He was our first casualty, not counting poor Bill, who was a sort of unfortunate accident.

Everybody went to the memorial service at Christ Church. Crestoners began to realize that war wasn't just flag waving and fine speeches. Men were getting killed, even men we knew.

Christmas was long past and the war hadn't ended, as everyone had predicted it would, and now it looked as though it wasn't going to end for a while yet either.

In August, Creston observed the first anniversary of the war with prayers for victory. Letters from our boys in France came and were passed around, some even printed in *The Review.* One soldier wrote, "Little old Creston on the flats would look like heaven to me now as I sit on a box of ammunition and wish that the bally war was ended. Another complained that he'd like some shirts and socks. "I haven't had a change of socks for three weeks – we generally get a bath and a change of sox and shirt every two weeks – but not always." One said that he and his mates felt they'd done their stint and would like to see some others taking over. He hadn't had his boots off for five days. He was tired of the war and he'd like a rest from it.

Alphabetical sent long letters directly to *The Review*. He too complained of poor organization at the front. They had body belts and bully beef enough to burn, he wrote, but a shortage of socks and tobacco.

I was sent up to the station with two cents every day at train time to buy yesterday's Nelson paper with its wider and more current war news. Gran and Gramps Little and Uncle Andy pored over the news and maps and had long discussions about how the battles were being fought and what the generals were doing wrong and how they could improve. Gramps began to mutter about useless tactics and the waste of lives. "If Britain can't do any better than this, the Hun will win," Andy said when he read about the Somme offensive.

Mum overheard. She would not tolerate criticism of the British army. "Britain will win. She's won every war she ever fought," she said.

Andy grinned. "She didn't do so well in the American Revolution."

"England didn't want the American colonies," Mum said grandly.

She was annoyed too that Andy had not yet volunteered. "My husband is fighting. Alphabetical is fighting, and dozens of your friends. Why aren't you there? You could show them how to do it right, instead of criticizing from afar."

Andy flushed and folded up the newspaper he had been reading at Gran's kitchen table. "I have a wife and four young children dependent on me," he said. "I have a ranch where fruit trees are growing and need tending. I've my duty as fire-warden to protect the forest. I'm a lot more use here than I would be in France getting myself blown into smithereens for the Empire." He would not be goaded into fighting a war on another continent.

All over the country other people in other towns were realizing, like our war experts, that the Germans were a much more formidable enemy than they'd thought. Either that, or the British army wasn't as fine and efficient a fighting force as we'd been led to believe. It was now admitted that this war would be a long one, though Germany's ultimate defeat was inevitable.

Attitudes hardened against the Germans. In England the King changed his German name to the English Windsor, and in Creston Mr. Weissenthal took his mother's maiden name of Jones. Gramps Little, who had had a difference of opinion with Mr. Weissenthal-Jones on a financial transaction, made a point of continuing to address him loudly and at every opportunity as "Herr Weissenthal."

Across the country, thousands of enemy aliens were interned in camps. Patriotic Canadians refused to buy from businesses with German names and wouldn't give work to anyone of German origin. The miners of the Crow's Nest refused to work underground with enemy aliens. It was too dangerous, they claimed. Under threat of boycott, the town of Berlin in Ontario changed its name to Kitchener. German was no longer taught in schools, and some musicians refused to play works by Beethoven or Wagner or other German composers.

My mother had a hard time with this. She didn't mind so much about Wagner but she loved to play Beethoven sonatas on Aunt Olive's piano. Eventually she found the solution in the name Beethoven. Who had ever heard of any Germans named Beethoven, other than Ludwig van himself? Therefore it couldn't be a German name. Even if he had been born in Germany, the family wasn't German. They must have come from Belgium, Mum guessed. So it was all right, it was even patriotic, for her to play Beethoven songs and sonatas and peasant dances at the Ish Kibiddle Club's musical evenings.

Some bad boys threw stones at Mrs. Baker's dachshund. "That's going too far," my mother said. "Poor innocent dog! He's not German. Mind you," she added, "I've always thought those dachshunds are a ridiculous looking breed. I would never have one myself."

The war went on and on because it couldn't stop until one side won. Britain would win in the end, of course, but victory was taking much longer than anyone had imagined.

The knitting and the bandage-rolling continued. There was talk of conscription.

I finished the scarf. Mum helped me wrap it up and we took it to the Red Cross meeting and it was added to the Creston women's parcel for the war effort.

We got something called a field postcard from Archie Murdoch. "Going up to the front now," was scrawled in pencil. "Hurrah! Will write later."

Only a few days later the news reached us through a letter from Alphabetical Smith. Archie had been killed in action on his first day in combat.

Mum cried and wrote a letter of sympathy to his mother in Edinburgh.

"What will we do about Bobby?" I asked.

"We'll keep him," Mum said. "It's what Archie would have wanted."

Poor Bobby. I stroked his thick furry ruff. "Mr. Murdoch died for King and Country," I told him. I wondered if the dog knew his master was dead. Myself, I could hardly remember Mr. Murdoch by now. "Don't worry, Bobby. I'll look after you," I promised.

At the memorial service we sang,

We by enemies distrest
They in Paradise at rest;
We the captives – they the freed -
We and they are one indeed.

I was sad about Mr. Murdoch's getting killed, especially on his very first day fighting. But now Bobby was going to stay with us forever. I couldn't help but be happy about that.

"Stop grinning like a Cheshire cat," Mum hissed to me.

On the way home we stopped at the Mercantile to buy wool for my next scarf. Would this war never end?

The war didn't end. It was costing unheard of amounts of money – four million dollars a day it was reckoned. Prices were going up. The Department of Agriculture urged us to grow fruit and vegetables and raise livestock to help feed Britain. Fundraising was more or less constant now. We collected for the Patriotic Fund, the Red Cross, the Belgian Refugees, the tobacco fund, the machine gun fund. We were urged to "make our dollars fight" by buying Dominion of Canada War Savings Certificates. Soldiers invalided out of the army gave lectures. Admission fifty cents. Proceeds to the Patriotic Fund. A Red Cross tea will be held at the home of Mrs. Mallandaine. Admission ten cents. A garden party to be held at Rosebank, home of Mrs. M. Young. The Creston Band will entertain. Admission twenty-five cents. Proceeds to the Belgian Refugee Fund. Aside from monetary contributions, women were expected to knit socks and scarves and body belts, sew shirts and pajamas for the Red Cross, and provide sandwiches, cakes and squares for the refreshments tables at the fundraising events.

Just about when we thought we couldn't knit another row or wave another flag or sit through one more presentation, it was announced that a forestry service unit was to be raised and trained right here in Creston under the command of none other than Captain Mallandaine, who became Major Mallandaine for the job. Since this was a service unit, men who did not meet the medical requirements for combat service would be accepted. You could be up to forty-eight years old and less than five feet tall, you could be partly deaf, flat-footed or disabled in a variety of other ways and still get in. It was a splendid chance for those who had been disappointed in previous attempts to enlist for fighting service to step in now. Men did step forward. Recruiting was brisk. From January 'til April of 1917, Creston streets were full of marching men, shouted orders, military salutes. And in April we turned out in force to see them off to Ontario from where they would go on to service in France. The band played, the people cheered. The sad news of battles and deaths was forgotten for a while. These men were going out to do a useful job of work they knew how to do well. They would be in no great danger. They would build roads, fell and saw trees for huts and field hospitals and duckboards, all to help the war to its conclusion, which surely must come soon.

In the new spate of enthusiasm I knitted my second scarf to a satisfactory end.

Chapter 5

Fear of Falling

Later that year Creston was rocked by a scandal that surpassed even the war news in interest for a few weeks. Mrs. Dixon, a prominent member of Creston society, had run off with Steven Hunt, and – this was said in hushed whispers – she was going to have his child. Most people in town clucked and shook their heads sanctimoniously. They'd always known that clique of socialites, the group Gramps Little called the codfish aristocracy, was a fast bunch. The women smoked and drank. And now their leading figure, Mrs. Dixon was in trouble like a hired girl. That's what came of fast living. Hunt wanted to marry her. At least that much could be said for him. But first she'd have to get divorced.

Divorce was a scandalous business then in Canada, which had one of the lowest divorce rates in the western world. Few were willing to go to the trouble and shame of proving adultery, virtually the only grounds for obtaining a divorce.

In the U.S., however, divorces were easier. So Mrs. Dixon moved across the border to Bonner's Ferry in Idaho to establish residence there, and get her divorce more quickly and easily.

Mrs. Dixon was a good friend of Mum's, and so was Steven Hunt. Perhaps Mum sympathized with their illicit romance. Perhaps she had been unhappy in her own marriage and so was more liberal than her contemporaries on the issue of divorce. Perhaps she was simply fed up with Creston, and the dreary atmosphere of a small town with its good men gone to war, some of them never to come back. Whatever her reasons were, Mum packed us up and we went to Bonner's Ferry to keep Mrs. Dixon company and to try life in the U.S.A.

The U.S. had just entered the war that year, so when we arrived in Bonner's Ferry we found ourselves plunged into the same flurry of flag-waving and patriotic speeches and fundraising that we'd known in Creston for the past three years. Only now the flag was the Stars and Stripes and the music was "Oh say can you see?"

As it happened, most Bonner's Ferry people had been pro-war since the beginning and welcomed the chance to get in on it. The Bonner's Ferry doughboys were one of the first contingents of American soldiers to embark for Europe. Reporters and photographers from all over the nation came to record the send-off. There was even a team of camera men to take a moving picture that would be shown in movie houses all across America. Talk about excitement!

The Bonner's Ferry ladies, like the ladies of Creston, wanted to give their departing heroes some "small token of esteem". They decided on a kit box for each soldier filled with oddments: a little sewing kit, shaving soap, letter paper, cigarettes, chocolate. As part of the ceremonies on send-off day, each soldier was to be presented with his kit by a school girl of the town. I was one of the school girls.

We wore starched white dresses and white stockings and we each had a huge white satin bow tied flat on our heads.

"I know two soldiers who already got killed," I boasted to the girl next to me in line.

"No you don't," she began to argue. "They can't get killed 'til they start to fight in France, stupid."

"These were British soldiers. Lots of them have got killed already. One of them gave me his dog to look after, and now that dog is my dog. I'll show him to you if you don't believe me." The American kids didn't know anything about this war.

"No American soldiers are going to get killed because they're the best," the girl said.

I could never get the better of these kids in argument.

"Girls, stop talking!" A teacher shushed us up. "Listen for the start of your music."

"Some of them will get killed just the same," I whispered the last words of the argument. "Bound to." This knowledge didn't make me any less excited about being part of the grand send-off spectacle.

When the music started I marched proudly forward carrying the little tin box in both hands, like a bouquet of flowers, the way we'd been shown how to do.

The band played. The soldiers stood in a long straight line and we girls marched smartly up to form a line opposite. When the music stopped, each girl handed her kit box to the soldier partner across from her.

"Thanks, sugar," my soldier said. "What a nice present! What's your name, honey?"

"Olwen," I said to his polished boots where the reflection of my white bow bobbed up and down.

"What? I didn't catch the name." He leaned down close to me.

Shutters clicked and the movie camera rolled

"Olwen," I repeated. People never caught my name. What was so complicated about it anyway? But people never got it right. I hated that name.

An officer shouted something, the band began to play again, and my soldier straightened up and marched away. We little girls ran to our proud mothers. But before I could reach my Mum, a very angry lady marched up to me and yanked the white ribbon on my head.

"You bad girl!" she said. "You were supposed to hand over the kit, not strike up a conversation. You've ruined the picture. What do you think you were doing, chattering away to my boy? All the other soldiers were standing straight and tall, the way soldiers should, smiling for the cameras, but my son had to lean down to listen to your nonsense. You ruined the whole thing. You're a very naughty girl."

I tried to tell her I wasn't chattering. "It was him who was talking to me," I tried to say, but she wasn't listening.

"A very naughty girl," she said again and flounced away.

"I didn't talk to him; it was him who talked to me," I wailed when Mum found me.

"What did he say?" she asked.

"He asked me about my stupid name," I said.

"It's not a stupid name," she said with a sigh. This was an old argument. "Never mind. It wasn't your fault. He should have stood straight like a soldier instead of talking about names.

"It's too bad that woman wasn't going off to fight the Germans herself. Wouldn't she give the Kaiser what for!" she added to try to joke me out of my shame, but it was too late. The soldier's mother had convinced me that I'd ruined the ceremony.

When the pictures came out, it was just like the woman said: a row of soldiers, straight as bowling pins, facing the cameras of America, except for only one in the line, bending down to talk to a naughty little girl in a stiff white dress.

When we went to the movies to see the newsreel I had to hide my eyes at that part. I'd ruined the whole thing, and it was all because of my horrible name.

Our family went in for ridiculous names. The funny thing was that most of them had chosen those names. Uncle Took's real name was a perfectly ordinary Henry but he chose to be known instead as Took. Worse still was Aunt Boo, who could have used her real name of Elizabeth. Then there were those who had changed their given names for good reason. My brother's official name was Eifion, a name even worse than mine, but he was sensibly called David. My cousin Hirell Talbot was known as Noonie, though in her case Noonie wasn't much of an improvement, I thought. Only I was left with my original horrible name, that Mum pretended to believe was a beautiful and distinctive name that I should be pleased to have. "Shall I call you Boo instead?" she'd ask when I complained. "Or Anghararadwyllnwll?"

She'd do one of her imitations of what she thought Welsh sounded like and I'd have to laugh. I was stuck with Olwen.

In Bonner's Ferry, the excitement of the doughboys' send-off faded in the months of war that followed. War, the women of Bonner's Ferry were learning, as the women of England and Canada already knew, was more than marching bands, and waving flags, presentations of useful kits and fund-raising socials. Lists of American casualties began to come in. Some of those men who stood straight that festive day of their departure were now fallen.

Then, in 1918, as if war hadn't brought enough of death and suffering, a new scourge devastated the country – the Spanish influenza. There was no cure for the sickness; some pulled through and some didn't. All that could be done was to try to prevent the disease from spreading. People avoided going to public gatherings, and when we did have to go out, we were warned to wear gauze masks. Some said wearing a hot mustard plaster or a hot bread poultice would protect you. Others took hot milk spiced with ginger. Despite these precautions, the flu came to Bonner's Ferry, and deaths. The school was closed. All meetings were cancelled.

My mother was especially worried for me, because she considered me a delicate child. Thinking I'd be safer in a smaller place, she sent me to stay with Gran in Creston.

Although I'd travelled back and forth to Creston several times, this was my first trip alone on the train. I would have preferred to face the danger of catching flu in Bonner's Ferry to that of getting on the wrong train when I had to change at Yahk, and being carried away helpless across the continent.

"You'll manage," Mum insisted. "You're quite capable of undertaking a two-hour train journey on your own. "Everybody in England rides trains all the time," she added. "I used to ride the train to school every day."

"But did you have to change?"

"No," she admitted. "But I daresay I could have done it. Tell you what," she suggested. "I'll write down the names of all the stations, and you can cross out each one as you come to it, so you'll always know where you are."

Not only did she give me the card, but she also introduced me to the conductor, a Mr. Hooper, who promised to keep an eye on me. He did too. He stood right beside me when he called out the stations, and I marked them off on my card. At Yahk he walked across the station platform with me, and told the station master to see that I got on the Creston train.

I completed the journey safely.

One of the first cases of Spanish flu in Creston was Gran. And then I caught it too.

We were both dreadfully ill. Gran's neighbour, Mrs. Spaulding, and Mrs. Mallandaine prepared food for us, brought it to our door, knocked to let Gran know it was there, and left. They could not enter the house for fear of infection.

Gradually Gran got better and, even more gradually, I did.

Then the day cook at the Creston Hotel came down with it. The hotel manager came round to Rosebank. Would Gran consider filling in during the emergency? Certainly she would.

Since there was no school because of the epidemic, I was allowed to go to work with her. We got up early and walked up to the hotel in the cool morning as the sun was lightening the sky behind the Purcell range to a yellowy- greeny-blue, while the Selkirks to the west remained in deep purple darkness.

In the hotel kitchen Gran tied on a long white apron and covered her hair with a white kerchief that made her look like a Duokobor, though she didn't care for the comparison when I made it. She oiled the gas range-top and got the coffee going. "First order of the day!" she called to me.

"Two eggs, sunny side up, bacon, toast and coffee," I read from the menu. I always got to order first and I always ordered the same thing. It was the best possible breakfast, I decided, and when I grew up I would eat exactly that every morning. I ate at the end of the enamelware table where Gran mixed the batter for pancakes in a big yellow bowl, and where she kept her own pot of tea so she could sit and sip a bit and nibble some toast between orders. After I'd eaten, I watched the toaster for Gran and helped the kitchen maid with the dishes and she or the manager usually gave me five cents for my work. I was sorry when the regular cook recovered and returned to work and Gran and I lost our jobs.

One afternoon just when we were beginning to believe life was getting back to normal, Aunt Charlotte's neighbour, Mr. Compton pounded on Gran's door. "Andy's sick bad, and the kids, and Charlotte too," he said. "She says can you come out to the ranch and help them out."

"Of course," Gran said.

"Olwen," she turned to me, "run and ask the doctor to drive out. If he can come before dark, you wait and go with him. If he can't, go to Aunt Olive's for tonight, and walk out to the ranch tomorrow. I'm going to go right now with Mr. Compton."

I ran up Fourth towards Doc Henderson's house. My black pigtails bobbed up and down as I ran and I thought of Gran's story of her famous run for the doctor through the dark and dangerous streets of London with her beautiful golden hair streaming behind her.

It was only late afternoon, and Creston was not the sort of place where one feared getting kidnapped or captured for the white slave trade. Still it seemed to me that because of the war and because of the flu epidemic, I was running through a world that had grown as dangerous as the dark streets of London had ever been in Gran's beautiful youth.

Doc Henderson was in, and he hitched up and we drove in his buggy to Aunt Charlotte's.

"Gran," I asked that night as I was being tucked up to sleep on the couch in the front room, "You know when you ran through the dark and dangerous streets of London with your golden hair streaming behind you to fetch the doctor for Lucy?"

"Yes?"

"Well, what happened to Lucy?"

"Ah, that's the sad part of the story. She died, poor girl."

Aunt Charlotte and all the children pulled through. It was Andy who died. He died on the tenth of November, 1918, the day before the armistice.

Gran took me aside and told me what had happened. Uncle Andy! Dead! But he was a Dad. He was a man who saw to it that no harm would come to us. Now the worst harm had come to him. It didn't seem possible. Old people died, and soldiers in battle, but not Dads. Aunt Charlotte and the cousins wouldn't be a family without Uncle Andy. Of course, my family didn't have a Dad either, but that was different. He wasn't dead, only away in another country, and we were used to his absence. We'd had Uncle Andy as his substitute. Only now we didn't.

Gran said I must not tell anyone about this. My cousins were not to be told of their father's death. "They, and their mother, are too weak to sustain the shock," Gran explained. "You must carry on as you have been and not say not a word, not even to Noonie." Noonie was the cousin closest to my own age and she and I were involved in an intense love-hate relationship.

It was a hard secret to keep, not so much at first when Aunt Charlotte and the kids were too sick to talk to or play with anyway, but later, when Noonie was well enough to get up and sit in the kitchen by the stove for an hour or two in the afternoons. One day she and I were sitting there, squabbling over a game of checkers. We were both restless and out of sorts.

"I know something you don't know, All-Went," Noonie said.

She always called me All-Went when she wanted to make me mad. "You do not," I answered back.

"Do so!"

"Yeah, what then?"

"Your father's dead. That's what. He got killed in the war. Blown up by a bomb."

"Did not!" I said, but somehow I knew what Noonie said was true. I'd noticed certain looks exchanged between adults when the subject of the war came up. I remembered half sentences overheard as I came into a room. Noonie had only told me what I already knew, but hadn't allowed myself to acknowledge. I was filled with rage at her for telling, for making me stop pretending.

"I know something you don't know too!" I cried.

"Do not!" she countered.

"Do too!" I remembered then what Gran had told me. The news of her own father's death could make Noonie sick again and she could die too. I'd promised I wouldn't tell. And besides, she probably already knew, or half knew. That's why she had told me about my father.

"What are you two girls bickering about?" Gran came into the kitchen with an armload of dirty sheets and stuffed them into the huge washing copper on the back of the stove.

"Nothing," I muttered and put on my coat and ran out to the barn. Noonie wasn't allowed outside yet. I sat in the dusty hayloft and cried because, even though I could scarcely remember my father, it was a terrible thing not to have one. And I cried for Uncle Andy, who'd sometimes seemed like a father to me, even if he wasn't, and for Noonie. Now neither of us had a father, neither of us had a real family anymore.

My mother came back to Creston for Uncle Andy's funeral. She told me then that my father was dead, and I cried again, but not very much.

There were many deaths those last months of the war. Hardly a family was not in mourning for a soldier fallen in battle overseas or for a victim of the terrible flu. All the hats Gran made were black.

There were no wild celebrations in Creston to mark the end of the war. People were too tired and too sad to celebrate, and besides, public gatherings were still prohibited on account of the flu.

After the war was over, and the flu epidemic, after Gran at last began making hats in fuchsia and lavender and blue again, there were two more deaths in Creston.

Aunt Charlotte had been much affected by her beloved husband's death. She had always had a goitre problem, and the stress of her grief seemed to exacerbate the condition. She was operated on and died on the operating table. She was twenty-nine years old. My six Talbot cousins were now orphans.

And then there was one more death.

The Spauldings lived on a small farm down the hill from Rosebank. There were four children in the family, of whom Sally, a girl a year younger than me, was my special friend.

The Spauldings kept a dairy herd and supplied most everyone in town with fresh milk. Every morning before school the Spaulding kids would walk through the village with covered pails of milk in a handcart. There were no bottles. You brought out a jug or a lard pail and the Spauldings filled it for you.

Mrs. Spaulding did the milking. The kids delivered the milk and helped with the separating and washing up. Mr. Spaulding kept the accounts.

Mr. Spaulding couldn't do the milking on account of his hands, which had been crippled when he was an infant. He'd been sitting in a high chair by the kitchen fire and the high chair toppled over, straight on to the fire. His hands were burned so badly that they could never be healed, but remained small, stiff, red claws.

The other permanent effect of the traumatic accident on Mr. Spaulding was that for the rest of his life he was terrified of falling. He hated ladders and was in a panic when anyone stood on a chair. He warned all parents of young children to beware of high chairs. He wouldn't have one in his house. He designed and built a small table and chairs for his children to use when they were little to protect them from the fate that had befallen him.

Mr. Spaulding was a gregarious fellow. He liked to walk uptown and have a cup of coffee with the salesmen who were passing through town and staying at the hotel. Then he might go on to hang around the Mercantile for a while and talk to the locals as they came and went. He knew everyone in town and everything that went on. Whenever you were asked about anything going on in town and didn't know the answer, you'd say, "Ask Spaulding!"

One early spring evening, Mrs. Spaulding was in the barn doing the evening milking. Mr. Spaulding had just sent the youngest child, Fred, off to bed. It had been a warm day, and they'd let the fire out in the kitchen range but it would be needed now for heating water to wash the separator and pails after the milking. Mr. Spaulding shook out the ashes, and laid in a twist of newspaper and built kindling in a pyramid. He filled the reservoir with fresh water. He set a match to the kindling and went out to fetch wood. On his way back from the woodpile with an armload of logs, he saw a car chugging up the hill towards town. There were only about a half dozen cars in Creston then, and this wasn't one of them. Spaulding was curious. Who could it be? American tourists come up from Bonner's Ferry? Or had Mr. Dixon gone ahead and got the automobile he'd been talking about buying? Spaulding wanted to walk up to the hotel and find out.

He dumped a couple of logs on the fire. "I'm just stepping up the street for a minute," he called towards the front room as he hurried off. Sally was in the front room, learning her spelling words.

Suddenly she heard a scream from the kitchen. She dashed in to find her youngest brother on fire. Flames were licking up his long flannel nightshirt. He ran towards her and the flames burned brighter.

Sally grabbed the drinking bucket, and dumped it over the boy, but the water seemed to have no effect on the flames.

"Ma! Ma!" She ran screaming to the barn and Fred ran after her, a torch of burning flesh and hair and cloth.

"A blanket!" Mrs. Spaulding shouted when she took in the scene, and ran to push her boy to the ground and smother the flames in the damp grass and her apron. By the time Sally returned with a blanket, the flames were out. "Fetch Doc Henderson," her mother said. "Quick!"

There was little the doctor could do. Fred lived for a day of pain, and died.

Sally was tormented with guilt. "I should have kept an eye on him," she said. "When Ma and Dad are out, it's my job to keep an eye on the little ones."

"It wasn't your fault. Fred was supposed to be in bed," I tried to comfort her.

"I should have kept an eye on him. I should have heard him coming down stairs and playing around in the kitchen. And I was too stupid to think of a blanket for the flames. If I'd thought of the blanket, I could have saved him, and I didn't."

"You can't be sure. I think it was your dad's fault for going out and leaving the matches on the table. And it was Fred's fault for playing with the matches. He was old enough to know better."

But Sally could not be comforted.

My mother took me and my brother to the funeral. As we looked at the small coffin, my mother whispered to me, "Let this be a lesson you never forget. Fire is dangerous."

That was a lesson I already knew. I looked now at the faces around me and learned other, deeper lessons as well. I saw the shocked grief on the face of Mr. Spaulding who feared falling more than he feared fire and thought he had sufficiently safeguarded his family, and I learned that it is not always what we fear that destroys us. Sometimes I saw a look steal across Mrs. Spaulding's face when she looked at her husband that taught me that there are some things that cannot be forgiven, even of those we love. And I saw Sally's guilt and grief and learned that responsibilities can fall upon us without our agreeing to them or even knowing they are there, and they can crush us, even so.

Chapter 6

A Love of Trees

Mum was staying at Rosebank again, having had to give up the house in Bonner's Ferry. My father's pension hadn't come through and she had no money at all. David and I were there too, of course, and Margie, the youngest of the six Talbot orphans. The older Talbot children shuttled back and forth between Rosebank and their uncle's house. Rosebank was overflowing. Some of us were sleeping on feather ticks we rolled out on the shop floor at night. At meals we crowded around the table, two children to a chair. Gran's dream of a little house for herself was long gone.

And then came the news that Uncle Bob was coming for a visit.

Bob was Gran's blind brother. He had been sent to Canada to be educated at Brantford School for the Blind in Ontario, and then he had gone to live with Uncle Percy, a clergyman in Edmonton.

Now Uncle Percy had three almost grown up daughters that he and his wife wanted to see well married. Rightly or wrongly, they felt that the presence of a blind and somewhat eccentric family member in the household was jeopardizing the girls' chances of finding suitable husbands. Their solution was to send Bob on to Gran. "We've done our duty by him; it's time you took a turn," Uncle Percy wrote. "All your daughters are safely married."

When Gran heard of Bob's imminent arrival, she held her hand, palm outward dramatically on her brow, as she liked to do in moments of tension, and wondered how we would all manage to cram into Rosebank. The answer came from Gramps Little, who had a gift for finding generous solutions to problems of all kinds. "He can stay in the shack down by my barn," he offered. "No one's been using it since the hired man joined up."

Gran was grateful. She simply couldn't fit one more body into her little Rosebank. "Thank you, dear Fred. You are always a kind friend to me."

Embarrassed, Gramps busied himself with his pipe. "Well, I've no use for the place. Someone might as well get the use of it before the roof caves in."

Crestonites made a careful distinction between a shack and a house or cottage, though there was often little outward sign of the difference. As far as I could see the main difference was that a shack didn't have curtains on the windows and a house did.

But Gran and Mum hung curtains on the shack that Uncle Bob was to occupy, swept it out, made up the bed and put a clean cloth on the table. Gran even put a vase of spring flowers on the little table by the bed. "Bob is very fond of flowers," she told us, "even if he can't see them."

And so one day in April 1919 Uncle Bob tapped his white cane down the steps of the CPR train westbound from Fort McLeod and into Gran's waiting arms. "Sooo thiiiis is Creeeeston," he said, sniffing the air, turning to face each direction as if to admire the view. He spoke slowly in a high-pitched screech. He was a peculiar looking man, small and thin with bright red hair. Though he'd be close to fifty then, he looked much younger.

"Come along. I'll take you home, Bob." Bob took Gran's arm and easily hefted a battered leather suitcase almost as big as himself, and they set off down the hill to Rosebank and then across the road to the shack that was to be Bob's home for the duration of his visit.

Just as Gran had told us he would be, Bob was very pleased to find the flowers by his bed. He knew immediately that they were daffodils and narcissi. He could identify flowers, trees and all kinds of plants by touch and smell. In a matter of a few days, he could find his way around Rosebank and Creston. He knew the apples trees and the plums and the cherries in the orchards, their scents, and the textures of their bark, and later their blossoms and growing fruits. He especially loved the red cedar by the door of his shack. "Like feathers," he said, stroking the soft needles, "like seaweed." He knew the soft feel of the path through the spinney to the barn and he knew the rows of vegetables in the garden. He knew his way up across the tracks and through town, and down the hill to the flats. He walked with a bouncing step, tapping his cane in front of him, and often humming a dirge-like tune. He soon became a familiar figure in Creston, tap-tapping his way along the wooden sidewalks and the muddy roads.

"Good morning, Bob!"

"Goooood moooorning, Mr. Spaulding."

"Helloooooo, Louis!"

Once a month he fetched from the post office a parcel of books in braille from the lending library of the Institute for the Blind. He loved to read poetry and could recite reams of it in his terrible, screeching voice: Kipling and Tennyson, Longfellow, Thomas Hood. He loved to read and he loved to be read to. David and I took to reading our schoolbooks aloud to him. When we fell in love with the poems of Robert Service, Uncle Bob fell in love with them too. Soon we were all three able to recite long passages of the swinging *Sourdough Ballads* to each other.

Service's poems infected David and me with gold fever and a desire for the rugged outdoor life. We wanted to travel deep into the wilderness and camp out and have many adventures and in the end find an unknown creek bright with gold nuggets and pan them out and come back to civilization bronzed and hardened by the rugged outdoor life, and immensely rich.

"Don't be silly. You're much too young!" was the response we got from both Mum and Gran when we suggested we take a camping trip in the bush.

"Well, if you came with us..." we suggested.

"No."

"Or Gramps?"

We were too young but Gramps was too old, we were told.

Despite our discouragement, we studied maps and made plans, to be ready just in case an opportunity came along and Mum relented and let us go.

And one day opportunity did come. Packrat Robinson was in town, advertising his guiding services. He was the best guide in B.C. If anyone could lead us to the river of our dreams, he could.

Still Mum wouldn't hear of our going. "We couldn't let you children go off into the woods with only Old Packrat to look after you," she said. "And anyway, we couldn't afford it."

To our astonishment, Uncle Bob piped up, "Perhaaaaps I could go with them, look after them, like."

How Mum thought blind Uncle Bob could protect us in a wilderness emergency, I don't know, but when Bob cinched his argument by saying, "I still have tweeeeeelve dollars from the travel money Percy gave me, so I could paaaay Packrat's fee," Mum gave in and said we could go.

"What for would a blind man want to go walking around in them mountains?" Packrat asked when he came round to discuss terms with us.

"I'm foooond of trees," Uncle Bob replied. "I'd like to live amongst them just once in my life."

"Maybe you won't be so fond of 'em when you walk into them, crack your head on 'em, trip over 'em," Packrat said.

"Oh he can walk real good," I assured Packrat. "Show him, Uncle Bob, how good you can walk." Uncle Bob obliged by walking through the Rosebank garden, neatly avoiding trees, wheelbarrow, flowerbeds and baskets. Of course he knew the layout of that garden as well as he knew his own shack.

But Packrat must have been impressed. Or maybe he was in bad need of clients. There weren't so many sportsmen and tourists in the Kootenays, not like there had been before the war. He tugged at his white beard, pushed his leather hat back to scratch his head for a while and finally said, "Well, if that's what yez want, I guess I could take yez up to Clear Lake."

"Hoorah!" Bob gathered David and me up in one of his bone-crunching hugs.

"This ain't no stroll in the garden," Packrat warned us. "You be ready for some hard walking. And don't pack up no feather beds and parlor organs and such. I ain't got but the one hoss."

"Only the one hoooosss," Uncle Bob repeated.

And I burst into one of my renditions of a Service verse:

This is the law of the Kootenays and ever she makes it plain:
Send not your sick and your feeble
Send me your strong and your sane
Sane for the battle before them
Strong for I harry them sore...

"That's a pretty verse," Packrat said in surprise.

"I know more," I said. "I know 'The Shooting of Dan McGrew' and 'The Cremation of Sam McGee' and 'The Man from Eldorado'."

"You'll be an entertainment around the camp fire," Packrat said. "Meet me at Kootenay Landing station from Monday's train." He shook our hands.

Mum and Gran made us up bedrolls, and we borrowed fishing gear and early on a brilliant August day we took the train to the Kootenay Landing station where Packrat and his "hoss" were waiting to take us out into the wilderness.

We walked all day on a forest trail, up a long, steep incline, then down into a cool, damp valley, and then up again. Packrat led the horse, Bess, and we followed. I held Uncle Bob's hand, supposedly to guide him, but after a few hours he was helping me along more than I was helping him.

At noon, on a height of land with nothing but forest all around, we lunched on the tomatoes and hard boiled eggs and jam sandwiches Mum had made for us, and drank water from our canteens. "Faaaar from the maaaadding crowd," Uncle Bob said with satisfaction.

After lunch, we followed a trail only Packrat could see winding down into another valley. Gradually this valley widened and the woods thinned out. There were patches of open meadow now. The land began to slope upward again. Not another ridge to climb! I thought. We were following a small stream which led us up to a lake, little bigger than a pond. After following the lakeshore for a short way, we came to a grassy promontory shaded by a huge old pine tree. The lake water was still, almost black in the late afternoon light. "Here we are, folks. The Kootenay Ritz!" Packrat pointed at a fire ring of blackened stones at our feet.

But he wouldn't let us flop down on the soft grass and enjoy the view. He said, "Matter of fact, I guess maybe this ain't the Ritz 'cause there ain't no dining room staff. We got chores to do."

Tired as we were from our trek, we set about getting the tent up, finding firewood, and unpacking the bedrolls and cooking utensils. Well, you had to be tough to survive in the wilderness, we reminded each other.

"Make a lot of noise while you're working, lads, scare off any of them rattlers or grizzly bears might be hanging around," Packrat warned us with a scary leer. You also had to be brave to live in the wilderness.

Packrat hobbled the horse and walked along the lakeshore to a fishing spot he knew of to catch our supper, while we got the fire going and put a pot of water on a flat stone to heat.

In a surprisingly short time Packrat was back with a mess of bass. He showed us how to lace them on green sticks to grill. We ate them with great chunks of bread off tin plates, using only knives for cutlery.

After we'd eaten, Packrat brewed up a billycan of thick green tea and lit up his pipe. We sat quiet, cradling enamel mugs of the hot tea, and listening to the sounds of the night beyond our campfire: the splash of a fish in the lake just a few feet away, or, more disturbing, a swish of branches as though some animal was moving through the brush. I was glad Packrat was with us.

"Have you ever actually seen a grizzly?" Dave asked, as if he were thinking the same fearful thoughts as I.

"Seen a grizzly! I'll say! I've seen 'em, and I've shot 'em, and one time I recall I was dang near caught by one. Chased me up a tree, he did."

"How did you escape?"

"Well, I'll tell you how. I was a-chewin of tobaccy at the time, do you see. Now when that bear came up the tree after me, I waited 'til he got so close I could feel his breath on my heels, then I looked down, and waited just a tad longer 'til the brute opened his mouth to bite off my feet, than I took my aim, and splat! I sent that tobaccy juice right into his maw. Well didn't he yelp and holler! I sent a couple of squirts more down, hoping to get him in the eye, but I won't swear I did. I couldn't take proper aim, do you see, cause the critter was tossing his head this way and that, and backing out of the tree. When his feet touched the ground, he shambled off, looking for water, I doubt.

"I don't never go out in the woods without my tobaccy ever since. You never know when it might be needed."

Uncle Bob and David and I all began to wonder if maybe we ought to take up tobacco chewing.

The fire was dying down. When Uncle Bob suggested it was time to turn in, none of us argued.

Packrat slept outside by the fire; he got to feeling crowded up in a tent, he said. I was glad he was out there, his mouth full of tobacco, guarding us from the dangers of the night.

The bedrolls were not quite as comfortable as they'd seemed when we tried them out on the floor at Rosebank, but we were so tired we could have slept on the bare ground, or even standing up.

The days that followed were as perfect as our dreams. We woke to the smell of bacon and coffee, and, shivering as we breakfasted close to the fire, we watched the sun burn the mist off the little lake. David and I spent the daylight hours swimming and fishing and panning for gold in the stream that flowed into the lake. While we panned, Packrat sat against a tree and smoked and thought up stupid jokes, like "Poor old Bess. How the deuce is she going carry out all the gold you kids are finding. Heh heh." And "You kids become millionaires on this trip, I'm a-going charge you double rates, I give yez fair warnin'. Heh. Heh."

We didn't mind the teasing. We were finding lots of rocks that looked like they might have gold streaks in them. Anyway, it was fun standing in the cold, clear river water or sitting on the bank, our feet and hands blue with cold while the sun baked our backs and we sifted through likely-looking gravel and sand.

While we worked, Uncle Bob whittled or played his harmonica or walked around touching trees, stroking their bark, feeling their leaves or needles. Sometimes he told his stories or recited poems to Packrat who listened attentively, not minding how long it took Bob to get through a story with his slow voice.

We ate bacon and bannock for breakfast, cold bacon or cold fish and bannock and dried apples for lunch, and grilled fresh-caught fish for supper. Uncle Bob was the best of us at the fishing, because he was patient enough to wait quietly 'til he felt a tug on the rod. Of course he wasn't as good as Packrat though.

After supper we gazed at the fire or up into the night sky where the stars blazed with a brightness we'd never seen before. We listened to Packrat's stories and then Packrat would get us to recite the Service poems over and over. Or we'd sing to Uncle Bob's harmonica: "Clementine," "My Darling Nelly Grey," "John Peel," and the new song from the war, "It's a Long Way to Tipperary". Packrat said it sure was some different from guiding fellows who came out to the woods to drink themselves drunk.

On the morning of the fourth day we folded up the bedrolls, took down the tent and loaded up old Bess, choosing only a few of our very best rocks to carry out, and began the long walk back to the real world.

It was the best holiday of our lives, we all agreed. For me, those few summer days remain etched in my memory as the last perfect days of my childhood. Never again was I so purely, so unthinkingly happy as I was then.

For Uncle Bob, it was the greatest adventure and probably the highlight of his life. He talked about it as long as he lived. "When we were caaaamping at Cleaaaaar Laaake," he would begin.

His "visit" to Creston went on for years and years, almost to the end of his life.

Chapter 7

The Return

It was a cool summer evening and Rosebank was strangely quiet. Little Margie was asleep; the other Talbot children were at their uncle's ranch for the day, and our David with them. Gran and I sat at the kitchen table hulling strawberries for tomorrow's jam making. This was the moment Mum chose for her announcement.

First she filled the blue granite-wear tea pot and set it to steep at the back of the kitchen stove. She set out cups and saucers. "I have come to a decision," she announced. She poured milk into each cup and added a spoonful of sugar to mine. In our household, any momentous news called for a ritual tea drinking.

Gran pushed the basin of strawberries aside. "Yes?"

Not 'til she had poured the tea and taken her place at the table did Mum reply. "I shall return home to England."

"England? Home?" I was astonished. Though to be sure England was always referred to by Mum and Gran as "home", to me it was as unreal a place as "our heavenly home" in church services and prayers. Creston was home.

It seemed that Gran too was baffled. "Home! To England! Do you really mean to go?"

"I do." Mum sipped her tea calmly. "You know I've always intended to return."

Gran clasped her red-stained hands to her aproned bosom. "But this is so sudden. I had thought that you meant to remain in Creston for some time."

Mum smiled. "You can hardly say we haven't had a good long visit! It's going on nine years we've been here. High time to take our leave, I'd say."

In the face of Gran's handwringing and my open-mouthed astonishment, Mum marshalled her reasons. "I want to have my own house at last. All this time I've been crowding in with you – not that I'm not grateful – or renting places. I'd like to settle down for good in a home of my own, and now that the pension money has come through at last, I have the means to do it."

"But not here in Creston?"

"No. England's *home*. I want to go back before it's too late. I want the children to go to proper English schools, to have cultural opportunities they're not getting here. I'd like them to get to know the family, and Tom's family in Wales too. They have no idea of their heritage, growing up here. If it hadn't been for the war, I'd have returned ages ago. Creston's all very well, but, well, it's a backwoods place."

"In any case," she pointed out, "one of us will have to take the Talbot children over to Boo and Took and Walter." It had been arranged that three of the Talbot children were to be given new homes with aunts and uncles in England, while Mum took in the youngest, Margie, and Gran took the oldest two, Andrew and Noonie. "I see," said Gran. She looked sad.

"I can't think why you want to stay here yourself, now that Charlotte's gone. Think of it. Once the children and I are back in England, your whole family will be there: Boo and Took and Walter, and almost all your grandchildren as well."

"Yes," Gran agreed. "But I shall have Noonie and Andrew here. And Uncle Bob. And Olive is close by, and many, many dear friends." She looked over towards Gramps' house. "And Mae and Percy not an unreasonable journey from here should I wish to travel, which I doubt I shall."

"You must do as you think best," Mum said.

"As must you," Gran agreed. Each of the women thought she was doing the right thing; each was disappointed that the other disagreed. The parting would be painful.

We children were excited at the idea of the coming adventure. We talked of nothing else but The Return. Mum showed us on a map the route we would follow all across Canada to Montreal and then across the Atlantic Ocean to Liverpool, England, and then by train to London, the centre of the whole British Empire.

England, we children knew, was a wonderful place where everything was exactly the way it should be. We knew this from years of comments from Mum and Gran. If, for instance, the Creston sun was too hot on a July day, or the train bringing the newspaper from Nelson was late, or there appeared a spelling mistake in that paper, Mum or Gran would remark that such a thing would never happen "back home". If anything broke or wore out too fast – the handle off a tea cup, the kitchen clock, a pair of shoes – then the most likely reason was that the item was of shoddy foreign manufacture. "Canadian quality," Mum would sniff. She always tried to buy products with "Made in England" stamped on them. They were bound to be the best.

David and the Talbots pestered me with questions about this marvellous England that we were to see at last. I pretended that I remembered England, though really it was as much of a fairyland to me as it was to them. I repeated what Mum and Gran had told us and described what I'd seen in the photographs in the *Country Life* magazines Aunt Boo sent us.

"The roses are magnificent. You have different money and it's worth a lot more than Canadian money. The grass is always green. London, which is where we'll be, is the largest city in the world. There are no mountains. It rains a lot. Everyone talks like Mum and Gran. Children are always polite and obedient."

"And I'll be going to a boarding school, and I'll have a cap with my school's crest on it," David put in.

This was a sore point. There was no question about David's getting to go to a boarding school and wear a smart uniform, just because he was a boy, and all nice boys in England went to boarding schools, according to Mum. But girls did too, I reminded her. I had read all about them in the Angela Brazil girls' boarding school stories that my English aunts sent me at Christmas. I longed to go to a school like the ones in those stories. I wanted to wear a gym tunic and a tie and a hat with a rolled brim, and live in a dormitory and have friends with names like Penelope and Daphne. I was going to be furious if I didn't get sent to a boarding school too, I warned.

"We'll see, after we talk to Uncle Will about our financial situation." That was as far as Mum would promise.

After my father's death, his brother Will had taken charge of financial matters for Mum. She had given him power of attorney to facilitate the signing of documents, since he was on the spot in London. There was an insurance payment, and a generous pension from the army. It seemed that Mum would be richer as a widow than she'd ever been as a wife. She was grateful to Will for his help in sorting things out.

She was to have one of the new houses the government was providing for officers and officers' widows. "Houses for Heroes" they were called. Mum applied for the lease of one in Havering, a small town in Essex close to her brother Took's home.

"That will be most convenient for you," Gran said. "You will be not far from Boo and within half a day's journey of Walter as well."

In all the excitement of anticipation, it was not 'til our suitcases were packed up and we were making our round of farewell visits that I realized that going "home" meant leaving home. A sense of loss overwhelmed me. Gran was a second mother to me and Rosebank the only permanent home I knew. Mum had moved me and David to Bonner's Ferry and back and in and out of rented houses from time to time, but Gran and Rosebank had remained the same, always welcoming us "home". I could hardly comprehend what life without Gran close in the background would be. And Uncle Bob. Who would read to him and listen to his slow, screechy recitations? And the Talbot kids. Even if Noonie and I had our spats, we were close as sisters, and now we would be half a world apart. And there was Sally Spaulding down the road: she and I were writing a play together. Now we'd never have a chance to finish it, let alone stage it. Yes, I wanted to go to this wonderful place called England, but I wished we could take everything and everyone with us, or that we could go and take a look, and then come back to Creston. It was sad and frightening to think of a life in which Rosebank and Creston would be far, far away. I wondered if I didn't envy Noonie and Andrew, even though they said they envied me.

And then there were last minute changes in the plans. Uncle Took wrote to say that much as he'd like to take in and provide for one of the Talbot boys, he really couldn't. He and his wife had four children of their own and were barely managing. Then Fred said that if Bob wasn't going to England, he wouldn't go either. He'd run away if they tried to make him. If they put him on the train, he would jump off. If they got him as far as the boat, he would jump off that. He and Bob were sticking together. They'd get jobs. They'd look after themselves. They wouldn't be a trouble to anyone, but they were staying here.

Their protest threw Gran and Mum into a dither. Gran alternately wrung her hands and pushed the news away from her troubled brow with open palm. Mum was thin-lipped with anger at first but soon looked more sad than angry. She and Gran and Aunt Olive, and the rector from the church and others held long conclaves at Gran's kitchen table. I overheard snatches of their deliberations. "The children must stay in the family." "Charlotte and Andy would want their children to be happy above all. Money wouldn't matter to them." "Too much change will not be good." "Those two boys are so close." The upshot of the talks was that Fred and Bob would remain in Creston under Gran's guardianship. Olive and Alphabetical and others in the community would help out. Crestonites would see to it that those four Talbot kids always had a roof over their heads and food to eat. They'd be all right.

That left only two Talbots, Margie and Charles, who would travel with Mum, Dave and me to England. Margie, who was too young to know where she was going, would stay with us, and Charles was to be delivered into his Aunt Boo's keeping. He was a little uncertain about his future in England, as were David and I, but full of excitement about the journey and all the new experiences that lay in store for us.

Any misgivings were forgotten as plans progressed until one day in August, dressed in smart new clothes, we boarded a Pullman coach on the CPR, heading east. We travelled in style. We sat on plush velour seats that at night a porter transformed magically into comfortable bunks with heavy canvas curtains pulled across and net hammocks for holding our clothes. It was like sleeping in a moving tent. You could push up the stiff brown blind and look out on the night sky with clouds scudding by and now and then the lights of a town or a lonely farm winking far away.

During the day we could walk through the swaying coaches to the open observation platform at the back of the train. We travelled through the beautiful and exciting Crow's Nest Pass, the train seeming to be suspended on the edge of precipitous slopes. We would plunge suddenly into the thundering darkness of a tunnel, cross chasms on high trestle tracks, catch sight of the engine as the train turned back on it itself and then lose it again on a straighter stretch. When we passed through towns, we waved to children who stood on station platforms and stared at us enviously.

Three times a day we swayed through more coaches to the dining car with its two rows of tables covered with spotless stiff white damask cloths. The white-coated waiter held Mum's chair for her with an obsequious bow, and flicked out a large starched white napkin for each of us, while Mum decided what we would order.

She insisted on plain food. "I don't want any of you falling sick on me." But even plain food tasted exotic when served with such elegance.

At our last dinner on the journey, as a special treat, Mum let us order whatever dessert we wanted and I chose chocolate cake. I was eating my way slowly through the large piece on my plate, savouring each delicious mouthful, and, as was my custom, saving the best part, the icing, for the last.

Just as I was about to plunge my fork into its sweet, creamy chocolate thickness, a hand reached out and whipped the plate away from me. "Never save the best for the last," a deep voice above me said.

Immobilized and struck dumb by the swiftness and the unexpectedness of the action, I watched a white-haired gentleman in a black suit stride on along the aisle between the tables and disappear behind the swinging door at the end of the coach. I put my empty fork back on the table. David and Charles turned to stare down the aisle after him.

"Did the waiter take that away before you were finished?" Mum asked. She had been spooning the last of an ice cream sundae she was sharing with Margie into the child's eager mouth and hadn't noticed the quick scooping away. "Really! He might have asked."

"It wasn't the waiter who took it away," I answered.

"I imagine it was. They want to hurry us along and get ready for the next service. I'll ask him to bring it back," Mum raised an arm, but I tugged it down.

"It wasn't the waiter. It was just a man. An old man. And I think he passed the plate into the kitchen."

"Well of all the nerve!" Mum was up on her feet, ready to fight for my lost bit of cake.

"Please don't," I urged her.

It wasn't just that I didn't want her to make an embarrassing fuss. It was because I saw in a sudden flash of recognition that the old man was right. It was silly always to save the best for the last. It wouldn't taste any better then. I wouldn't do it again. It was like that poem we learned in school. "Gather ye rosebuds while ye may."

"Eat your icing while ye may." I muttered this aloud. I would make it a rule of my life.

David heard me. "I've already eaten mine," he said.

"Me too," Charles said.

"Too," Margie crowed, and beamed at us. She didn't know what we were talking about.

I was the only hoarder, but I never would be again.

"Sit down, Mum," I said.

And Mum, though she ranted on for a bit about perfect strangers who make bold with other people's dinners, sat down and drank her tea.

I have remembered the strange man's lesson all my life.

Our journey from Montreal to Liverpool on the *SS Metagama* was even more luxurious than the train had been. The *Metagama* was one of the CPR's cabin class steamers, boats designed for the increasing number of middle-class travellers who wanted comfort, but who were a little too modest or too parsimonious to choose the aristocratic first class. All the accommodations in cabin class steamers, the advertisements said, were of first-class standard, at a reasonable rate.

I enjoyed the first few hours of the journey. I ate a grand dinner in the palatial dining room finishing with a "*gateau surprise*" from which I ate the icing first. Then I got seasick. From then on the luxury and delights of the journey were wasted on me. I stayed in our cabin or, at Mum's insistence, out on a deck chair, wrapped in a blanket and benefitting from the sea air. I consumed almost nothing but dry crackers and tea. The boys made me even sicker with reports of the meals the rest of them had just eaten and the great games and entertainments going on. Even little Margie tried to tell me about a wonderful rocking horse she rode on in the playroom. The thought of riding a rocking horse on this rocking boat made my stomach heave over again.

I was furious with myself to think of what I was missing. I wish I could have packaged up the trip to enjoy it on dry and steady land.

We arrived at Liverpool in a heavy rain. A porter found our bags and conducted us through the din of a huge echoing station to the London train and we moved out into an afternoon that was almost as dark as night. We had tea in the dining car, but here the table cloths were not so stiff and white, and the waiter was not so attentive as what we had come to expect on the CPR. I still couldn't eat anyway. Back in the compartment, the boys and I put our faces against the damp windows to see what we could of England but we saw only darkness and rain and sometimes a dim-lit station.

Chapter 8

Orphan

Aunt Boo didn't know what to think. Long after Clary had left for work and Percival gone to school, she sat on at the breakfast table in her North Finchley home. For the third time she read the letter that had come in the morning post from her sister Sarah and still she could not quite believe its news. Sarah was proposing that Boo and Clary adopt one of poor Charlotte's orphans. Actually, she wasn't proposing, or suggesting or asking. She was bringing the child to them. They were almost on their way. They would arrive in a month's time. "Charlotte's last thoughts were for her children. She was most anxious that they should remain in the family," Sarah's letter said. "We thought Charles would fit in best with your family as he is almost the same age as your Percy."

Another child would not fit into Boo's family. Her family was complete. She and Clary were not among those people who adore children, dogs and playful kittens indiscriminately. They had the one child – a miniature adult really, was young Percy – and that was quite enough.

Another child, a child they did not know and did not want, would disrupt their life. Boo really didn't see how she could cope.

On the other hand, how could she disregard the dying wishes of poor Charlotte? Grief at her sister's death overcame Boo once again.

How could it be that Charlotte, the youngest and the dearest of the family, would die at such a young age? And her husband before her. And six children left orphaned. Of course the family must care for them now. Of course she would take one of those dear little children and care for him as if he were her own. She must. It was her duty.

But really, it would be so terribly inconvenient for her and Clary and for Percival too. It was too much to ask of them. She'd never be able to cope. She and Clary weren't good with children. Their nerves weren't up to it. Couldn't Sarah take the boy? After all, she too had a boy more or less the same age. Why couldn't Charlotte's boy fit in with her family, instead of with Boo's? Furthermore, Boo didn't like the way Sarah had decided the child's fate without consulting with her. Perhaps she might have preferred to take in one of the girls instead of the boy.

Charles, the boy was called, after his mother, poor Charlotte. Boo wept fresh tears. She folded the letter back into its envelope. She would see what Clary had to say when he came home from work this afternoon.

What Clary had to say was this: "How dare your family foist an unwanted child upon us? 'They've decided this boy is to live with us,' they write. Write back at once and say he can't come. We won't have him."

"I dare say that would be the thing to do," Boo said. It was what Clary wanted. In truth, it was what she herself wanted. It was the most sensible way to deal with the problem. But Boo couldn't make herself write that letter. Every time she thought of doing so, the image of her dear, dead sister came before her, weeping for her little boy. If the roles had been reversed, Charlotte would have taken in her Percival without a moment's hesitation, she knew. But Boo was not so loving and easy-going a person as Charlotte and not so fond of children either. Imagine Charlotte's having had six of them! She really shouldn't have had so many. The mere thought of another child always underfoot gave Boo nervous palpitations. And Clary, she knew, would be at the end of his tether if a noisy little boy should create mischief around their beautiful house, which this boy would no doubt do. Colonial children, Boo believed, were generally an undisciplined lot.

If only she could say a clear "no", they wouldn't have to deal with the problem. Their little family could go on undisturbed in its ways.

But if Boo wrote that "no" letter, her mother would never forgive her for her selfishness, nor Sarah, and worst of all, Boo would never be able to forgive herself.

She didn't know what to do.

Every day she determined to write the letter of refusal, and every day she couldn't bring herself to do it. She needed to think about it more. Perhaps she could come up with an alternate plan that would suit everyone. Was the child too young for the navy, she wondered. She seemed to remember hearing that midshipmen were taken on at a very early age. Or there were live-in apprenticeships with chances for a boy to advance: gardener's boy or under-footman for a ducal establishment. How old was the boy again? Boo calculated. He'd be nine or ten, she thought: too young then for apprenticeship. Boo turned over ideas and thought and fretted and did not write the decisive letter. To make no decision is preferable to making the wrong decision was one of the maxims by which she directed her life. Sometimes, she had found, the problem solved itself; sometimes Clary solved it for her; and sometimes it proved to be not a great problem at all. So perhaps the arrival of Charles would be no problem. Or perhaps Sarah's plan for him would change and he would go elsewhere.

Boo fretted and thought until it was only a week before Sarah and the boy were to arrive and then it was too late to do anything. The problem had not been solved but at least the agony of making a decision was over. Boo broke the news to Clary at breakfast time when he wouldn't have time to rage at her for long because he'd have to leave for work.

Understandably, Clary was furious. "I could not do it," Boo said. "It would have been quite wrong." She took the moral high ground in her defence. "It is my duty – it is our duty – to give my orphaned nephew a home."

Clary folded his newspaper carefully. "I should have written the letter myself. I might have known you wouldn't be up to saying no; you've always been too soft-hearted." He sighed dramatically and stood up from the table. "The die is cast. Let him come, if he must." He picked up the folded newspaper. "I'm taking this to read on the tube." He leaned over to give his wife a cold kiss on the cheek. "Just don't expect me to be pleasant and fatherly to the boy."

"But you are never pleasant to anyone, dear!" Boo smiled. "Except to myself and dear Percy."

"I don't *need* to be pleasant to anyone. I supply the funds for you to be pleasant," Clary fired a final salvo, and left for work.

That was just Clary being cranky, Boo knew. He'd be good to the boy, not overly friendly, but correct and fair. That's what a boy needed really, not a chum who played cricket and built model boats with him. Look how well their Percy had turned out under Clary's parenting. Boo just hoped she could fill the role of surrogate mother as effectively.

While she prepared a bedroom for the new family member, the doorbell rang. It was the telegraph boy with a wire from Sarah. When she had deciphered the cryptic message between the "stops" Boo ascertained that Sarah and her children would be staying for an indefinite time "to help Charles settle in". This was worse and worse.

"Sarah's lot won't stay long, of course," she offered as comfort to Clary when she told him at tea time of the added trial they were to endure.

"How many children does Sarah have?" Clary asked, rolling his eyes.

"Two, I believe. Possibly three." Boo stirred two precious teaspoons of sugar into her tea. "Let us hope that it is the lower number."

"Does that woman think we're running a residential hotel here as well as an orphanage?" Clary asked.

Boo laughed in her peculiar high-pitched sort of whinny, and Clary continued, "Does she know food is still rationed here? Who does she expect to feed and house her and her brood while they're here? Good old Clary, of course! She has an infernal nerve, she does. Traipsing across the Atlantic the way you or I might undertake a trip across London! She should stay in Canada, the silly woman. And all the rest of your family with her."

Clary was working himself into one of his rages. It was so bad for his heart. It was up to Boo to calm him down. "There really is no help for it. We can't, we really can't, put my own sister out on the street, no more than we can refuse to give Charles a home. Besides, you used to quite like Sarah, I remember."

"I may have, but that was before she was in charge of an infant army needing homes."

"I expect Charles is a lovely little boy," Boo said.

"Do you, indeed?" Clary stomped out of the room.

"...and will be a good companion for our Percival," Boo called after him to the closing door.

The day came. The visitors were to arrive on the late train and take a taxi to the house. Boo would wait up for them alone. At nine o'clock, his usual time, she tucked Percy into his bed. "When you wake in the morning you will have a new brother. Won't that be nice?" she asked with false cheerfulness.

Percy considered. "What if he's a naughty boy?"

What indeed? Boo wondered even as she assured Percy that Charles was his own cousin and therefore sure to be a very nice boy.

"If he isn't, I shall bite him," Percy decided.

"Oh no, dear. That will hardly be necessary. Good night now." Boo turned off the light and closed the door half way, as Percy liked it.

Clary went to bed at ten, as he always did. As was his custom, he turned off the electricity in the house. "It's too risky to have electricity running into the house when I'm not up and alert," was his belief. "Fire might break out and the house burn to cinders while we slept."

"Tonight I could turn it off before I come up to bed," Boo suggested.

"You wouldn't know how to cope." Clary left her two candles.

Boo waited. There. The sound of a motor on the street. Yes, stopping. A door slamming. Footsteps. Boo took up a candle and hurried to the front door.

"We're here!" Sarah's well-remembered voice called in greeting. A sudden vision of their girlhood came to Boo and she held her sister close for a long, sweet moment. "Sarah, my dear!"

Then she recollected herself. "And the children!"

Sarah put an arm around one of the boys. "This is Charles."

Boo looked at the pale, solemn boy who stared back at her with her dead sister's round grey-blue eyes. She had not expected the boy would look so much like Charlotte. It was almost frightening.

"And this is Margie, Charlotte's youngest, poor little mite." Sarah turned the baby she held in her arms for Boo to admire. Boo glanced at it without interest. All babies looked more or less alike.

"Well now, come in, all of you," she waved them in. "These other children are your own?"

"Yes. You remember your Aunt Boo, don't you, Olwen? And David?" Olwen and David stepped forward to be kissed.

"Well, I expect you'll be tired as that little one." Boo nodded at the baby sleeping on Sarah's shoulder. "You'll want to go to bed straightaway. We'll talk in the morning. Don't come down until I call you." She was too tired to visit tonight. She didn't want to know anything more about Charles or about Charlotte's death or about the rest of the family. She couldn't cope. She wanted only to sleep.

She showed her visitors to the attic room she'd readied for them. Sarah and the girls could share the bed. The boys would sleep on the floor. "Boys don't mind a hard bed," Boo told them. It would not do to make them comfortable here. Lord knows how long they'd stay if she made things too agreeable. She left them a candle and bade them good night.

Four children in the house! Five, counting Percy. Oh dear, oh dear! Boo was tired of the company of them already. She pulled on her nightgown and slipped into bed beside Clary who was snoring in that soft soothing hum he had. She told herself that perhaps the situation would look more normal in the morning, although, really, she didn't believe that it would. She wished that boy didn't look so much like his mother.

In the morning, after Clary had left for work and Percy for school, Boo called the troops from Canada down for breakfast. She gave the three older children slices of bread and dripping and sent them out to play.

"What will we play?" Olwen asked, looking out at the mournful grey street.

"You'll think of something," Sarah said.

Charles immediately set out to climb the tree in next door's garden. "Come down out of that!" Boo shouted, but too late. Her neighbor Mrs. Briggs was already at her door threatening to call a bobby.

"Sorry!" Boo called to appease Mrs. Briggs. This was even worse than she had feared. The child hadn't been out for two minutes and already there was trouble with the neighbours. Mrs. Briggs nodded, offered a brief "good morning," glared at Charles 'til he was off her property and then retreated, slamming her front door behind her.

"Stay on the pavement and don't go past the corner either way." Boo closed her own door against the three unhappy children slouching against her garden fence.

In the sitting room Boo addressed her sister. "Now then. Put that infant somewhere where it can do no harm. You and I must talk."

Sarah's account of Charlotte's death was heart-rending. "She was weakened by her own bout with the flu and with nursing the children, and then Andy's death nearly finished her. If it hadn't been for the children, I think she would have turned her face to the wall and died with him. But for the sake of those children, she fought for her life through the pain. When she knew she might die, she was frantic with worry for them, pleaded for them with her dying voice. We promised her we'd look after them, see that they would be loved and cared for and that they would have the best lives they could have.

"Telling the poor little souls their mother was dead was the hardest thing I've ever had to do. They were in shock for days afterwards.

We've all been trying to do our best for them and I think they're coming along. Charles is a grand boy," Sarah finished. "He'll be good company for Percy."

"I suppose," Boo said. She was moved by Sarah's description. She too wanted to do her best for the little boy. "But I honestly wonder if my nerves are up to the strain of another child. It comes as such a shock to me. I have never been as strong as you, Sarah."

"Nonsense," Sarah replied to that. "You are perfectly well. And two children are no more trouble than one. They amuse each other."

"Percy has never been a trouble," Boo reminded her.

"Nor will Charles be. He's a good boy. Once he's been here with you for a couple of months, you won't know how you ever got along without him, I'm sure."

"You're sure of too much, Sarah. Clary, I tell you straight out, is not at all pleased at the thought of another child in our household."

"Clary will come to love Charles as much as you will."

Boo doubted if that was how it would be. But they would at least do their duty by the boy.

Clary greeted his visitors upon his return from work at tea time.

"Well, well, here's our orphan from Canada," he shook Charles' hand. "Lost both parents. Dear, dear. You know what Oscar Wilde said: 'To lose one parent may be regarded as a misfortune; to lose both looks like carelessness.' Ha!Ha! Ha!"

"Ha! Ha! Ha!" Cousin Percy echoed.

Charles flushed red, balled his fists. "I didn't lose them. They died."

"Yes, dear. Your uncle was joking." Aunt Boo gave him an awkward little hug. Not a very funny joke, Charles thought.

Everyone sat down to tea then, and while the adults talked family, Charles and Percy eyed each other suspiciously over plates of fish paste sandwiches and walnut cake.

"Percy will show you the room we've chosen for you," Aunt Boo said when Charles had refused a third piece of cake to be polite, though he would have taken it if he'd been urged.

Percy led the way. It was a grand house, huge by Creston standards. Charles was impressed as he followed Percy, lugging his case down from the attic bedroom, careful not to bang it against furniture. Percy opened a second-floor door to a room with a neat wooden bedstead and a chest of drawers and a table and chair by the window. It would be the first time Charles had ever had a room to himself.

"How do you like it?" Percy asked.

"Skookum," Charles said, overawed, "real skookum."

Percy snorted. "What on earth does that mean?"

Charles set down his case. "It means 'very nice'."

"Indeed," Percy said with another snort.

Charles had a bad feeling that despite the grandeur, he wasn't going to like his new home. He thought it might be lonely sleeping all alone in a room.

And he didn't much like Percy.

"You'll get used to life in England," Aunt Sarah had said. "Soon, you'll be so busy, you and Percy, that you'll forget about little old Creston and your friends and family there. And you must always be grateful to Aunt Boo and Uncle Clary for taking you in and giving you a home."

Well, he would do his best. He'd already noticed Aunt Boo was going to be pretty fussy about tidiness and wiping his boots when he came in and about exactly where he could play and where he could not. He wasn't used to that. There weren't many rules in their house on the ranch. Mostly he and his brothers and sisters got on with their chores and with whatever games they wanted to and only got yelled at when they did something really stupid or dangerous or mean, and that was only fair. He wondered how he'd get on with Aunt Boo and her rules, and Uncle Clary who made strange jokes and this boy who wore a tie all day long and talked like a grown-up.

As for England, Aunt Sarah had made it out to be the greatest place on earth, but so far he wasn't much impressed. England was grey rain and tiny little fenced gardens with trees you weren't allowed to climb and dirty, crowded streets.

He didn't think much of it. And he'd never forget Creston, no matter what Aunt Sarah said.

Chapter 9

A Hero's Home

Our stay at Aunt Boo's house was not pleasant. Every night when Mum tucked me and Margie, way too early, into our cold bed in the cold bedroom, I'd ask," When are we going to move into our Hero's House?"

"As soon as it's ready," was her reply. "And let us pray that will be very soon," she'd add with a wink.

I envied David who had left for his boarding school the day after we arrived. He wore his new cap and blazer with the school crest on them and he had a tin trunk with his name painted on it. I felt sorry for myself and little Margie because we weren't going anywhere for a while, and even sorrier for my poor cousin Charles who was to stay at Aunt Boo's forever. I wondered if he was wishing he'd made a protest about leaving Creston too. At least he got to go to school during the day though, and I didn't.

After a week or two of boredom, Mum left Margie in the care of Charles and a reluctant Aunt Boo and took me on a trip to Wales to see Uncle Will and my father's family. We broke our journey in Birmingham to see Uncle Wyatt, another of my father's brothers, and his new wife, Oliver.

Oliver? That was a strange name for a woman, and another to be added to my list of strange names in the family. Oliver herself was also strange. She was more than six feet tall and thin as a rake. She wore trousers and high boots and smoked like a man.

They were packing up, Wyatt told us in apology for the disorder of boxes and crates that filled the room where they received us. They were going to emigrate to Australia. "England is finished," Wyatt told Mum. "The war has done for us. You should never have come back."

"I should say Australia is the right place for those two nuts," Mum said when we were back on the train to Wales.

Uncle Will met us at the train station in Caernarfon with a hired car and driver to take us up into the hills to the little village of Llanaelhaearn, where grandfather Evans lived. In contrast to morose Uncle Wyatt, Uncle Will was all smiles and charm, and he was very good looking as well. He embraced Mum and me and gave a tender speech about the sadness of our loss, and how all Tom's family mourned with us and what a wonderful man Tom had been. Then he got us into the car and asking solicitous questions about our health and the rigour of the journey, tucked a rug over our knees and squeezed mine as he did so. He complimented Mum on her hat and me on my beautiful hair. Before we'd gone far, Mum was chatting happily and I was thinking Uncle Will was about the most glamorous uncle a girl could have.

"I'm afraid I had to use some of poor Tom's money," he apologized to Mum when the subject came around to the business affairs he'd handled with power of attorney.

"That's quite all right," Mum replied graciously. "I realize you will have had certain expenses to meet, bills to settle and so on."

"Ah, good. You know how it is then." Will smiled. We drove on into Llanaelhaearn.

Wales was better than England. The weather was just as wet, but there were mountains, although nothing like as high and wild as the Kootenays around Creston. There were no orchards and no forests; only green fields dotted with white sheep and separated by low stone walls. In grandfather's small grey-stone house in the village, a huge crowd of Evanses were always hanging about: aunts and uncles and cousins and half-cousins. Once you got used to the crowded conditions and the lack of light and the din, the cottage was a friendly place. All day long, it seemed, men argued, babies cried, women and children shouted to be heard and sometimes everyone broke into song. There was always washing festooned around the kitchen range, and meals of bread and tea and bacon were served at all hours on the long blackened table that nearly filled the rest of the room. Mum spoke in a loud clear voice and the Evans answered her in lilting sing-song English.

Among themselves and to me they spoke Welsh, and I found I could understand what they said, though I always answered in English. I had forgotten my father, but some memory of his language had remained in my unconscious.

A few days after our arrival, Mum asked Uncle Will to show her Tom's papers, and explain where she stood financially.

I noticed the nervous glances that flew around the room among the Evans' and then Grandfather –Taid as I was to call him – took my hand and said, "Will you walk along to the church with me, Olwen, and I'll teach you how to play the harmonium? Would you like to play some hymns? "

I would.

Taid sat on the high stool in front of the harmonium and, pumping the two wide pedals vigorously, he pounded out "Guide me, o Thou great Jehovah". "There now. You try it," he said after a couple of run-throughs.

I sat and pumped the pedals and laid my hands on the keys. "Which ones do I press on?"

"Why, the ones for the tune," he said. "The tune I just showed you. Sure you know it well yourself."

I did know the hymn. We sang it sometimes in church, but I couldn't understand how that would tell me which keys to press. "Could you show me again, please?"

Taid played the tune another couple of times. "Now then."

I peddled and let my hands move over the keys but all that came out were moaning discords, nothing like the tune.

"You must sing it to yourself so you'll know what to play," Taid advised.

I sang, but still the wrong sounds came out of the instrument. "When my mother plays, she uses a book with the notes written in it," I hinted.

"Ah yes," Taid conceded. "Some play with the books. But there's easier it is just to play what you hear." He was puzzled. "I taught your father thus, and he had no trouble."

Then we went home, both of us disappointed that I had not inherited the Welsh gift for music.

We found Will gone, and my mother fuming. "He spent all the money!" she was raging at poor Nain Jane, who held out a cup of tea to her with one hand and tried to wave her onto a chair with the other. "Every last penny! The cad! Out of the hands of widows and orphans! And for what? Gambling and carrying on, I shouldn't be surprised! The cad!"

She noticed our entry and shouted at Taid, "What sort of a family is this where a man steals from his own dead brother?"

Taid looked down at his feet. "Will is not a reliable man in matters of money, I fear. You did not do well to trust him with Tom's."

"Fine advice *now*," Mum shrieked. "Why didn't you say anything before?"

"It was too late when I heard of it. I am sorry, sorry, Sarah. Will has a weakness for the horse racing, you see. He was not on a winning streak, else he would have the money for you, sure. I'd pay myself if I could, but..." He held up empty hands. It was evident that he and his new family had no money to spare. "When his luck changes, Will will pay you back, I am certain. Sit down now and drink some tea."

"Tea and promises will do me no good," Mum said but she sat down and took the cup that was offered her and drank from it in sharp, little sips.

My mother and I left Wales the next day. And that was the last we heard or saw of the Welsh side of the family for more than forty years. Except for a Christmas card and letter every year from that strange Aunt Oliver and morose Uncle Wyatt.

When we got back to London, we were pleased to hear that our Hero's House was ready. We moved in. Located in the village of Havering in Essex, the house was one in a row of grey stucco cottages with a bare strip of grass in front. There were two rooms downstairs and two up. The plaster felt damp to the touch and the rooms smelled of fresh paint. But there was electric light, and a bathroom with an amazing gas-fired machine called a geyser that produced hot water. There was a big kitchen with a shiny black range for cooking and heating, and a scullery with a sink and tap.

And it was ours. We settled in, Mum and Margie and myself, a small family, I found, being used to the crowd at Rosebank. I missed them all. I missed David and Gran most of all. I began to write letters and watched for the postman's arrival every day. The replies were disappointing. They were mostly addressed to Mum and were never as interesting as I expected them to be. David wrote that he was fine. He was learning Latin and playing cricket. Could Mum send him a cake? Charles wrote that he was fine, the weather was wet, and Aunt Boo was kind to him. I didn't believe that last bit. Noonie wrote that she'd made eight dollars picking apples and was going to buy a new winter coat. Gran wrote that she was preparing for her autumn show and putting up plums and that she missed us, and so did Uncle Bob and Gramps who sent best regards. Uncle Bob particularly missed our poetry readings.

The only people we knew in Havering were Uncle Took and Aunt Georgie and their four children. They lived a half mile down the road towards Romford. The children were all younger than I, babies, almost, and I considered them rather naughty and not much fun. We walked down to visit them most afternoons. While Mum and Georgie talked, I'd be sent out to "play" with the children. I was thirteen years old. I didn't want to play with four-year-olds and infants.

I was too old to make friends of my own age in the village. Girls of thirteen didn't just go out and stare at other girls until they were asked to play, which was the way Margie made friends with the toddlers in our row of Heroes' Houses. There weren't any kids of my age in the row anyway. I sometimes saw girls walking to or from the village school, but they didn't speak to me and I was too shy to speak to them. I needed to get to that school if I was going to have any friends at all in this country. After Will dropped the bombshell about Mum's money being all gone, I'd given up hopes of a boarding school and said good-bye in my heart to my imaginary friends Penelope and Daphne. Now I would settle happily for the village school, but Mum still had higher standards for my education and would not let me go. "Have patience," she told me. "Wait 'til I clear up this financial muddle we're in. It won't be long."

But it was long. The "financial muddle" continued, as did my loneliness.

Some days we'd take the bus to Romford and have tea at a café or in one of the department stores. Mum or Aunt Georgie would ask me to keep an eye on the children on these outings. This was no easy task as the kids were quick at grabbing at things on the counters in the shops, or running off into the crowds, or dipping their fingers into iced cakes in the tea shop. These outings were more like work than pleasure for me.

In compensation Mum would sometimes arrange to leave Margie with Aunt Georgie and organize an excursion into London or a visit to a stately home for the two of us. We visited the Tower of London, Westminster Abbey, Hampton Court, Blenheim Palace. I was awed to see places where history had taken place so long ago. In Creston there was hardly a single building that was any older than I was. Those were wonderful days, with Mum as excited and moved by what we saw as I was. Then England was a wonderful place.

But most days we spent in Havering, where the grass was indeed greener than any we'd see in Creston except maybe in May, and it was already October here; and the roses in the small front gardens were maybe superior to Gran's, though I didn't think so; and there was a village green and an old pub, but we never went in there; and a very old church that we attended every Sunday and I tried to feel the history of it, but really it was very much like the church in Creston and the sermons just as boring; and a school that I was not allowed to go to because we were waiting to get back the money from Uncle Will to send me to one of those schools with gym tunics and girls called Penelope. Havering was boring and I was lonely. I longed to go school. I waited and waited.

"Are you crazy?" Noonie wrote back when I complained to her in my weekly letter. "You are so lucky. No school and all holidays." She didn't know what she was talking about.

Mum bought me a bicycle to cheer me up, so that I'd be able to get out on my own. Where could I go? A bicycle was not what I wanted. I wanted to go to school. I couldn't learn how to ride that bicycle. I've never in all my life known anyone else who was unable to learn to ride, and now, looking back, I think what I was doing was subconsciously refusing to learn to ride. I was never a rebellious child, but this was my protest against the decision my mother had made for me. I would not ride a bicycle that was given to me as a substitute for school.

We began to go into London more often. We called on some of my father's Welsh friends. They talked and talked of publishing a book of his poems, but nothing came of it. Mum couldn't read the poems for herself because they were in Welsh, but she was sure they were worthy of publication and was disappointed to be told that there were too many collections of the work of poets killed in the war and not enough paper to publish them. We called on Aunt Boo and, if Charles was around, he and I would walk up and down the dreary street and have a good commiserating talk about how much we missed Creston and everyone there.

At about this time a terrible thought came to me, so shocking in its disloyalty that I did not dare to say it aloud. The thought was that, so far, I didn't like England. Even if it was the land of hope and glory, the mother of us all, the proud centre of the Empire on which the sun never set, the strongest nation on earth, I didn't like it. Canada was much nicer. Canada was home.

I sensed that Mum too was not enjoying England as much as she had thought she would. Long absence from the country must have made her forget some unpleasant features of London, such as the dirty and crowded streets, trains, and buses; yellow fogs thick with coal dust; and days and days of rain. She had expected to find a happy prosperous country celebrating victory. She had not reckoned on seeing so many people dressed in black and with sad faces. She had not expected to see soldiers, officers even, selling pencils and apples on street corners or struggling by on crutches or in wheel chairs or with empty sleeves. These were men who had served their country and were now, it seemed, unappreciated. It was not right. The reality of England in 1920 had more the atmosphere of defeat than victory.

Everything was much more expensive than Mum remembered it to be, and in short supply too. There wasn't even enough paper to publish a small volume of her late husband's beautiful poems. The pension from the War Office, that had seemed generous back in Canada, was only enough to live on in England. Mum was not as rich as she had expected to be.

Many others were in the same plight. Jobs were scarce and pay was low. There were strikes. People's spirits seemed as grey as the rainy grey skies.

It was the Hun that was to blame for this, Mum and Aunt Georgie agreed. The war had spoiled everything. "To think England should win, and then come to this!" They shook their heads.

Slow months dragged by. In the mornings we went to the shops. Mum talked about the terrible quality of the goods for sale. The bacon was streaky, and the butter was "off" and the leather on my new shoes was thin, cheap stuff. "This bread I got at Johnson's this morning is half stale," she complained as she buttered slices for our supper one evening. "And here's another letter from David came this morning asking for a food package. He says they don't get enough to eat at Amberley. Considering what I'm paying to send him there, I think it's shocking, I really do. I've a mind to write to the head master."

Another day it was the quality of the fruit available at the green grocer that raised her ire. "He's asking a shilling for a half peck of apples and hard, miserable little things they are. In the Kootenays we'd throw fruit like that to the chickens." We left the shop without buying any.

"Do you remember the apples from Gran's tree at Rosebank?" I asked as we walked back to our Hero's House with the shopping basket almost empty.

"Those were the best apples I've ever eaten, bar none," Mum said with regret.

"And the apricots," I reminded her. My mouth was watering.

"And the raspberries and currants." Mum was walking faster and faster. "I've put up no preserves at all here, not a single quart. There is simply no decent fruit to be had in the shops. We've had to do without all winter. Do without. I think that's become England's new motto."

We turned into our Hero's Home. "Well, then," I ventured aloud the idea that had been with me for weeks, "why couldn't we go back to Creston? I think it's nicer there than here."

Mum looked at me sharply but she did not argue against what I'd said. After that, on our visits to Aunt Georgie's, I noticed the two women talking in urgent whispers, sometimes arguing. I suspected something was afoot.

Mum went in to London alone "on business". She came home with steamships tickets. We began packing straightaway. We would be ready to go as soon as David's school term was over.

We left England on a day as dull and wet as the day we arrived. We had been "home" for a year and a half and now we were going back to our real home, Creston. We were all very glad.

Chapter 10

The Black Sheep

Long after we got back to Creston, Mum continued to write letters to solicitors in England trying to get back her widow's money that Uncle Will had made off with. Whenever an answer came to one of her pleas, she'd call in Colonel Mallandaine – he'd been promoted to that rank during the war – to look the letter over and give her his advice. The answers were always the same: it was most unlikely she would ever recover the money. The Colonel agreed with the English solicitors. "I'm sorry, Mrs. Evans, but there it is. And even if, by some fluke, you won your case, you wouldn't get the money because the man would have spent it all by now. There's no use suing a man with empty pockets." The Colonel sipped his tea with a calm Mum must have found annoying.

"He could be made to pay in instalments," she argued. "If those solicitors had any sense of justice, they'd make him."

"Well, they can't find him, for starters. And their advice is it's not worth paying out money to try to locate him, given his record." Mallandaine pointed to the latest letter. "And you did give the man power of attorney."

"I didn't give him the power to rob me!" Mum snapped. She paced back and forth, letting her tea get cold. The Colonel sat back and winked at me as she raged. We both knew that Mum was continuing her argument strictly as a matter of principle; she knew the solicitors and the Colonel were right. Her letters were a waste of time and postage. She just kept on because she hated to give up what was hers by right and she did hate to lose an argument.

For myself I found it hard to believe that the handsome, charming man who'd driven us to Llanaelhaearn, who'd spoken so lovingly of his dear brother, my father, could have done such a wicked thing as rob us, and if he had taken the money, well, perhaps there was some reason we didn't know about that had driven him to it.

Many years later I heard the whole of poor Will's story from a cousin in Australia. According to him, Will had certainly taken the money and gambled it away. He was a blackguard through and through, a con artist you might call him. Even after hearing that condemnation, though, I kept a soft spot of sympathy for Will. He was a man of great charm and many talents, and his life might have been different had he not been afflicted with one unfortunate and embarrassing handicap. He was incontinent.

He'd been a bed-wetter since childhood. No beating from his dad could cure him, nor no medicine his mam bought when the peddler made his rounds in the little village of Llanaelhaearn.

By the time Will was eleven years old – this was in 1899, the year his mam died – he was still wetting himself like a baby, almost always at night and sometimes in the day as well. He wouldn't curb himself. He wouldn't learn sense. Perhaps in self-defence, perhaps because he really didn't care, he took on a defiant attitude to his problem. Who cared about a bit of spilled pee? He didn't.

After their mam's death, aunts and uncles descended upon the bereaved household to take the younger children away and give them new homes. It was the Reverend Uncle Thomas and Aunt Mair from London who chose young Will. Graceful and fine-featured with deep blue eyes and tawny gold hair, he enchanted them with his beauty and his angelic smile.

His dad, our Taid, might have warned the Reverend Thomases about Will's problem, only they'd made him cross the way they'd examined the children and discussed their features as though they were choosing a Christmas goose.

Anyway, the change might be just what Will needed. He'd enjoy the excitement of life in the big city. Living as a gentleman in a grand house and wearing fine clothes would maybe teach him the self-restraint he needed. If it didn't, then maybe the holy preacher could knock some sense into the boy and cure him of his filthy habit.

"If you behave well, you will have a good life and many opportunities," Taid advised his son.

"I'll behave," Will promised. Promises came easily to him.

"Be of use to your Uncle Thomas. Try to earn your keep in his house."

"How could I be of use to a preacher?"

"You must look about you to see what's to do. Run errands. Shine his boots for him. Read him sermons in the evenings.

"And, for God's sake, remember to pee last thing before you go to bed."

"Ah, that's not a problem for me now." Lies also came easily to Will.

He had no sense of shame.

The reverend uncle and aunt had no more success than Taid had had in teaching Will restraint. And, as he grew older, Will picked up new bad habits as well: drinking, gambling, betting on the horses. By the time he was seventeen, the parson and his wife had lost all patience with him and his sinful and disgusting ways, and they sent him home to Wales in disgrace.

In the meantime, Taid had married again and he and his new wife were raising a second family.

Will arrived back in Llanaelhaearn in a fine suit and shiny top hat.

"A gentleman you've become, is it?" Taid greeted him.

"I suppose I have, rather," Will answered in English. He'd forgotten his Welsh, he said. He looked about him as if he'd never seen the cottage of his childhood: the stiff parlour with its lace-curtained window; the steep stairway leading from the front door to the tiny bedrooms above; and the kitchen with its great, blackened fireplace.

He treated his young stepmother with elaborate courtesy. He rose when she entered the room, pulled back her chair for her when she sat down to her tea, offered his arm and carried her shopping basket when she went up street to the shop.

He delighted his little half-brothers by conjuring sweets out of their ears, like a real magician.

And he was not too proud to take his old Dad around to the pub for a drink and to sing the old songs with the men there. His Welsh came back to him better then.

But the little brothers, who shared his bed, were soon complaining to their mam about wet sheets. Will said, "It's themselves who are doing it, only they don't know, the poor loves."

And his stepmother found that though Will was a great one for opening doors and fetching her shawl for her, bowing as though she were the Queen of England, he couldn't seem to understand her at all when she asked him to dig up the potato bed or fetch water from the stand pipe for the washing.

She wrinkled her nose at the smell of his wool trousers. "It's the sea you are smelling, and the sheep," Will insisted, and with his pocketknife he snipped off a wild rose from the hedgerow by the gate and tucked it into her hair. "There's the scent of the flowers of the fields will surround you now this day." He smiled his winning smile and she had to smile back. It was hard to stay angry with Will.

In 1914 when the war came, Taid saw in it a great opportunity for his older sons to better themselves. "Enlist," he told them. "Try for the officers' training. There's gentlemen you could become."

Tommy joined up, and Wyatt. But not Will. "I'll not go and get myself killed for King and Country," he said "That's a mug's game."

Even when conscription came in 1916, Will wouldn't go. He got himself declared unfit for service. " 'It's my kidneys,' I said to the medical blokes," he reported to Taid. " 'I have no control.' Then I pissed all over the floor to prove it. They chucked me out soon enough."

"The army might have cured you, if you'd behaved better," Taid grumbled. "They'd know what to do with a problem like yours.

"And isn't it your duty to serve King and Empire? That's Tom's opinion."

"Oh, piss on duty. Piss on the Empire. Come on down the pub." Will had won on the horses while he was in town at the medical board.

Even if he didn't join the colours like his brothers, Will made a pretty good thing of the war. He got down to London often. There he knew how to find his way into clubs where card games went on 'til late late at night, where a clever fellow could win enough to drink champagne and dance with beautiful women and bet on fast horses and live in hotels where the servants would never dare to remark on the state of the sheets on the beds.

Sometimes he came back to Llanaelhaearn with money for drinks at the pub, sweets for the little ones, a trinket for his stepmother. Just as often he came home with his head in his feathers, as Taid would say, and his pockets empty.

Then Taid would urge him to find a proper job. "There is work at the quarry. I could speak for you to the manager."

"Swinging a sledgehammer, is it? Thanks, but I think not."

"And there are jobs down the pits in the south."

"I have not the strength for the coal mines," Will said.

"Your brother Llewellyn is earning good money at the coal," his stepmother reminded him.

"Llew was always the better man." Will had no false pride.

"Now, Dad, I'm expecting a money order in the post any day. I wonder if you could you see your way to letting me have a few pounds to tide me over?"

Taid lent him a pound, and Will was away.

He was soon back.

"When will I have back that pound I lent you?" Taid asked.

"Well, now," Will said, "didn't I meet a poor, shoeless beggar on the street, and seeing his great need, I gave him the pound. I knew you'd have wanted me to."

"Ah, hush with your storytelling. You gave the money to no beggar."

"All the same," Will grinned, "it went to a man in need. Don't worry. I'll pay you back. Soon."

And after a lucky card game with some soldiers on leave, he did. And then he was off to London again.

In 1918 the war was over. Wyatt was wounded and never the same man again, and poor Tom killed at the very end.

Will looked prosperous though, when he brought Tom's English widow and her daughter home to Wales.

"Will's been kind enough to see about dear Tom's money for me," the widow told Taid. She sat on a stiff chair in the parlour and gestured towards a stack of official-looking papers on the table. "The insurance and the officer's bonus. It's all so very confusing."

"You've been handling her money, Will?" Taid blanched as he turned to his profligate son who stood by the feeble coal fire, twirling a new silver-handled walking stick.

"Yes. Investing it for her, don't you know?" Will said,

Taid turned away. He knew how this would end.

When the widow discovered that it was horse races Will had been investing in, she fell into a fury. "Thief!" she shrieked. "Blackguard! I'll have the law on you for this. Don't think I won't." Her shouts could be heard all up and down the village street. Grandmother Jane hovered over the visitor, offering a cup of tea to try to soothe her. Jane spoke no English and had no idea what had made the English lady so angry, though anyone would know Will had something to do with it.

Will thought it best to slip away that night.

Australia was the place to go. He had family there: his two sisters, Megan and Ruth, had emigrated there. Yes, Australia would be the best bet.

Pity about the money. He wouldn't have put so much on Heart's Folly except he'd had a sure tip on her. Just bad luck all round. The winnings would have been a great thing for Tom's widow and her little family. She was a pretty woman, with lots of spirit to her. He liked her. If he made his fortune in Australia, he'd pay her back, every penny, she could count on that.

Will signed on as a waiter on the *Sophocles*, bound for Sidney. The first day out of port he talked the steward into letting him give tango lessons in the first class salon. He danced with professional grace, and he knew how to charm the rich war widows who were travelling to new and warmer climes to restore their shattered spirits. He danced those lonely, grieving widows across the wide, wide southern ocean, guiding them with seductive steps, exciting them with melodious, whispered flatteries, daring them to let go of their sorrows in the breaking bubbles of bitter-sweet champagne.

He very nearly caught himself one of those widows for a wife through his lessons. He might have done it, too, if his old problem hadn't caught him out once he'd inveigled himself into her bed.

Truth was, he was not entirely disappointed. He was not the marrying type.

In Sydney, he jumped ship.

He was ready to seek his fortune in the new world.

Considering the size of the country, the first thing he'd need was a car. He paid ten pounds cash, and signed a paper agreeing to pay eight pounds per month for many, many months to come. But he needn't worry about that.

The salesman shook his hand to close the deal. "Were you by any chance at Gallipoli?" he asked.

"No, I'm afraid I never got past France."

"I hear it was no picnic there either."

"It was not." Will looked solemn.

"That's the DSO I see you have," the salesman nodded at the row of Tom's medals on Will's jacket.

"Oh yes. Ran into a spot of bother at Cambrai, and some Colonel or other mentioned me in a dispatch." Tom had probably been at Cambrai, Will thought. Or some place near it.

"We owe a lot to you fellows. Don't think we don't appreciate it, those of us who didn't get a chance to serve," the salesman told him.

"Only doing our duty. A man can't do more. Or less." Will let his hand be shaken again. He liked being a war hero.

He liked his new car too.

He drove along to a pub and stopped for a celebratory drink. There he got into a card game and won ten quid. Not bad for his first day in the land of opportunity.

When he was ready to apply for a job, he wrote himself a nice letter of recommendation on a page of War Office stationery he'd pilfered when he'd gone to sign for Tom's insurance. The letter and the medals worked on the first try. He was hired to work in an insurance office, a stuffy old place, as he soon discovered. He wrote dull letters and filled in forms. There was no excitement in it. He couldn't stick it. He left at the end of the month. No hard feelings.

He dropped round to the place where he'd bought the car and made his first payment in cash. A person had to establish an honourable reputation before he could get away with much.

Now that his money was gone, he thought about visiting his sisters.

Will drove up to Megan's place in Cooma in his swell car.

"Do I have the pleasure of addressing Miss Megan Evans?" he asked the woman who answered his knock at the door.

"Miss Megan Evans that was; Mrs. Harry Prentice now," the woman said.

"Ah Megan, my dear, do you not recognize your own brother, Will?"

She did then, though she swore she could have walked past him on the street and never have known. You could knock her over with a feather.

"I knew you right away," he said. "You don't look a day older than when I last saw you."

"I was twelve then, Will. And you did not recognize me." Megan had always been a sour one.

"Well now that I've come all this way, are you going to invite me in for a cup of tea?" he had to ask.

He came in and met Harry. They drank beer and Will told his stories of the widows and the tango lessons. He whirled Megan around the kitchen to demonstrate and told her she could dance rings around any of the first class ladies in their golden slippers.

"Hark at your foolishness!" Megan scolded, but she laughed and blushed and half believed his flattery.

Will talked about his job in insurance, and how he was looking for something better now. Harry was a teacher, and Will wondered if there might be anything for him in that line. He could teach dancing, history, English, singing, card tricks. Whatever was required.

There happened to be a vacancy in the junior school staff.

"But Will, you're never qualified to be a teacher," Megan said.

"Sure I am." He showed her Tom's M.A. diploma. Nobody would ever look at the exact name in all that Latin, and it wasn't doing old Tom any good now, was it?

He got the job. But it didn't last. He was a grand teacher. The children loved him. It was only that there was some trouble with the secretary, and questions about a cash box. He left in a hurry.

Megan gave him Ruth's address in Sydney. They were a matching pair, Will and Ruth, she told Harry. "Lord knows what they'll get up to, the two of them together. And it's she can wash his smelly sheets!"

Ruth and her dull little husband were no use to Will. Fred had some menial job at the hospital, washing floors, or bedpans. He offered to put in a word for Will, but Will thanked him and said no. Catch him scrubbing floors for a living! Not bloody likely!

Ruth was out most days. She said she was looking for work, but Will knew a person didn't get that happy glow on a job search. He'd bet his last penny Ruth was getting something on the side, and enjoying it too.

Well, and more power to her. Will wasn't the man to blow the whistle on someone having a bit of fun.

He took her to the horse races one Saturday afternoon. She told him some tall tale about how she'd learned fortune-telling from the gypsies, and he let her choose the horse to bet on. Damned if the nag didn't win.

He bought her a pint and let her pick for the next race. Another winner.

Maybe there was something in this gypsy claptrap.

"Who'll it be in the third?" he asked.

"Sweet William."

How could Will lose on a horse of that name?

Sweet William lost.

"Damn you! We've lost the wad." Will and Ruth stood by the rail and Will searched through his empty pockets, hoping he might find a forgotten pound note.

Ruth was not going to stand quietly and be shouted at. "Damn you! I didn't say put it ALL on Sweet William. And he would have won if the stupid jockey hadn't run him into the fence."

"You don't know what you're talking about, you daft gypsy." There was not a penny in any of his pockets.

Ruth searched through her handbag and found a shilling. "I know I'd have saved enough cash to buy us another drink."

They drank one last beer at the refreshment stand and quarrelled and laughed all the way home.

Fred cooked beans and toast for their supper and Will found enough change in the pockets of his other trousers to buy more beer.

Through the meal he and Ruth talked about what they would have done with the money if Sweet William had won.

"I'd have bought ten new dresses," Ruth said.

"I'd have bought a decent pair of shoes and spent the rest on drink," Will said.

"Not you. You'd have bet the lot on the next race and lost it."

That set them laughing again. They laughed 'til Will wet himself, and then Fred laughed too. Will left the next morning.

He went to Tenterfield where he got a job selling farm machinery, but the farmers were maddeningly slow to make up their minds whether or not to buy, and when they did buy, they drove a hard bargain. The police caught up to him then about the car and took it away. Piss on it; the clutch was shot anyway.

Without a car he couldn't be a salesman and that was a good thing too. He was getting sick and tired of the job.

He called on Megan again, but she said he'd never get anything in Cooma now, not after the business at the school.

Well, piss on the working life. He could make his money gambling. The Aussies, bless them, would bet on anything.

Sometimes Will won; more often he lost. Occasionally, he worked. He ran a taxi service for a bit. He fell in with a fellow who was studying aboriginal music and they got a programme going on Australian radio. The programme lasted a few months. Will liked the Abos; they didn't take work so bloody seriously either. He liked the Aussies too. Anzac Day he'd put on old Tommy's medals and walk into a pub and everyone would shake his hand and buy him drinks 'til he passed out.

He liked the country with its wide spaces and its hot sun and its friendly people. It was a good life he was having. Better than he'd ever have had in old Llanaelhaearn, with its one narrow street of grey houses and Taid telling him to get a job of work and his stepmother complaining about the smell of him.

From time to time over the years that followed, Will visited his sisters. Sometimes he arrived with nothing but a swag bag on his back. Then he'd try to touch them for the price of a new suit or a stake to get himself started again.

Other times he'd drive up in a fancy car and peel bills out of a fat wallet, buying everyone drinks.

They never knew when he'd show up or what state he'd be in.

Then, in 1956, Megan saw an article in the newspaper: the body of a man by the name of William Evans, a gold prospector, had been found bludgeoned to death in the shack on his claim near Bloomfield, on the Cape York Peninsula. Theft was the motive suspected. On the evening preceding the slaying, the victim, a man known to the police, had been seen and heard in the Southern Star Tavern boasting about having struck pay dirt.

Megan sent copies of the article to Ruth and home to Wales, but none of the Evans family went to claim the body. They didn't dare.

This was just as well because, about ten years later, didn't Will show up again like the proverbial bad penny?

Hippies discovered him. When they moved into the remote Cedar Bay area, seeking an alternate lifestyle, they found an old fellow called Will Evans already living there in a driftwood shack. Will, they soon learned, could tell them a thing or two about dropping out, hanging loose, finding inner peace, and letting the answers blow in the wind. That's what he'd been doing all his life.

The hippies loved Cedar Bay Bill, as they called him. They made him their guru. When he died in 1972, they gave him a real groovy funeral with flowers and incense and prayers for his soul wafting up in smoke.

To this day people still bring flowers to his grave. Not the Evans family though. They said you'd never know what Will might be trying to pull off this time.

But when I eventually heard the end of Will's story, I promised myself that if I ever got to Australia – though it seemed most unlikely that I ever would – I'd visit that grave and lay a wreath of white lilies on it, for forgiveness. Will was indeed a rogue, but he was not a vicious or mean-spirited man. And, after all, we'd managed without the money that he took.

Chapter 11

Coming Home

Although Charles was living with Aunt Boo and Uncle Clary and cousin Percy, he didn't go to the same school as Percy. This was because Percy's school, as Uncle Clary explained, cost a lot of money. Charles didn't mind a bit. Fancy paying out money to go to a school where you had to wear a pink jacket and knee pants and a stupid little beanie hat! Charles thought that was about the limit. The lads back home wouldn't be seen dead in duds like that.

The state school was not bad, as schools went, although even there, it turned out you had to wear a tie. Charles made some friends, fellows who knew a lot more about fun than cousin Percy. He learned how to play the English games: cricket and football and rounders. The music master told him he had a very good voice and that he should join the church choir. This pleased his aunt who began to talk of Charles' going into holy orders, which made Percy snigger, and Charles too, this time. At choir, he made more friends. He kept busy.

He kept away from his aunt and uncle as much as he could. He thought that would please them best. He had heard Aunt Boo complaining to Clary about her nerves, stretched to the edge with that great boy to take care of.

In this family, he couldn't seem to get it right. If he cleaned his plate at mealtimes, Uncle Clary complained about being eaten out of house and home. If he left something on the plate, Uncle Clary was likely to say something about picky eaters. If he invited Percy to play snakes and ladders or catch or tag or even cricket, Percy complained that he cheated or was too rough or didn't know how to play properly. "And you needn't expect me to coach you, because I won't." If he stayed in his room, Aunt Boo accused him of skulking and not being any company for Percy. It was not easy to be an orphan and to know you were not behaving right in the house you were told was home.

The best thing was to keep busy at school and in the choir and stay out of the way as much as possible.

Despite Aunt Sarah's assurance that he'd get used to England, Charles didn't. Aunt Boo took him to the Tower of London but it was dark and grey and all about history. The changing of the guards was better, but you didn't go to the changing of the guards every day. Mostly you just went back and forth past the same rows of yellow brick houses with their tiny little squares of green grass in front of them.

Every day was the same. The menfolk went out after breakfast and Aunt Boo stayed home and did whatever she did. They had tea at exactly five and went to bed at exactly the same time every night. Aunt Boo and Uncle Clary never went out, never had friends in. Everybody kept themselves separate.

Charles missed his family and the ranch. It was always busy there, people coming and going, work to be done, different things going on every day. In the summer the kids worked alongside their parents in the orchard and afterwards they'd run down for a swim at the creek, all of them together. Saturday afternoons they'd get up a game of baseball and maybe have ice cream at the drug store for a treat. In the winter the small frame house was crowded and snug. After supper they'd play cards or have a singsong, or friends would come calling. Often the friends would stay all night and the kids would get to stay up as late as they wanted and then sleep on the floor. Sometimes his parents went out dancing and the kids would stay at Gran's, and Uncle Bob would recite long, long poems for them, or Gran and Gramps Little would tell stories. Charles missed his family so much he sometimes woke up at night crying for them.

He missed Creston too. He missed the wide river flats, and the woods above the town and the pools along Dead Horse Creek and the baseball diamond by the school. He missed the cold, clear winter days, and the heavy haze of hot summer days.

But he was doing all right. For an orphan, he was doing all right.

He wrote to Gran once a week.

"Dear folks:
How are you?
I am learning how to play cricket.
We went to Kew Gardens and looked at flowers."

It was hard to be an orphan in a strange country. He kept forgetting to do things the way Aunt Boo and Uncle Clary liked. He was supposed to polish his shoes every day, every single day! He was supposed to wear a tie to eat in the dining room. He couldn't see the sense in that. He was not supposed to get dirty, never to get in fights with other boys, not to say "Skookum" or "jake" or "zowie".

Maybe it was hard for them to get used to having him around, too. He could see that they were trying to be nice, or at least Aunt Boo was. She took him and Percy to that Tower place and to watch the guards and to the greenhouses. She came to his school concert and said he'd done his part well. When he did a solo at church, she told him he sang beautifully and asked was he still thinking about going in for holy orders. Uncle Clary didn't have much to do with him, but he left pocket money for him every Monday morning on the breakfast table, same as he did for Percy. Percy was never nice, but then Percy was a drip; he'd known that right from the start.

Charles remembered what Aunt Sarah had told him about being grateful for being given a home, so he tried his best, but he never really felt that this was his home.

Things didn't get better. Through the winter he caught colds and bronchial coughs in the damp, sooty air that smelled of coal fires. He wondered if he would die too, like his Mum and Dad. His aunt complained of the germs he was picking up from the common children at the school and made him wash his hands far too often.

The last straw came when Percy stole his pocket money. For two weeks there was no sixpence at Charles' place. He didn't like to ask about it; perhaps Uncle Clary was running short of the ready. His father often had. Not that Charles or any of the other kids had ever had pocket money at home. Pocket money was one of the advantages Aunt Sarah said he'd have in his new home.

The third Monday he entered the dining room just in time to see Percy pick up and pocket the sixpence at his place. This was too much. "You dirty sneak!" He lunged at Percy, intent on recovering what was his by rights.

Percy wouldn't fight, but crammed his fist into the pocket into which he'd slipped the coin and lay on the floor and howled. Charles tried to drag him to his feet.

Aunt Boo entered the room. "Charles!"

Charles let go of Percy who ran to his mother. "What has he done to you, darling?" she asked.

"Hit me and tried to take my pocket money, but I wouldn't let him," Percy cried.

"That's not true," Charles started to explain.

"Please leave the room at once," Aunt Boo said.

Charles left.

Percy was not hurt, Boo ascertained. She managed to soothe him and send him off to school in time.

Then she sat in her well-ordered drawing room and wept. Her worst fears had been realized. It had come to fighting in her once peaceful home, fisticuffs even. And theft. Boo couldn't bear the way Charles had looked at her when she sent him out of the room. His eyes, Charlotte's eyes, had accused her, even though it was he who was the thief and the brawler.

She'd known all along that there would be trouble. Her peace of mind was shattered; Percy was threatened; and Clary had never taken to the boy at all. His coming had ruined their happy home.

For Charlotte's sake she had tried to love the boy, but she couldn't. He was not at all like her Percy. Whenever he looked at her, she fancied she saw her dead sister looking through his eyes, accusing her of not really wanting him, of not being kind enough to him. In Charles' look she could see that he was not happy here either, and that increased her guilt. They'd been a comfortable family – she and Clary and Percy – 'til Charles had been foisted upon them and spoiled everything. The arrangement wasn't working for anyone, not for her or Clary or Percy, and not for Charles either. He simply didn't fit in.

"Send the boy back to Canada. That's my advice," Clary said when Boo reported the incident to him that evening after Percy had gone to bed. "Young Charles is too much for us. We've given the boy a fair trial, and look where it's got us. Your nerves are shattered. The only solution is to send him back to the place whence he came. He'll be better off there, happier. It's what he's used to and where he belongs. That's my advice."

Clary had his faults, but he was a sensible person. Boo thought over his suggestion. He was probably right. If she'd followed his advice before Sarah arrived with the boy, this would never have happened. She had half a mind to write to Ma and tell her she must take Charles back, for his own good, as well as theirs. The climate here obviously did not agree with him. He'd had some shocking colds this winter. His school work was not up to standard, his teacher had told her. He was not getting along well with Percy, and it was evident that he was still missing his own brothers and sisters. Boo's mind was busy gathering arguments for sending the boy back to Canada.

If only the decision could be made, it would be easy to make the arrangements. Dear Clary helped her; he took care of everything.

"He's to leave on August 11th," he said, "on the *Empress of Scotland*. There's a special third class rate going for boys and men, as they're in need of harvesters to work on the prairies."

"Will he be all right, mixed in with farm labourers?" Boo worried.

"The lad knows how to look after himself," Clary assured her. "I'll see him on to the boat train, and he'll be fine from there on."

The surprise was that Charles didn't seem to mind at all when he heard he was to leave almost immediately. He actually grinned from ear to ear at the news he was to go back to Canada "I'll get my things packed then," was all he said, and bounced away.

"He doesn't realize what's happening. It'll hit him at the station," Clary predicted. "You'd best not come. It'd be too hard on your nerves."

"I've never cared for stations anyway," Boo agreed. "So noisy. I don't want Percy going either. I think he may be coming down with something. He's feeling his cousin's departure."

Following Clary's advice, Boo made a label of strong pasteboard and tied it around Charles' neck on a string. "Charles D. Talbot," it said. "En route Southampton, England, to Creston, B.C. Canada. In event of emergency, please contact Mrs. M. Young, Creston, B.C."

"You look like a parcel," Percy said when Charles stood ready to go.

Charles realized that a parcel was exactly what he felt like. Aunt Boo and Uncle Clary were going to ship him off to Canada like the parcel of old magazines and outgrown clothes that they didn't want any more that Aunt Boo had packed up at Christmas time for the others back in Creston.

Well, he didn't care. However he was going, he was glad to be going. Lord, if he'd known attacking Percy would have this effect, he would have punched him all around the house months ago.

He was so pleased to be saying good-bye to the little drip that he shook his hand and said, "Goodbye, old chap!" That was one of those silly expressions the English boys liked to use.

He walked through the tiny green garden and out through the dinky little iron gate for the last time, careful to latch it behind him as Aunt Boo liked. She and Percy waved from the front door and Charles waved back.

At the station, Uncle Clary looked in at each third class carriage of the boat train until he found a decent-looking family. He addressed the father: "I'd be obliged if you'd keep an eye on this young man for the journey."

"Right you are, govn'r." The man tipped his cap and Clary handed him a pound note which the man stared at in some surprise 'til his wife signalled him to put it in his pocket and help the boy stow his case on the luggage rack. Then the three children shifted over on the bench so that there was a place for Charles to squeeze in.

First he turned to Uncle Clary. "Good bye, sir," he said without a tremor in his voice. A brave little lad, in the end. The stay in England had been good for him. Clary tipped him half a crown, shook his hand, and stepped out on to the platform. A guard slammed the door. Charles was on his way.

The family who were to keep an eye on him were called the Carvers and they were going to Toronto. One of the children, Stephen, was the same age as Charles and the two of them were soon on the way to becoming fast friends. The Carvers had accents that Aunt Boo would call common and Percy would make fun of, but they were jolly people and easy to talk to, as excited as Charles was to be on their way to Canada. When they learned they had fallen in with a real Canadian before they'd even got on the boat, they were delighted. They peppered him with questions about Toronto, refusing to believe he wouldn't know, being a Canadian himself.

"Creston is quite a distance from Toronto actually," Charles explained.

"Still it's in the same country, inn't?"

Charles named all the provinces and their capitals, surprised that he remembered them from Grade Four, when he'd left. He explained Canadian money to them and laughed when they found it more difficult than their own complicated shillings and pence system that he'd had such a hard time with at first.

At tea time Mrs. Carver opened a bag and unpacked thick bacon sandwiches and handed him one just as if he was a member of the family. Charles realized he felt more at home in a couple of hours with the Carvers than he'd ever felt at Aunt Boo and Uncle Clary's.

The train made a stop and the children clamoured to be allowed to get off and run on the platform and the parents reluctantly agreed. "But none of yez goes out of my sight or I'll crown yez all," Mrs. Carver threatened. She included Charles in her admonishing stare.

The children hopped up and down on the platform and then the whistle blew and Mrs. Carver shouted and stormed until everyone was packed in again and she said her nerves was played out, but she must have had a different kind of nerves from Aunt Boo's because her attack included fits of laughing.

When they reached Southhampton, there was great excitement getting off the train and on to the boat and poor Mrs. Carver began to cry and everyone patted her on the back and said, "There now, lovie, it's all for the best," so Charles did too. Then the band began to play and a tremendous whistle sounded somewhere above them and scared them out of their wits, but only for a minute, and Charles flung his cap high in the air and shouted, "Hurrah for Canada! Hip hip hooray!" And the Carvers, and all kinds of other families gathered along the rail, joined in on the "hoorays!"

Gran sat in Creston, sewing yellow straw ricking on to a buckram hat form and worrying about Charles. What could Boo have been thinking of to send an eleven-year-old child to cross an ocean and then a continent alone? He'd be kidnapped, Gran fretted. Such people as there are in the world today! He would be robbed, taken advantage of in ways she couldn't bear to think of.

Boo had never been noted for her good sense, but this latest foolishness of hers verged on the criminal, in Gran's opinion. It was no doubt Clary who had put her up to it. If only she had realized what their plans were! "Impossible keep Charles," Boo's telegram had said. "Sending him Creston. Dates follow."

And they sent him off on the first boat available. She thought they'd at least wait until someone from the family was travelling. Or that they would entrust him to the care of an emigrating friend. Someone would be sure to be going sooner or later. If only they'd waited. She would have found the money and gone herself to fetch the boy, if she'd known what they were planning, Gran thought.

If anything happens to that boy, I shall never forgive Boo. Never, Gran vowed to herself, even if she is my own daughter.

She picked up the hat again. While she set tiny stitches into the buckram form, she imagined her grandson boarding that huge ocean liner, all by himself. If he'd managed to reach Southhampton safely, that is. What if he lost his ticket? What if he got on the wrong boat? Set off for India, or China? And if he did reach the boat safely, would he find his way around? Those ocean liners were huge. Would he find the dining saloon? Would he get anything to eat? She imagined him sitting on the third class deck, staring out an empty sea, alone and afraid.

On the *Empress of Scotland*, Charles was having the time of his life. The third class kids played tag and hopscotch and rounders and other games they made up as they played.

He sat with the Carvers in the dining room and they all ate their way happily through the huge meals. Corned beef hash for breakfast and porridge and all the bread and jam you could eat. Fish *and* meat for dinner. A meat tea as well. And a supper of bread and cheese if you could stay awake long enough to eat it.

He shared a cabin with three taciturn farm lads from Somerset, going to the Prairies to work at the harvest. But Charles spent very little time in his cabin and with his roommates. He and Stephen and the Carvers were together all day, eating and playing and talking about Canada. He hadn't had such a good time since before his parents had died.

At last the *Empress* docked in Quebec and they had to part – the Carvers to take the CN line to Toronto, and Charles to board a CPR train bound for Winnipeg, Calgary, Fort McLeod and Creston. The Carvers saw him on to his train and passed on the pound note Uncle Clary had given them to the Somerset boys who would be travelling on the same train as Charles, along with many instructions to see that the lad came to no harm. "And you write to us, the minute you get to your Gran's, you hear?" Mrs. Carver ordered Charles. "You've got that address in your case and don't you lose it!"

"I will," Charles promised. "You write to me too."

The five days on the train were ten times as long as the six days on the boat. There were no other children in the long third class carriage, only babies that howled and stank.

The seats were hard and pulled down into berths that were harder. He and the farm boys were too shy to eat in the dining car. They changed Uncle Clary's pound to Canadian money and bought bread and tinned beans that they cooked on the little stove at the end of the car. They bought cups of tea at the stations. They were afraid of spending too much of their small supply of money too fast. Charles was hungry all the time, and tired, and so were the Somerset boys and many others on the train. They were all orphans here.

At Regina the Somerset boys got off and handed over to Charles the rest of Uncle Clary's money. There was just enough to buy a package of chewing gum and an American comic. Charles was tired but didn't dare to fall asleep, in case he'd miss Fort McLeod, where he had to change for the Crow's Nest Pass Line.

A kindly farmer's wife going to visit her sister took the seat beside him and when she opened her lunch bag, she handed him a tomato sandwich. The thick slices of bread were soggy with the juice from the huge slab of the tomato. Charles realized he hadn't had a tomato like that all the time in England. 'Tom-ah-toes' they called those hard little red fruits they ate there. He devoured the sandwich hungrily.

Seeing his appetite, the woman gave him a handful of sugar cookies too.

She was nice, but a bit of a fusser. "All the way from England you've come! My! My! Aren't your folks worried about you all alone?

"An orphan – ah now that is too bad."

Soon everyone in the coach knew his plight and fed him sandwiches and cookies and candy bars 'til he was well and truly stuffed.

At Fort McLeod they handed him into the care of the station master, who passed him on to the charge of the conductor on the Crow's Nest train. He didn't have to worry about a thing.

Soon after he got on the Crow's Nest train, he could see the mountains with clouds hanging over their peaks. Ah yes. This was the way a country was supposed to look. He hadn't realized how much he'd missed the mountains 'til he saw them now and remembered the way they turned purple as the darkness came down fast on autumn nights; and how they sparkled after a winter's snow; he remembered them pale blue against the pink sky of an early spring morning when he set out for fishing down on the flats.

Yes, and he'd be able to go fishing again, and swimming in the cold clear water of the creek. He could play baseball and pick sweet plums and apples warm off the trees, and slide down the Fourth Street hill in winter and build snow forts. How good it was to be going home.

He'd get to play with his brothers again, and kids from school. He'd even be glad to see his bossy old sister Noonie again. His mother and his father would not be there, not ever again. But Gran would be.

A sudden fear clutched him. Would he feel the same sense of not being welcome at Gran's as he'd felt at Aunt Boo's?

He thought about the Carvers and how they'd made him forget he was an orphan when he was with them. They made room for him at the table, in their games, in their family conclaves. Aunt Boo and Uncle Clary and Percy weren't like that; their little circle was so tight, he reckoned, there was no room for anyone else to fit in, no matter how good he'd been. Even Little Lord Fauntleroy probably couldn't have got it right with them. They were like a secret club, all tied up in the rules and schedules and likes and dislikes they'd made up for themselves, the only three members.

What would it be like at Gran's, he wondered. He remembered how it was when he'd stayed there in the past. Gran was always busy, sewing her hats, pottering around the garden, cooking, baking. She had no time to fuss. People came and went, staying to visit for an hour or a day or a week or months: Uncle Bob, Gramps Little, Aunt Sarah, Olwen and David, he and his parents and brothers and sisters. Gran just set another place at the table, found another straw tick or a feather mattress to roll out on the floor at night. Gran was like the Carvers. She would make room for him. He'd be all right at Gran's. Surely he'd be all right at Gran's.

Fernie. Cranbrook. Yahk. His excitement grew. Here was a mountain that looked familiar. Could it be Goat? Yes. Yes. That was surely its peak. And here was the siding for the mine. Then the trainman came along the aisle shouting, "Creston! Creston is the next station stop. Creston next." He took the ticket out of the window blind above Charles' seat and handed down his case.

They crossed Goat River Canyon and Charles thought he could hear the river roaring down below. Even in the train he could smell the raw, hot scent of the forest. Then he could see ordered rows of orchard trees, and then there were the Flats, and then the first houses, and the squat white steeple of the church.

The whistle sounded. Charles stood on the open platform between cars, straining to see around the trainman who blocked the door. They were slowing down. There. The hotel. The Mercantile.

Now, now there it is. The station! And on the platform a little old lady under a huge hat. Gran!

The train puffed to a standstill, sending out clouds of white steam. The trainman set the nobbled brown stool on the platform, and reached up to give Charles a hand, but the boy was already running along the platform towards outstretched arms. "Gran! Gran!" he was shouting, "I'm home!"

Chapter 12

Saving the Grand Piano

The first my brother Dave and I knew Mum intended to marry Mr. Hooper, the train conductor, was the morning she took us to Christ Church, sat us down in a front pew beside Gran, and handed us a prayer book open at the page headed "Sacrament of Holy Matrimony."

This was back in 1922 when kids were seen and not heard and their opinions never asked for. Anyway, even if we had been consulted, we would most probably have said, "Fine. Go ahead." Mr. Hooper was okay. He was very good-looking, blond, quite a lot like the movie star Douglas Fairbanks. He'd taken Dave and me fishing a couple of times at Kootenay Lake and swimming. We couldn't remember our own father so we weren't able to make unkind comparisons and had no old loyalties to fight. Mum seemed to like him a lot. "Good idea," we'd probably have said if we'd been asked.

None of the Hooper family attended the wedding. This upset Gran. "It's not as though it's an arduous journey from Cranbrook to Creston," she grumbled to Mum while we three "ladies" were "freshening up" in the Creston Hotel washroom before the wedding lunch.

"Rodney says his people don't like travelling," Mum explained. "And there's no afternoon train; they'd have to stay overnight and they don't like doing that."

"I'd say they can't think much of the match if they won't travel a hundred miles to see it solemnized," Gran maintained.

"Oh, no; they're ever so pleased. They've given us over their house for a wedding present. It's a beautiful cottage with four bedrooms, modern kitchen, indoor bathroom, electric light, and right in town, close to the shops. Fancy! A house! So very kind of them."

At the lunch in the dining room, Colonel Mallandaine gave a speech and Mr. Hooper saw that Dave and I got the biggest pieces of the strawberry shortcake. "Call me Rodney," he said. There was no question of our having to call him "father".

The cake was delicious. Rodney was all right.

Mum and Mr. Hooper had a three day honeymoon and then we moved out of Creston to our new home in Cranbrook. Mr. and Mrs. Hooper senior and Rodney's sister and brother-in-law stood on the front porch, waiting to meet us.

Clinging to Rodney's arm, Mum walked towards her new in-laws, a beautiful bride, smiling, ready to like and be liked. She was well turned out, as always, in a new navy blue suit and a hat with one magnificent drooping feather flashing emerald and wine red.

Behind the bridal couple followed the rest of us: myself, a shy, slouching fourteen-year old; David, eleven, with a bouncy step and mischievous eyes alight with interest in these new people and surroundings. Gran had advised leaving Margie with her at least temporarily, to which Mum had agreed. Two older children would be enough for Rodney to cope with for a start. We did however have our dog Peppie, successor to the beloved Bobby. He barked and bounded about us as we approached our new home, glad to be out of the train. A wagon load of goods, including a cat yowling in a wicker basket, lumbered up the street behind us. This caravan was probably not what the Hoopers would have imagined when they pictured their Rodney bringing home a bride.

Still, they applauded with a show of enthusiastic good will when Rodney picked Mum up and carried her across the threshold of our new house. Dave and I looked away in embarrassment. It was quite mortifying to be attached to a couple so sloppily in love.

Our Peppie became the first target of Hooper disapproval. He left his "calling cards" in the garden, Rodney's sister complained.

"Calling cards!" Mum rolled her eyes, and Dave and I giggled.

Next came the *contretemps* of the curtains. Rodney's mother was aghast when Mum took down the lace curtains in the front room and replaced them with flowered chintz. "They make the house look like a booth at the fair," she said. "What will the neighbors think?"

"It wouldn't be any of their business, would it?" Mum answered pertly. "So why should we worry? I'm fond of the flowered look myself."

"What do you think, Rodney?" Mrs. Hooper appealed to her son, and he – the traitor – said he didn't like those flowery things either.

Mum's face took on a stubborn cast, and the chintz curtains remained in the sitting room, waving defiance at the senior Hoopers, who were well placed to observe all changes taking place in their old home, as they had moved only as far as next door. Rodney's sister lived in the house directly opposite. It was a Hooper family compound. And the Hoopers found many things to complain about in it.

The cat scratched the wallpaper. My posture was terrible; I should be made to wear a brace and take ballet lessons. Mum should put less starch and more blueing in the water when she washed Rodney's shirts. Dave and his friends should not be allowed to play baseball on the lawn. It was only a matter of time 'til they would break every window.

And there was the care of the Chickering grand piano. The Hoopers had been good enough to leave their most prized possession in the big house for the use of Rodney and his new family. It was a wonderful piano. The tone was exquisite. Percy Grainger had played on it once, which made it almost a sacred object.

Now Mrs. Hooper worried that it wasn't being treated properly. She thought she might have heard David banging on the keys one day. Children should not be allowed to touch the piano, much less bang on it, she told Mum. And when she dusted it, Mum should be sure to use lemon oil – not too much – and a clean flannel cloth dipped in milk for the keys. Mrs. Hooper gave a demonstration as she instructed. During the performance, Mum wiped picture frames at the other side of the room and cast only an occasional glance towards the lesson.

Mrs. Hooper left, after bestowing on Mum a bottle of the best brand of lemon oil and a handful of clean flannel cloths. Immediately Mum turned on Rodney, who had been reading the paper throughout the demonstration. "Why didn't you stand up for me?"

"Well, you know," Rodney drawled, "I guess Mama has a good system figured out. She's sure kept that piano looking like new all these years."

"And you think I can't?" Mum demanded. "I too have owned pianos," she sniffed.

"She's only trying to be helpful," Rodney said. "There's no need to get upset."

Rodney's family were all musical. His father had been an organist and choir master until he went deaf as Beethoven, and had to give up his profession. Rodney's mother and sister were talented pianists and singers. So was Rodney. His tenor, everyone said, was every bit as good as John McCormack's. All the Hoopers loved to perform, so on many evenings we had musical gatherings around the Chickering grand.

Occasionally Mum was accorded the honour of playing the accompaniment for one of the singers. She was a good pianist, though not as good as the Hoopers. One evening she began the intro for

"Danny Boy", one of Rodney's favorite solos. She rolled the opening notes.

"Oh you never get that right!" Rodney's sister suddenly exploded. "It's la la la Lah, not la Lah la Lah. Here, let me show you." She plopped down on the bench and pushed Mum aside.

Mum said nothing. She came and sat beside me and Dave on the sofa. She had a dangerous set to her mouth and a steely glitter in her eye.

We listened to Rodney sing "Danny Boy" to his sister's accompaniment. Then they did "The Rose of Tralee".

"'The Ash Grove,'" old Mr. Hooper called out then, no doubt meaning to be kind. "The Ash Grove" was one of Mum's favourites.

Rodney's sister rose to surrender the bench.

This was Mum's moment. "My playing has not been found satisfactory," she declared. "I will not offend you with it again."

No amount of persuasion would move her. She declared she would not play the piano that evening, or ever again.

Later, after the in-laws left, Mum fought it out with Rodney. "She pushed me off the bench like an unwanted cushion, and you let her. You didn't say a word in my defence. You let them insult me and order me around. You never stick up for me."

"I don't know why you're making such a fuss," Rodney said. "Belle was only trying to help. You did have the dynamics wrong." He ran a hand through his beautiful wavy hair. "I tell you, all this bellyaching gives me the pip. It's bad for my nerves."

"Playing the piano in this house is bad for *my* nerves," Mum said.

As the weeks went by, Mum's annoyance increased. She was used to running her own household. She valued independence. She did not take kindly to advice and what she called interference. "I can't make a move in this house without those women noticing and commenting," she complained.

The Hoopers inspected the laundry Mum hung on the line; they saw when the lights went off at night and when they came on in the morning; they watched Mum go downtown to shop and came over when she got back to see what she'd bought and to ask how much she had paid for it. If she went out alone when Rodney was at home, they rushed over to see if he was all right. If Mum and Rodney went out together, the Hooper women had to know where to, and get a full report afterwards.

They knew Mum was pregnant almost before she herself did and rushed over two and three times a day after that with concoctions or advice for the expecting woman and for the coming baby.

Mum hated having such a fuss made. She felt fine and didn't want to be treated like an invalid. "I have borne and raised two children already," she reminded them as they darted about with cushions and footstools and shawls for her. "Neither of my children suffered from colic," she said when they offered recipes for gripe water. "I doubt any kind of remedy will be needed." She accepted more hand-knit bootees and bonnets and matinee jackets than one baby could possibly use. She packed them away in a dresser drawer. "Shall we give these to the church sale?" she asked me with a wink. "Or save them for your babies to wear some day?"

"Can't you get them to leave me alone?" she asked Rodney after they'd brought her some foul-tasting tonic from the drugstore to build her up because she wasn't gaining enough weight. "They're acting as though it's going to be their child, not ours."

"They only mean to be helpful," Rodney explained. "They're excited about the baby. So am I. We wouldn't want anything to go wrong." Mum knew that, but still she found the hovering of the elder Hoopers irksome. "Why don't they stay in their own house and knit more bootees and matinee jackets then?" she asked Rodney. "Can't you tell them I don't want them hanging about in here?"

"I couldn't say that." Rodney was shocked at the idea. "They mean well. It's their way of showing how much they care for you."

"Well then I wish they didn't care for me so much," Mum said. "I don't like their interfering." Then she and Rodney quarrelled about the difference between "caring" and "interfering."

Later they made up with apologies and assurances of undying love on both sides. This was the way of their marriage. It followed a pattern of ups and downs. For a while they'd be happy as honeymooners. They laughed and flirted. Rodney sang, though accompanying himself now, for Mum stuck to her resolve never to play that piano again. They danced. Dave wound the gramophone for them and I would try to copy the steps

Then the in-laws would annoy Mum again, and again she and Rodney would quarrel. You could tell the marital temperature of the household by the music being played. When Rodney and Mum were getting on well, it was dance music on the gramophone and sentimental songs and Rodney's sweet tenor at the piano. When Rodney and Mum were having a disagreement, Rodney would play Bach, hour after hour of quiet fugues intended to demonstrate what a reasonable and restrained man he was. After an all-out fight, the gloomy, dramatic music of Liszt or Gottschalk would thunder through the house, rattling the dishes on the shelves and the pictures on the walls.

"Music is Rodney's greatest solace," his mother told us one afternoon while Rodney pounded the Chickering. We had taken refuge in the kitchen where we were drinking the peppermint tea Mrs. Hooper had recommended, and not liking it very much. "Rodney's nerves have never been strong. It's so bad for him to be subjected to aggravations." Mrs. Hooper looked at Mum.

"Well, I'm sure he has no aggravations from me," Mum bristled. "And my nerves must be considered as well, especially given my condition. It's outrageous the way Rodney hammers that piano for hours on end. I shouldn't be expected to put up with it."

Now Mrs. Hooper was offended. "For my part, I have always enjoyed Rodney's playing. He has a masterful touch."

Mum referred to Rodney's masterful touch as "infernal hammering". After Mrs. Hooper left, Mum marched into the sitting room. "I can't bear that infernal hammering," she shouted at Rodney, who was bent over the keyboard banging out Liszt. "I cahn't bear it." She still spoke with an accent as strong as it had been the day she left England. The accent infuriated the plain-speaking, proudly Canadian Rodney. "La de daaah," he stopped playing to say. "Why don't you talk ordinary?"

"I cahn't help my accent," Mum insisted. "It's the way I was taught to speak." She and Gran were the only people I ever knew who actually pronounced the gh in 'taught.' "Tawgggghhht." It was a long drawn out sound. Rodney went back to Liszt.

Mum shouted again, "I caahnn't bear that racket. It gives me a dreadful headache." Rodney continued playing. Mum found some cotton wool and stuffed her ears full and paraded past the piano. Rodney closed his eyes and went on playing.

Mum, defeated, put on her hat and gloves. "Let's walk downtown," she shouted an invitation to me. "We'll leave himself to the solace of music and we'll solace ourselves with ice cream."

Once in a while we solaced ourselves with a trip back to Creston to see Gran and to keep up with events there, like the dedication of the war memorial, for instance. That monument had been the cause of a little war of its own among the townsfolk of Creston, and Gran had kept us apprised of its progress. Some had wanted a stone and mortar cenotaph like those being built in cities and towns all through the Empire to honour the war dead, while others had argued for using the money that had been collected towards the building of a hospital or clinic with only a bronze plaque to commemorate our heroes. In the end, the "right side" as Gran put it, prevailed, and a granite monument was erected. When it was learned that the Governor General himself, Baron Byng of Vimy and his lady were to make a special trip to Creston for the dedication, differences of opinion on the appropriateness of the monument seemed to vanish. Everyone wanted to be there for ceremony. Mum was certainly not going to miss it.

Canyon Street was decorated with evergreens and a triumphal arch. Colonel Mallandaine and the town councillors were delegated to meet their Excellencies at the station and escort them through the evergreens to the monument. Schoolchildren and veterans marched, Piper Ross played a lament, Baron Byng laid a wreath. Creston's war was over at last.

Back in Cranbrook, domestic battles continued and peace accords were celebrated. Dave and I didn't dare to bring school friends home. There was no telling what might be going on: irate shouts and pounding music, or an amorous idyll. The one state of affairs was as almost as embarrassing as the other.

The first baby was born, an adorable little girl, and a year later there was a boy. They were sweet little creatures with white blond hair and blue eyes. Dave and I loved them, and they adored and hero-worshipped us, but we felt more like aunt and uncle than sister and brother. And who else of our friends had to stay home babysitting on Saturday nights while their parents went to the Gyro's dance?

The quarrels and the romantic idylls alternated in the usual pattern. Sometimes, while a quarrel was raging in the front room, Dave and I would sit at the top of the stairs, eavesdropping, and reminiscing nostalgically about the peaceful old days. We wondered if Mum regretted her decision to marry. "She didn't know what she was getting into," Dave said. "She can't have known Rodney all that well; she married so soon after we got back from England."

"She knew Rodney from before, from way back when we were in Bonner's Ferry. Don't you remember?"

Dave couldn't remember, but I could. Mum used to go down to the station when his train came through. Anyway it wasn't so much Rodney that was the problem. It was his mother and his sister, I thought. "They start most of the arguments and they egg Rodney on. Rodney tries to please everyone and winds up pleasing no one, and then he gets mad because his nerves are bad."

Mum also blamed her in-laws and, after three years of living in the family compound, she took steps to escape. She persuaded Rodney to move away from Cranbrook and take up fruit farming. Rodney could still keep his job with the railway as he was on a schedule of three-day runs to Spokane followed by four days off, which would leave him plenty of time to manage the ranch. Mum would help too of course. Rodney's nerves would benefit from the physical work in the open air, Mum maintained. Her own mental state would improve in direct ratio to distance from the Hoopers. The ranch would be a money-maker. Everyone would be much happier.

They found a beautiful little ranch with a clapboard house and a small barn and thirty acres of fruit trees in the Kootenay Valley, very close to Creston.

A removals wagon was hired to carry all Mum's precious goods: her Axminster carpet, the black walnut dining room suite, dark paintings in gilded frames, Gran's old silver tea service that she'd passed on to Mum. Rodney's Chickering grand was delivered separately in a special conveyance by a firm of piano movers who came all the way from Nelson.

David and I changed from the Cranbrook school back to the Creston school again. By this time I was two grades behind my contemporaries, which was a little embarrassing, but I had learned to be grateful to be at school, whatever grade I was in. And I was in luck with my teacher, a man who loved poetry and recitations. Every day when we entered the classroom, there was a poem written on the blackboard. We copied it out and if we had free time through the day we were to memorize it. I memorized dozens of poems, short and long, and I could recite them all: "A garden is a lovesome thing," "Oh to be in England, now that April's here," "Lochinvar." "The Highwayman" "Shall I compare thee to a summer's day?" I loved them all. I was, for once in my school career, at the top of the class.

Our family settled into life in Creston and at the ranch and we were happy there for a while among the orchards. Another child was born, a boy named Rodney, like his father.

But by and by, troubles returned. Mum and Rodney began to quarrel again. Why had Rodney stayed at his mother's overnight in

Cranbrook instead of coming to his own home where he belonged? Mum might demand.

Why should he come home only to be shouted at? Rodney would answer.

Why wasn't his good suit pressed when he needed it?

How was she to guess when his good suit was next needed since he never kept her informed of his comings and goings?

When Mum was especially angry, she would pack up a suitcase and take us to Gran's. Of course she never admitted that she did this to get away from Rodney. The pretense was that she was in town to shop, or to help Gran with the spring cleaning, or the fall hat show. But Creston was a small town, and everyone knew what was going on.

After a few days at Gran's, Mum's temper would cool off and we'd go back. Or Rodney, grown lonely and penitent, would come to Mum, begging her to return. He could be very persuasive. Besides, there was strong social pressure to keep them together. In those times a woman who left her husband lived under a cloud of disapproval. Rodney might be a man with a temper, but he was never physically violent, he didn't drink, was a steady worker and a good provider. Therefore he was a good husband, and it was Mum's duty to stand by her man. Married was married, for better or worse. So back we'd go to Rodney and the marriage with its ups and downs, sharp and steep as the mountain walls around us.

It was during one of the times we were staying at Gran's that the marriage ended in a dramatic and unexpected way.

Colonel Mallandaine heard the news first, and he hurried to tell Mum. "Rodney had a truck out at the ranch early this morning and he's packed it full of your furniture," he reported. "The postman saw it! You've got to get out there p.d.q. Hurry!"

When Colonel Mallandaine said hurry, people hurried.

Mum tore off her apron, and she and I jumped into the Colonel's Ford.

"Rodney's got the contents of the house and you'll have the deuce of a time getting them back, I'll tell you that straight out," Mallandaine lectured as we drove towards the ranch.

"Possession is nine points of the law," he continued. He was county magistrate and knew about it. "You must take possession of the house or he'll have that too. Get in there and stay. No court in the land will put you out. We'll get the youngsters out there with you. Stay put. And don't let him in."

Rodney had taken everything: the Axminster carpet from the front room and the green and maroon velvet three-piece suite, the chintz curtains from the windows, the dining room set, and the dishes, all but Gran's tea set and a few things from Mum's first marriage. He'd taken the pots and pans out of the kitchen, and even the preserves off the cellar shelves: the raspberries, plums and cherries Mum and I had put up in the hot, steamy kitchen during the past summer, sweating over the kitchen range while Rodney played Chopin in the front room.

"That bastard," Mum said, running her hand along the empty shelves. "The bloody baahstard!" It was the only time I'd ever heard her use profanity. I knew right then that this fight would be worse than any of the others. This had the feeling of permanent rupture.

The one thing Rodney hadn't taken was the Chickering grand. "He'll come back for it," Mum knew. "He wouldn't risk it on an ordinary moving wagon. He'll have booked the piano movers from Nelson to come for it."

Sure enough, Rodney arrived the next day with the "Willis Pianos, Nelson" truck.

Mum was ready for him. She'd discovered he hadn't emptied the barn, and in it she'd found the shotgun used against marauding animals in the orchard.

She stood on the front steps waiting, with the gun cradled in her arm. She looked like one of the women in Rodney's family photos of tough Cranbrook pioneers, hard as nails and loaded for bear.

"I've come for my piano," Rodney said.

"You own no piano here," Mum answered.

"Come on, Sarah. That's my piano. I need it."

"The only piano here belongs to me."

"You know damned well that's my piano. I've got the men here to move it. We're wasting their time." He took a step forward.

Mum lifted the gun. "The only piano in this house is mine. You can't have it."

She spoke with quiet, deliberate fury. "You caahn't have it." Possession is nine points of the law. It was her furniture he'd taken. She pointed the gun at Rodney's chest.

"Put that thing down, woman!"

"Leave my property!"

"It's not your property."

"It is now."

They stared at each other in a long weighing up. Did he dare to walk on up the steps?

Would she fire?

The piano movers stood well back by their van.

Enter Colonel Mallandaine. You could always count on the Colonel. This time he rode on to the scene in an RCMP car. He was out of the car and running towards Rodney before the car came to a stop. "Now then, sir. Now then," he bellowed in his loud military voice. Two officers emerged from the car. The Colonel indicated that one should take charge of Rodney, the other disarm my mother.

"It isn't loaded," Mum told the officer who took the gun gently from her.

Rodney was being treated less politely, but he was making more of a fuss. "My piano," he was shouting. "She's got my piano in there and I need it. I have arranged to have it moved by professionals."

The officer nudged him forward towards the car and Mallandaine, swishing his military walking stick back and forth, made it clear to Rodney that he wasn't going to get his piano that day or any other day to come.

We never saw Rodney again. Mum was left to manage as best she could.

Our standard of living fell with a thud that echoed all through Creston. Mum sold the ranch and moved us into a cheap rented house in town. When the money from the sale was used up, my once proud mother with her stylish hats and her posh English accent had to take day work cleaning for the doctor's wife and the banker's and the dentist's. We ate potatoes and pancakes and the cheapest cuts of meat. We wore mended and re-mended clothes and hand-me-downs from Aunt Boo and Uncle Clary in England. We got by, barely.

I quit school. I was almost nineteen, too old for sitting in a classroom with younger kids memorizing poems and the dates of the reigns of English kings. My teacher had suggested I take senior matriculation and then go to normal school to train as a teacher but I didn't have time for all that education. I needed to learn something fast, something useful that would get me a job so that I could earn some money soon. A secretarial course was the obvious choice. Unfortunately there was no business college in Creston. I would have to go to Nelson, and we could never afford that.

I was in despair until the British War Office came to my rescue. Although Mum had lost her widow's pension when she remarried, she discovered that some funds were available for the education of deceased officers' children. She and I wrote letters and filled in forms and battled through red tape for almost a year and eventually I was granted an allowance to pay for a two-year secretarial course in Nelson.

Those two years should have been happy years for me, giving me a first taste of independence, but they were not. My allowance was adequate but not generous. I stayed in the cheapest boarding house I could find, crammed in a room with two other girls. Pittman shorthand, typing, and basic accounting were not as interesting subjects as poetry and history and geography. I had to study hard, always worried that I might not pass and thus disgrace myself in the eyes of the British government and of my family. Some of the girls in the class were local girls, putting in time before marriage. They wore nice clothes, smoked cigarettes at lunch hour, and talked about movies and boyfriends. The rest of us, easily distinguishable by the dowdier clothes we wore, desperately needed the jobs we were training for. We stuck together, envied the others, worked hard, spent as little money as possible and did not have a good time. Our graduation day ceremony was brief and businesslike. We hurried away to find jobs. We did not promise to keep in touch with our classmates.

These were hard years for Mum too, bringing up three children on her own. Perhaps she wished she had been less feisty, more tolerant of Rodney and his family and more amenable to their way of doing things. If she did have regrets, she never said so. "We're managing," was her invariable response to questions about how she was getting along.

We managed, barely. There were no luxuries – except for the grand piano. No matter how tough things got, Mum held on to the Chickering, even if she never did play it. It filled the small sitting room; it dominated the house.

And every week, no matter if we had to do without meat, or without stockings for school, even if we had to go to church or Sunday School without a nickel for the collection plate, Mum would manage to scrape together fifty cents for the children to have piano lessons from Miss Bailey, graduate of the Royal Conservatory of Music. "A beautiful instrument, this," Miss Bailey could be depended on to say at least once during the lesson and Mum, darning or mending in the cramped corner by the window, would nod in satisfied agreement.

Two of the children had inherited the Hooper gift for music. They played at school concerts, at church and Sunday School and at the Legion. In Kiwanis competitions and talent shows they almost always won for both duets and solos.

Whenever people congratulated her on her talented offspring, Mum had a ready answer. "Of course, my children have an advantage as musicians. They're used to playing on a concert grand, you see. We have a Chickering at home."

Chapter 13

New Shoes

"Any mail?" Mum called as soon as she opened the door. She was waiting as anxiously as I for replies to my job applications. "No letters," I answered. "Only the parcel from England." I nodded towards the large, brown-papered box on the table.

"The parcel from England!" Mum's tired features brightened. She stamped the snow from her galoshes and, with a puff of relief, sat in the rocker to unclip them. She'd been working at the Mathesons all day, "obliging" as she called it, polishing their silverware or waxing their floors or ironing, to earn half a dollar. "Did you think to call in at Rosebank to tell Gran?" she asked.

"Yes, she'll be along soon. Old Mrs. Hunt was in to get new ribbons for one of those bonnet things she wears."

"There you are then; blessings abounding. We'll wait for her before we open the parcel. Put on the kettle, will you?"

I hooked the round burner plate off the stove to check on the fire. The wood was smouldering again. That load of wood the hobo had chopped for us was too green. I went to the woodbox for newspaper and kindling.

"Gainful Occupation Instead of Relief Is the Aim of Your Government" was the headline on the paper I crumpled and poked in among the charred bits of wood. That was a promise good only for burning, I thought. I laid on a couple of sticks of kindling, banged the burner back and pulled the kettle over it.

Before the water boiled, Gran appeared, wrapped in her old plaid shawl. Her eyes darted to the parcel. "What will it be this time, do you suppose?" she asked. Her look suggested she thought it might be gold bricks.

I rolled my eyes. "Old clothes," I said. "Same as always." Every spring and autumn, Aunt Boo, over in England, went through the closets in her house and sent the things she and her family no longer wanted to us in Creston. For Mum and Gran it was a red-letter day when the box arrived. They treated those clothes as though they came from Worth of Paris. When I was younger, I used to be excited about the parcels too. Now I knew better.

There'd be a frumpy old wool dress in navy blue or grey. A tweed skirt. A silk blouse with a stain down the front or a tear under the sleeve. Maybe a cardigan with darned cuffs or elbows. A scratchy woollen vest. A housedress. Uncle Clary's or cousin Percy's old trousers or plus fours, shiny across the seat and bagging at the knees to be cut down for the boys. At least Aunt Boo wasn't sending any more of those awful grey kneepants English boys wore. For a few years the young John had had to wear them to the Creston school to hoots of derision, and calls of "bare-legged Englishman!" It was a happy day for him when Cousin Percy graduated to long pants.

I sighed. It would be so nice to have something new to wear. Something from Eaton's Catalogue, for instance. Eaton's always had the smartest things. But Eaton's was too expensive for the likes of us who had no regular wage earner in the family. Mum's work brought in only a few dollars a week. My brother David was making his keep and seven-fifty a month at a government work camp. The younger children were still in school. And I was a useless, unemployed weight on the family budget. In our household, we considered it a good month if we got by and a bonanza if we managed to whittle down our bill at the Mercantile a little.

I'd graduated from the Nelson Secretarial College at the end of 1929, just as the Great Depression was getting going, and in two years of job searching since, I had not been able to find work. I was not alone in my predicament. Thousands were unemployed. Thirteen percent of Canada's population was on relief. This depression was worse than any financial crisis there had ever been before.

Compared to many, our family had no great cause for complaint, Mum used to say. We had vegetables from our garden and eggs from our chickens. Fruit could be had free for the picking at Gran's or at some of the orchards around town. Down in the cellar were shelves full of canned tomatoes, beans, pickles, and fruit to help feed us through the winter. Sportsmen, like the Talbot boys, brought us venison in season, and brook trout. So we weren't what you could call "in want". We just didn't have any money.

There were many worse off than us. We saw them on their way through Creston: men riding the freights east, having heard there were jobs in the factories of Ontario and Quebec; men riding the freights west, following rumours of work in the lumber camps and mines of B.C.; men riding the freights because no town would let them stay and they didn't want to go home and be one more mouth to feed. We saw families packed into old cars with chairs and crates and mattresses and washtubs, looking for a new life. We saw pinched men and women waiting outside the relief office, furtive and ashamed. We saw men camping in the Hobo's Nest down in the ravine where the railway crossed Dead Horse Creek.

Sometimes these fellows came into town to beg at back doors for food in exchange for work. They weren't often turned away hungry. Even in homes like ours where there was little to spare, they'd get a bowl of stew or a plate of beans and a cup of tea. We all knew young men who were living like these fellows, and in a kind of faith in a mystic exchange we believed that if we gave to the stranger at our door, somewhere another stranger would be feeding our Jack or Tom or Fred.

We weren't on relief and we had enough to eat; we had much to be grateful for, Mum said, and I supposed that had to include Aunt Boo's old clothes.

Mum untied the string from the parcel and rolled it into a neat coil to put in the sideboard drawer. Gran folded the brown paper. String and paper would always come in useful. Then the two of them shook out each item of clothing, one by one, and examined it with minute attention.

"Feel the quality of this serge," Gran said. "Boo always buys the best."

"Look at the buttons," Mum exclaimed.

"Tweed," Gran crooned. "This will wear forever."

I couldn't see what they were so thrilled about. This batch of clothes was the usual mothball-smelling old lot, as far as I could see.

When they had finished unpacking and admiring, Mum and Gran drank their tea and got down to the serious business of planning which castoffs to allot to whom and how they could best be transformed into garments we could wear without too much shame.

"Two housedresses for you, Sarah, and perhaps I could have the serge skirt to go with my black jacket?" Gran suggested.

"Certainly. You ought to have one of the housedresses, too."

"I'm well enough for this season. Cut it down for Liz or Olwen."

"All right," Mum agreed. "The blue one would be pretty for Liz. And the flannels. I'll take this pair in for David. Do you think I could get two pairs out of these for John?"

Gran examined the old trousers carefully.

"No," she decided. "You'd have seams all over in the wrong places. They'd look terrible. You'd do better to get the one good pair out of them. And here are two shirts. We'll turn the collars and they'll be as good as new."

"But no overcoat this year." Mum sorted through the pile again just to be sure. "That's a pity; I was hoping for something to make into a jacket for John. The one he's wearing is far too small."

I pulled out a brown wool jacket she'd overlooked. "What about this?"

"That's a lady's coat," Mum said. "And here's the skirt that goes with it, do you see?"

Gran took the ugly jacket from my hands. "Why, this would be the very thing for you, Olwen, dear!" Her theory was that because I had brown eyes, I looked good in brown. I didn't. My colouring was sallow, and brown made me look drab as potato sacking.

"You see," Gran was saying, "we could take material from the skirt to set into the side seams here to get that new boxy look in the coat you like. A – what is you call it? – a swagger coat?"

I didn't see the possibilities, but Mum did. "Yes! It'll be perfect. Very stylish. Such fine material. You'll be the best dressed secretary in town." "Secetary", she pronounced it. This irritated me since I was not a secretary at all. I was an unemployed graduate of Nelson Secretarial College. My diploma wasn't getting me anywhere.

"With a peach-coloured silk blouse, I think," Gran decided. She was looking at an orangey–pink nightgown thoughtfully.

Oh, surely not. I turned away. "I won't need a suit and a silk blouse to pick strawberries and raspberries at Turner's ranch, which is about the only paid employment I'm ever likely to get," I complained. "If I even get that," I added darkly.

Mum poured me another cup of tea. "You'll get your office job. Just wait. Your ship is bound to come in one day, and it'll be very soon now, I expect."

She'd been saying that for the past two years. I didn't see how she could still believe it. She was putting on a front to keep me from discouragement. I wished she wouldn't bother because, in fact, I was discouraged, and bored and angry and ashamed. I'd applied everywhere. "Dear sir," my letter went. "In the event of a vacancy arising in your office (store) (company,) would you please consider my application for the position?" I'd written to every office, store and company in the Kootenays. But there wasn't a job to be found. Not in Creston. Or Nelson. Or Sirdar. Or Cranbrook. I'd tried them all. No one wanted to hire a typist, no matter how many words per minute she could type. No one wanted a stenographer, no matter how skilled at Pittman's shorthand.

I was almost twenty-four. I wasn't a schoolgirl and I wasn't a housewife and I wasn't a career girl. I was nothing. I was worse than nothing. I was another drain on the all too slender household finances. It was humiliating. It was enraging. I'd worked hard at business college and graduated at the top of my class. And all for nothing.

Mum pretended she needed my help looking after the younger kids, and doing the housework, but I knew they could easily manage without me. Most of the time I hung around the house and tried to make myself useful, cleaning or mending for Mum and Gran, helping Gran with her garden, helping my half-sister Liz with her homework. Sometimes I'd spend an afternoon with blind Uncle Bob. He seemed to be content with a life of unemployment. Perhaps I could learn from him. But reciting poetry had lost its appeal for me at that time. Nor did I care much for joining Bob on his walks around and around the familiar streets of Creston, even though I could see the views that he could not. I was grateful for the public library. I did a lot of reading, and a lot of dreaming of the time when I would have a job and a salary and a useful life.

In the summer, like most folks in the Creston valley, we'd all had a few weeks' work picking fruit, but the ranchers had grumbled that they couldn't afford to pay pickers and shippers, considering the prices the fruit was fetching, and the season ended early. Some were saying they would let the fruit rot on the trees this coming season.

After the harvest, I'd begged Mum to let me go in her place to the day jobs she had in town, but she wouldn't hear of it. "No, no. You're a qualified 'secetary'." She was proud that I had been able to go to business college and that I had acquired career skills; she didn't want me to squander them. "You'll get a job offer one day soon. Your ship will come in."

The bank manager's wife advertised for a nursemaid to look after her two small children. I wanted to apply, but again Mum restrained me. "You don't want people to think of you as a nursemaid, Olwen: you're a trained 'secetary'. You wait 'til you're offered a job suitable to your qualifications."

I would wait my life away. "Did you read the editorial in this week's paper?" I asked. "It said companies aren't hiring new young workers any more. If an opening comes up, it goes to someone who was let go earlier."

"I'm sure the editor is referring to young people with no professional training," Mum answered. "Your 'secetarial' diploma is your open sesame."

You couldn't squelch Mum's optimism.

Gran and Mum set to work straightaway, ripping out the seams of Aunt Boo's brown suit.

"Don't rush," I told them, as I cleared the tea things off the table out of their way.

"Suppose a job offer came for you tomorrow." Mum unpicked stitches with little jabs of the scissors. "You haven't anything suitable to wear. Gran is quite right. This will make up into a lovely outfit for you."

Over the next couple of weeks, working on days when Mum had no "clients" to attend to, Mum and Gran made the "secetary's" suit. Mum did the machine sewing and Gran did the finishing work. They took in the skirt and made a swagger jacket and a blouse of peach silk, and Gran made me a cloche hat of brown felt to match.

Considering that it was brown, and considering what they had to work with, the outfit wasn't bad. I wasn't pleased, really, but I was grateful. I knew that Mum and Gran had done their best for me. But the fact remained that when I tried on the finished ensemble, I looked a lot like the brown velour couch in the sitting room

"You look lovely, dear," Gran said.

"Like a real career girl," Mum added. "You could walk into any office in the country today and not look out of place." She looked down at my shoes. "Except for the shoes. We'll have to get you new shoes."

"Oh, these will do," I protested, looking down at my worn black oxfords. Why waste money on something I wasn't going to wear?

"Prospective employers always pay particular attention to your shoes," Mum said. "Your shoes and your collar. If those items are not spic and span, you have no chance of getting the job. If they are neat and clean, you will most likely get the position."

Mum had some crazy ideas. "What would you know about getting an office job?" I asked her rudely.

"It's what my father always said," Mum replied. "An employer chooses according to your shoes and your collar, he said."

I wished the formula for getting a job really was that easy.

Mum insisted, so we walked up town to buy new shoes to go with the suit. "It's you need the shoes more than I do," I pointed out. Mum's shoes were not just down at heel, like mine, but cracking at the sides as well.

"Oh not me," she laughed. "I won't be swanking off to a job in an office like you. These are quite comfortable for the sort of work I do. They give more room for my bunions."

In his store Mr. Speers showed us some brown kid pumps that had just come in, with cross straps and three neat buttons across the arch.

"They're lovely," Mum sighed, feeling the leather.

I didn't even touch them. I knew what I had to do. "I prefer oxfords," I said. I chose the cheapest pair in the shop: square, clunky things, but only a dollar seventy-five. "Just in case my ship hasn't come in by next summer," I said with heavy sarcasm, "these will do well for apple-picking shoes."

Mum ignored my remark. "Please put these on our bill," she told Mr. Speers with dignity.

Mr. Speers made a big to-do of rifling through the pages of his accounts book so that we'd be sure to notice all the money he was owed. "Absolutely No Credit" said the sign above the till. But that was there for any outsiders who might come in. Speers would give credit to his home-town customers; he pretty well had to. Creston was a small place. How could he refuse to provide tea or flour to the woman who sang in the same church choir as he did? How could he refuse seeds or a handful of nails to the rancher who was his lodge brother?

The one family we knew who were eventually refused credit was one who lived extravagantly. Every week they ordered sirloin roast and leg of lamb from the butcher. At the grocery, they asked for the best teas and coffees and imported biscuits and marmalade. Speers sent them bills and warnings and final notices. They ignored the bills and continued to order the same expensive items they always had until at last he cut them off. The butcher, emboldened, did the same. Finally the bank manager foreclosed on their house and they disappeared from town. "They ate their house!" Mum said of them in shocked disapproval.

Now Speers kept a pretty sharp eye on what people bought. He'd give credit on necessities but we wouldn't dare to ask it for luxuries. I bet he'd have made us pay at the very least half down on those six-dollar brown kid pumps.

He wrapped the oxfords in newspaper and tied the bundle with a bit of string.

"There now. Let's walk on to the post office," Mum said. "Perhaps there'll be a letter for you today."

"Sure," I said. I wished I could have afforded those pumps. I swung the parcel of my new shoes by its string as we walked along Canyon Street. These were the first new shoes I'd had since high school. It would have been nice to have a good pair that I could like.

We walked into the post office. "Letter for you today, Olwen," the postmistress called from behind the brass cage. She handed me an envelope with "Canadian Imperial Bank, Cranbrook" printed on it. I tore it open.

"Dear Miss Evans,

"We are pleased to inform you that a vacancy has arisen..."

Mum had to read the rest for me. The vacancy was for a clerk typist. I was to present myself next Monday for a second interview.

I'd gone for an interview last spring and I thought they'd forgotten all about me.

"A second interview!" Mum exclaimed. "That means they'll almost certainly hire you."

"Provided my shoes and collar pass inspection." I grinned.

"What a good thing we have everything ready: the new suit and the shoes and all," Mum said with satisfaction.

We called in at Gran's to share the good news and drank a cup of tea in celebration. By the weekend we'd managed to scrape up a dollar ten for the train fare to Cranbrook. I went for the interview and I got the job. The pay was to be fifty dollars a month.

I arranged to board with a family called the Somers. They were recommended by Mrs. Speers and they would let me pay the first month's rent in instalments. I started work the following Monday.

The whole world looks and feels different when you're employed, I discovered.

I walked along Baker Street to the bank in the crisp early morning air, glad to have a day of purposeful activity ahead of me. I walked between the imposing white pillars of the entrance into the hushed, high-ceilinged edifice, into the busy smell of ink and paper and brass polish.

I loved the work. In the mornings I typed letters for the manager. One of the first letters I typed was to the millionaire William Astor Drayton who lived nearby and banked with us. I typed his name the way it sounded: William Aster Drayton.

Two days later Mr. Drayton stormed into the bank, waving the letter. "I am not a flower!" he bellowed. I had never heard of the wealthy American Astors, had no idea who this man was and why he was so angry until my mistake was pointed out to me by the manager. I was terrified that I'd be fired for my mistake, but soon everyone, even the manager, was laughing. He admitted that he should have seen the mistake when he signed the letter. "But for heaven's sake, don't make the same mistake again!" he warned.

I told the story at supper that evening to my landlady's family. "I can't imagine anyone making such a fuss about the misspelling of a name," I complained. "Hardly anyone spells *my* name right."

"Well, yours is a tough one, Oliven," Mrs. Somers said. She still hadn't got it right, and never did.

There were three banks in Cranbrook at this time. Our business came mainly from the railway and from some big lumber companies of the area. Substantial accounts were also kept by Camp Skookumchuck in the Rockies, a posh summer camp for wealthy Americans, as well as by a few wealthy individuals like our Mr. Astor Drayton. I was astonished at the vast sums of money that flowed in and out of our establishment every day. I typed letters to our wealthy clients and to the poor ones as well.

These last were often reminders of overdue mortgage payments or threats of foreclosure. I soon came to learn that the manager would never actually fulfil the threats his letters contained. What would the bank do with another property no one could buy? Might as well let the poor folks in the place stay put. They'd pay when they could. Businesses in Cranbrook ran on the same principles as those in Creston.

At lunch time I walked along streets of shingled cottages behind whitewashed picket fences to my boarding house for a hot dinner, then back to work for the afternoon.

I counted up sums on cancelled cheques, clipped them together and passed them to someone else to count again. I added columns of figures the teller had already added, then I added them again and passed them back to him. Female employees always worked in the background. Only men could be trusted to count out money to customers.

My favourite assignment was to accompany a teller in the delivery of the day's clearings, that is cash and cheques for the other two banks in town. In case one of the tellers might be tempted to make away with the loot, the delivery was rotated among them on an irregular schedule, and the teller chosen had to be accompanied by another employee, sometimes me. One of us carried the leather bag with the clearings and the other carried a loaded gun in case we should be hijacked along the way. The fact that none of us knew how to shoot the gun was of no concern to anyone.

My co-workers teased me about liking the clearings job. They pretended to believe I was the mysterious thief who had held up the Creston branch of the Imperial Bank back in 1925. One of the partners in that famous robbery had been caught with half the loot. The other had eluded capture and disappeared with several thousand dollars. "Watch her carefully," my colleagues would warn the teller when he and I would set out with the clearings. "She's waiting for a chance for her next heist."

What I liked about the clearings job was walking through the business district of town, feeling the excitement of its commerce and knowing myself to be a part of it. Here was the business of the day, gathered into a leather bag, and entrusted to me, a working woman of independent means.

At work I wore the brown suit and I had three blouses to go with it. "Sweet blouse," one of the girls, Betty, said to me the day I wore the ex-nightgown orange-y-pink one. Betty became my best friend. She'd been working at the bank for three years. She had some beautiful clothes, and what really astonished me was that she was saving up to buy herself a car. A car! The possibilities of what a salaried worker could buy were dazzling.

At five o'clock, tired after my day's work, and so grateful for it, I walked back to my boarding house, dawdling past the shop windows on Baker Street, planning what I might buy with my first pay cheque at the end of the month. Well, not a car. Not yet.

On late shopping nights Betty and I walked around downtown and looked through Fink's department store and Doran's and Wilson and Haynes. So many things tempted me: a soft blue coat, a green silk crepe dress, a smart navy skirt with narrow pleats. I wanted to buy them all.

I also wanted to send something to help Mum. But she'd told me, "Buy yourself what you need. I've managed this far; I can manage a little longer without your help. You'll need smart clothes for the office. And some spending money for movies and concerts and things. You have yourself a good time." With me gone, too, there'd be one less spoon dipping into the stew pot. She'd manage.

Still, once I'd bought myself a few of the clothes I really needed, I would certainly send home a little each month. Even a couple of dollars would help.

When payday came at last, I had to keep telling myself to be prudent. I would have liked to ask for all the fifty dollars in dimes, so that I could take them home and count them and gloat over them like a miser. But I made myself take a business-like attitude, befitting a bank employee. I took the money in bills and counted them. I had room and board to pay. I owed my landlady for the coming month and half of the past month as well. That would come to thirty-three dollars. And it would be prudent to put something aside for an emergency. Say ten dollars. No, five.

That would leave me twelve dollars to put in my purse. I was rich.

I would go home to Creston for the weekend and show off a bit. I'd go shopping at the Mercantile on Saturday with Mum and Liz. Perhaps I'd go ahead and buy those smart brown pumps. I hadn't seen any nicer in the Cranbrook stores. There'd still be enough left to buy treats for Mum and Gran and the kids. Maybe ice cream, or Saturday evening at the movies. Or both. Oh, it was good to be rich.

Creston looked good. It was April; the cherry trees were coming into blossom, soft pink, like dawn clouds. Below, the flats shimmered hazy blue-grey, like a vast still lake among the dark mountains.

Mum was at the station to meet me. She wore her best housedress, gloves and hat, as she always did when she went up town. As we started for home, I noticed that, though the street was quite dry, she was wearing galoshes. They were tied around the ankles with black grosgrain ribbon but they flapped at every step.

"Why are you wearing galoshes?" I asked.

She answered indirectly. "Do you remember your great uncle Walter – the vegetarian pacifist, you know? Well, another of his theories was that shoes are bad for the feet. Going barefoot is much healthier, he always said. He made all his family go barefoot, everywhere. This was right in the middle of London, too. Just fancy. His eldest daughter was married in bare feet. A lovely wedding gown and bare feet. Imagine that. Anyway, I'm trying it out. I just slip on the galoshes for going uptown."

"Your shoes wore out entirely, did they?" I asked.

"To bits and laces," Mum admitted.

"But," she added as her optimism took hold again, "these galoshes are surprisingly comfortable. The ribbon was Gran's idea. Who knows? I may be setting a new fashion in footwear."

"Stop pretending," I said. "You know they're awful."

We walked along Canyon Street.

"Let's stop at the Mercantile," I said. "There's something I want to look at."

I bought Mum a pair of the best black leather oxfords in the store. They cost three-fifty and I paid cash. She wore them home and said they were the nicest shoes she'd ever had.

Chapter 14

Love Calls Me by My Name

A thin man on a thinner horse plodding slowly down a long straight road. Dust rises in clouds at each footfall and blows in gritty gusts around them, covers both in its fine grey powder so that they appear to be one substance, one creature. "Black blizzards" they call these dust storms here.

"Whoa!"

The man pulls a clean handkerchief from an inner pocket, takes off his wire-rimmed glasses and polishes them, then peers through them into the dun-coloured gloom.

Sky and land are merged in a featureless haze. Wheat fields lie on either side of the road, he knows well enough, although the grain can hardly be seen. All the fields look the same. There are no landmarks to guide him. He is lost, again.

No matter. The horse will know the way home. He lets the reins hang loose, nudges the ribby sides with his heels. "Ged-up!" The horse plods forward on the long straight road past the monotonous fields.

It is late August. Harvest time. The hymns of the season play through his mind.

Come ye thankful people come,
Raise the song of harvest home
All is safely garnered in ...

But in these fields, there is little to harvest. There has been no rain since May. The topsoil has blown away. What little grain there is stands short and thin and the kernels flat. Another bad harvest. They're saying it's hardly worth the effort of cutting and binding and stooking and drawing in.

"Plough it back into the land, might as well," most of the farmers are saying. "That is, if it ever rains so we could run a plough through the earth."

This is the third straight year of drought in southern Saskatchewan.

The first failure was bad, but farmers knew they had to expect some bad years. Most had some savings put by. They tightened their belts, and said, "Next year's bound to be better."

They needed a good crop of wheat, and they needed a good market to sell it in, like they'd had in the war years. But since 1929 the price of wheat had fallen from a dollar sixty-five a bushel to thirty-some cents a bushel. Prime Minister Bennett couldn't do anything about the weather, but he had promised them the price of wheat would rise again, and the farmers believed him. Bennett was a smart man; he'd started out poor and become a millionaire by his own hard work and good sense. He must know what he was talking about.

But the next year was worse than ever. The crop was bad, and the prices were worse. There was no money now for new machinery, no money for parts to fix the old, no money to buy gas for the cars bought in better times. Farmers took out the motors, hitched horses to the cars and called them Bennett buggies, poking fun at the prime minister's false promises.

That year there was real privation, but they survived.

They even made jokes. "My hired man's working to buy the farm off of me," one of their favourites ran. "When he gets done paying for it, I'll work to buy it off of him. That way we'll both keep gainfully employed."

They still had hope when they planted the third spring. "Third time lucky," they said. "You never get three bad years in a row."

At Sunday services they sang hymns of hope and faith:

We plow the field and scatter
The good seed on the land,
But it is fed and watered
By God's almighty hand.

They prayed for the yearly miracle of growth and harvest. But this year was turning out as bad as the last two.

Now the people had nothing left, not even jokes. Families were packing up and leaving. Most of the young men were already gone. They rode away on the freight trains looking to find work on the west coast or in the big cities back east. If they didn't find anything, at least there'd be one less mouth to feed at home.

To those who remained on the farms around the hamlets of Wyndam, Willow Bend, and Bell's Corners, Reverend Gordon McGuinness had been assigned as Presbyterian minister for a year's mission field service after his ordination last spring. It was his job to conduct Sunday services in the schoolhouses at the three hamlets – the congregations were too poor to afford churches – to minister to his flock's spiritual needs, and to sustain them in their faith.

"What can you preach to these people of faith and hope?" he'd asked his predecessor who had taken him around on his first Sunday to show him the ropes.

"I stick to the psalms," Reverend Halloran said. "There's comfort in the psalms."

So today instead of the harvest hymns that perversely would not leave his mind, they'd sung:

O God our help in ages past
Our hope for years to come,
Be Thou our guard while troubles last,
And our eternal home.

Only eight people had shown up for the eight o'clock service at Willow Bend. Fourteen cents in the collection plate.

More at Bell's Corners, of course. A dozen at the three o'clock at Wyndham.

A total of fifty-six cents for the young minister to buy food and tobacco this week. He'd manage. Not in abundance, but in sufficiency.

The horse stopped.

Ah yes. A pole barn, mud chinked, roofed with sods. Home sweet home.

He dismounted, pushed open a sagging door and led the horse into its stall. There he removed the bridle and bit, fetched a pail of water, scooped out a small measure of oats and tossed the grain and then a forkful of musty hay into the manger. "Good night, Beauty."

He latched the stable door, then walked around to the front of the building and let himself into his home. A beaten earth floor, a west-facing window curtained with yellowed newspaper, a wooden table and chair, a plank bookcase laden with books and papers, a straw mattress laid on an old door propped up on bricks, and a couple of wooden crates serving as kitchen cupboard and wardrobe.

He lit the kerosene lantern.

Supper time.

He wasn't hungry. The McLaughlins had invited him for dinner after the eleven o'clock at Bell's Corners School. They'd had roast chicken and potatoes with gravy and canned peas. A white cake for dessert. The food had nearly choked him for he knew the McLaughlins would be eating nothing but porridge for the next week after putting on a spread like that.

He'd pretended to enjoy it. They'd have been shamed if he had refused their hospitality, or if they hadn't been able to offer a decent meal to the minister when it was the Sunday of their turn.

He brushed the dust off a hard-boiled egg from the supply he'd cooked up in the morning and cracked it open. He ate a lot of eggs. Eggs were cheap.

There was just enough water in the pail to do for a pot of tea. Good. He boiled a kettle on the kerosene stove, and sitting at the table, rolled the first of the evening's cigarettes, a voluptuous pleasure, a self-indulgence he could not bring himself to even try to resist.

Monday morning, after he'd fetched water, and done his few barn and household chores, he began work on his sermon. He usually dedicated mornings to study and sermon writing. Afternoons and evenings were for pastoral visits and meetings.

He worked hard on his sermons, tried to make them interesting and inspirational. What could he tell these people to sustain their faith and their belief in God's goodness and mercy?

He wondered if he himself would be able to keep his own faith if he knew he was to share these people's future. Yes, he shared their hardships now, but he would be rescued at the end of the year, and go to a better parish. He remembered the look of joy and relief on Reverend Halloran's face when he'd climbed aboard the eastbound train last spring. He'd almost literally shaken the dust of this place off his shoes. And next spring, it would be his turn to leave. How then could he dare to talk to these people of keeping the faith, of trusting in the Lord? They had endured two failed harvests and were facing a third. And there was no new posting coming for them.

He had been here only half a year, though it seemed much longer. The winter hadn't started yet. How would he manage in this place through the long cold months? The parishioners were going to put in a wood stove for him, but the cold would come up from the earth, and in through the chinks between boards. There would be days, they said, sometimes weeks, when he'd be snowed in. Would he go mad with cold and loneliness and despair?

No. Surely with God's help and his own willpower he would endure. And he would be sustained by the knowledge that in the spring his trial would be over.

Meanwhile, what message could he preach without sounding smug?

Could he talk of Joseph's seven fat years and the seven lean? No. These people couldn't survive seven lean years. That story would be an incentive to despair. Despair was a pernicious sin.

Stick to the psalms. The psalms are always a comfort. "Why art thou cast down, o my soul? And why art thou disquieted in me? Hope thou in God."

His meditation was interrupted by a knocking on the door. It was the young Forster lad.

"Little Ellie is dying," he announced with no emotion in his voice. "Mum and Dad say can you come?"

"Yes, of course."

"Did you walk over?" he asked the boy.

"Yeah."

That would be a good seven, eight miles. "Sit down. Eat." He gave the boy a drink of water from the dipper and one of his hard-boiled eggs. He had nothing else to offer. "I'll get ready."

He put on his clerical collar, bridled the horse. He had no saddle. He hoisted the boy to sit in front of him. The boy was asleep before they'd gone a mile.

What to say? How do you comfort a bereaved parent? What did he, a young man who had neither wife nor child, know of such sorrow?

Mr. Forster opened the door to him. "She's gone," he whispered.

Reverend McGuiness took the father's hand. "The Lord giveth and the Lord taketh away. Blessed be the name of the Lord."

The mother and two children were sitting at the kitchen table, their hands folded, not knowing what to do.

He walked around the table, touched each of them, sat down on the chair beside the dry-eyed woman. He wished for a moment his church allowed some rituals, like the Catholics. He would like to busy himself with oil and candles, get these people down on their knees counting beads and murmuring comforting, familiar words.

He had only the Bible and his own awkward and diffident pity.

"The Lord is my shepherd," he read, "I shall not want."

When the psalm was finished, they seem satisfied that something fitting had been said, though the words about green pastures and still waters didn't seem right in this landscape.

"Would you like to see her?" the woman asked.

He rose and followed the woman into a curtained-off end of the main room. A child lay tiny and still in the middle of a large bed. Flies buzzed around, busy at the lips and at the corners of the closed eyes.

"She was too good for this world." The mother brushed the flies away.

"Let us pray," the Reverend McGuinness said. He watched the flies settle again as he spoke.

"You'll have a cup of tea?" the woman asked when he was done.

"Thank you."

While the tea steeped, they discussed the few details of the funeral. Then, because there was nothing else to talk about, he asked about their crop. They would harvest what they could, Mr. Forster said. "It'll feed the chickens maybe. Anyways, we might as well work as sit idle."

"Yes," the preacher agreed.

He was relieved when the tea was drunk and he could go.

At the funeral the next day a few neighbours and church people gathered round the grave. The dust blew in, covering the small coffin too soon.

Later that day he made another start on his sermon.

"Today," he began, "I buried a child of this parish." From that bald beginning, he wanted the sermon to soar upward to an affirmation of faith in God's goodness. The sermon refused to soar. Whenever he took it past that first sad sentence, it sank deeper. "And I will bury others before my year among you is over. Death is in your eyes as silent and empty as that small child's body."

Go back to the psalms. Always to the psalms. "Many a time have they afflicted me; yet they have not prevailed against me."

On Friday he stopped in at the general store in Bell's Corners to pick up the few grocery items he needed, and the precious packet of tobacco. "Mail for you," Mrs. Bell handed him two envelopes: one from the Board of Missions, one from home.

In front of the store he tore open the envelope from Ontario, lifted it to his face, and breathed in the smell of home that permeated the pages.

His mother's uneven handwriting spread all over the page. He imagined her writing it last Sunday, after the evening chores, sitting at the kitchen table, newspaper spread over the faded oilcloth, the coal-oil lamp spreading a shadowy light on the white pages of the writing pad.

"My dear son,

"Hope this finds you well. We are all well here.

"The threshers was here this last Wednesday. Many asked after you and send kind regards. The Hughes boys, the McFaddens, and Violet, who was kindly helping me with the kitchen work.

"The crop was good. John says near thirty-five bushels to the acre, we are thankful. The weather has held good.

"John and Dad go tomorrow to the Harrisons if it don't rain, which we hope not.

"This week I will pick and do down the blue plums. Also John is set to plough up the potatoes for me."

Potatoes and plums and a good harvest. Such good fortune seemed marvellous to Gordon now.

If he was back at home what he'd like to do would be to run out to the south pasture and roll in its greenness, like a horse let out in the spring.

Wouldn't that set the folks wondering! He smiled at the thought of it.

"I was sorry to hear how hard times continue for your people out there. They must be fearful disappointed and suffering."

There was not a word about her own hard time. Her bad leg would be swollen up from running around the kitchen with all the extra work of baking and cooking and cleaning up for the threshers. And now she was turning to and making plum preserves, and walking along the fresh-furrowed field stooping and gathering potatoes. It was too much for a woman in her sixties with no other woman to help her.

But maybe she was glad to have work, to have plums and potatoes to gather and food enough to provide good meals for her family. Here the women had the never-ending work of sweeping away dust and grime that settled again in minutes, of cooking meal after meal of porridge and eggs, and often not enough of those.

"Dad and John send their love.

"We think of you every day. Your loving mother."

Only when he was back at his place, unpacking his sack of groceries – another week's supply of rolled oats and eggs and tobacco – did he remember the second letter, the one from the Board of Missions.

"Dear Reverend McGuinness,

"This is to inform you that a change of assignment for your mission field service has become necessary.

"The church of St. Andrew's in Cranbrook, B. C. having fallen vacant due to the sudden death of the incumbent, you are to be transferred there, as soon as the arrangements can be made.

"Whilst it is not our policy to make changes of this sort, we feel that in this particular case, a move is imperative. St. Andrews has a congregation of about sixty families, while you are ministering to only thirty-two families where you are now placed.

"Services in your present charge will be taken by Mr. Lamb, a lay preacher from Yorkton. He will be in touch with you shortly."

Gordon glanced quickly through the rest of the letter, relief and joy pulsing through him. He was to leave, to leave this joyless place.

He would not have to spend a winter here watching the brown dust change to bitter white snow. He would no longer have to try to offer hope where there was no hope. The Lord had blessed him, unworthy as he was.

But why should he be spared? Was it not his duty to stay and suffer with the cold and hungry here? Or would that be pride? Who was he to think he could do a better job of ministering to these people than Mr. Lamb of Yorkton? And no doubt Mr. Lamb was in need of the pitiful stipend the Mission would pay him. Best do as he was bid.

Where was this Cranbrook place anyway?

Cranbrook was in the Kootenay mountains of British Columbia. Though it was the first of October when he arrived and snow covered the peaks round about, the town seemed marvellously green, as beautiful as the Promised Land. Truly, the Lord had delivered him. Ah, the sermons he could preach here of God's goodness!

He walked the first Sunday to the church along streets of shingle houses and tidy lawns and gardens bright with late blooming zinnias and geraniums. All this week he had savoured the luxury of living in a real room with plastered walls and wooden floors and curtains on the window and a real bed. He had enjoyed eating good meals cooked and served to him by a smiling landlady. He had delighted in seeing smiling people in the streets.

This morning the town sparkled in the clear mountain air. No dust, Lord, no dust. People on their way to the four different churches of the town greeted him. They looked content, even prosperous, not like the grim-faced people of Bell's Corners and Wyndham.

Of course he knew there was poverty here too, as there was all through the country. Many would have little more to put in the collection plate than the folks on the prairie. But at least they had enough to eat. They had harvested the fruits of their gardens and orchards. Why had the Lord not done as much for the farmers of Saskatchewan?

He had had no final inspiring message to leave with his congregations there.

> *God be with you 'til we meet again,*
> *Till we me -ee-eet*
> *Till we me-eet*
> *Till we meet at Jesus' feet.*

When they sang the parting hymn at his last service, the tears had come to his eyes, but not to theirs. He was just one more loss to them, and not a very significant one.

He preached his first sermon to the Presbyterians of Cranbrook and they listened with attention. Then he stood at the door and shook hands with the congregation as they left and many said his sermon was good. He was pleased.

After the evening service there was a reception with tea and cakes in the church basement and a big crowd showed up, even more than had been at the morning service, which was a good sign. People shook his hand and bid him welcome and he tried to remember their names and wondered if he could dare to light up a cigarette.

"Hello. I'm Betty Ferguson," a young woman said. "You've met my father; he's clerk of session."

"How do you do, Miss Ferguson. I'm pleased to meet you."

"And this is my friend Olwen Evans," Betty said.

"Olwen," he said. "What a beautiful name! Welsh, is it?"

For some reason that set the two young women laughing. Reverend McGuinness realized his mistake immediately. He should have said, "How do you do, Miss Evans."

Miss Evans rescued him from embarrassment. "It's because it's the first time anyone's ever said something nice about my name."

"And you pronounced it right first time," Betty said. "Took the rest of us ages."

Reverend McGuinness looked at the laughing girl called Olwen Evans. She was tall and slim, and her face was kind. He felt there was a great deal more he'd like to be the first to tell her. He'd like to make her laugh again, too. She had such a joyful laugh. All those months in Saskatchewan, he'd hardly heard any laughter.

Betty leaned closer to him. "I have to warn you, Olwen is not of the elect. She's an Anglican. You must try to convert her."

Reverend McGuinness smiled and, with a boldness he would never have thought himself capable of, said, "In that case, may I call on you later this week, Olwen Evans?"

"Yes," she said. "Yes, that would be very nice."

Chapter 15

We Have Done Very Well

I'd been working at the bank in Cranbrook for three years and liking it. Although I'd had two pay cuts instead of raises, that was nothing to complain of in these hard times. I had to consider myself fortunate to have a steady job and regular pay cheques, however small, when so many people had no jobs and no pay.

I was fortunate too in that I liked my work and I liked Cranbrook. It was a bigger town than Creston, and there was more going on. I had friends here now: Betty Ferguson and her fiancé, Jim; Ruby Somers, the daughter of the family where I boarded; her friend Frank; and Gordon, the young minister Betty had introduced me to recently. He and I had been going about together since we met and we'd been having a good time, or as good a time as a Presbyterian preacher was allowed to have. We went for walks, to the movies, to the occasional play or lecture when something came to town. I'd taken to attending evening services at his church, not so much out of piety as for the opportunity to gaze at him without shame for the full thirty minutes of his sermon. Some evenings we sat in the Somers's front room and read aloud to one another, or I did some of my recitations from Robert Service or from *Cautionary Tales for Young Children.* Gordon preferred Shakespeare and Browning to my favourites and I began to see that it was perhaps time for me to enlarge the scope and seriousness of my literary interests. In the secrecy of the Somers's kitchen, we occasionally played euchre with Ruby and her family, but we had to be careful that word didn't get out about that, as some of Gordon's parishioners did not approve of card playing.

We did not go dancing. Gordon said his church disapproved. I suspected this disapproval had as much to do with Gordon's disinclination as with church doctrine, but I didn't argue the point. I wasn't as keen on dancing as Betty and Jim were. They went to just about every dance going in Cranbrook and vicinity. They knew all the latest steps: the Black Bottom, the Turkey Trot, the Fleahop, jitterbugging, all of the crazes.

Betty was an energetic young woman who liked to keep on the go and have a good time, and she liked everyone around her to be having fun as well. She scolded Gordon for his refusal to dance and, when that had no effect, she started in on me. She chose a day when business was slow at the bank. She and I sat idle at our side-by-side desks, talking in low voices, with a stack of papers at hand to turn to should the manager walk in. "I don't know whether I did the right thing in introducing you to that preacher," she began. "I realize we can't expect Gordon to frequent the jazz bars, and frankly I can't see him doing a Charleston, but I don't know why he has to be so stuffy about good clean ballroom dancing. The Gyro's dances are very respectable; it's all fox trots and waltzes. Lots of Presbyterians go. Me, for example. It seems to me Gord could step out on a dance floor once in a while without endangering his immortal soul or shocking the elders to death. Myself, I wouldn't give ten minutes of my time to a man who couldn't dance."

"We can only be thankful that Gordon at least has nothing against movies or card playing, like the Baptists," I reminded her. Out of the corner of my eye I saw the assistant manager heading our way, reached for a form letter and put an end to our conversation.

I was much more concerned about our idle afternoons at the bank than I was about the ethics of dancing. If I lost my job, there'd be no more dancing for me at the Gyro's or anywhere else. The manager had been kind enough to explain to me that the pay reductions I'd had were no reflection on my work, only an unfortunate but necessary step in view of the business slowdown, but I worried that if business slowed down any more, the next unfortunate but necessary step might be my dismissal. It had happened to plenty of others.

Betty, who lived at home with her wealthy family, was not so much affected by the pay cuts. She was able to spend her whole salary on herself. She bought beautiful clothes and recently she'd actually bought a car. Like old Gramps Little in Creston with his Pioneer motorcar, Betty was convinced that the automobile was a necessity of modern life. Everyone should have a car and know how to drive it. She wanted me to try it out.

I'd never be able to manage it, I told her. I was a person who was unable to learn to ride a two-wheeled bicycle and could therefore not even hope to be able to control a four-wheeled vehicle. And anyway, I could never afford to buy a car, so what was the point of trying to drive?

"Because you'll have a car, sooner or later. You'll have to. And then what are you going to do? I can't see you as Lady Dum-Dum sitting in the back seat giving orders to your chauffeur. Do give it a try. It's not at all like riding a bike. It's easy. You'll pick it up in no time."

I knew that there were some people who just instinctively knew how to drive. My brother Dave was one of those. At his work one day the manager asked him to take his car and pick up some documents in Nelson, and David, with typical Young self-confidence got in the car and drove to Nelson and back without mishap and never let on it was the first time he'd ever driven a car. You didn't need a license back then, just the confidence that you could manage. Unfortunately, I didn't have that confidence. Full of doubts and trepidation, I got behind the wheel of Betty's Buick and, at her urging, set the vehicle in motion. I was appalled but not really surprised when I immediately crashed into a nearby fence post.

Betty took the mishap calmly. "This is not a problem; it's just a small dent." She took over the wheel, backed the car out of the fence and drove back into the Somers's laneway where we got out and examined the fender.

Mr. Somers came out of the house to offer his opinion and began the teasing about my driving that I feared might go on for the rest of my life. He also fetched a mallet and banged out some of the crumpling. It did look better after that, but I wanted to have it fixed properly for Betty. Even a small dent, I knew, could cost a lot of money to repair. I hoped I would have enough to cover the cost.

Betty ran her hand along the dent. "Actually," she said, "I kind of like it. It gives the old girl character. We'll leave it as it is." I thought at first she was saying that out of generosity to spare me the expense of the repair. But eventually I came to believe she really did become fond of that dent, the way one can come to love the imperfections in favourite things: the ink stains on a desk, the broken spine of an often-read book, the hollowed place on an old kitchen table worn down from years of use. And Jim said it was a good warning to other drivers to give Betty a wide berth on the road.

But for weeks I flushed with shame every time I looked at Betty's car, and it was twenty years before I dared to get behind a steering wheel again. I did it then only because, just as Betty had predicted, I did need to drive. Eventually I even managed to acquire a driver's license. But I never did like driving.

Betty loved that dented car of hers. She drove it with panache. She tore along the mostly unpaved and precipitous mountain roads around Cranbrook at speeds I found alarming, taking the hairpin curves with verve and often on two wheels. She drove us on wonderful excursions to Moyie Lake or St. Mary's Falls and the surrounding countryside. She drove to go shopping, to go to the movies; she even drove to work sometimes, though it was only a distance of less than a mile.

"I don't know how we ever managed before I got my old flivver," she said one Saturday afternoon when she was driving me home from downtown. She and I had just spent several hours on Baker Street looking at the shops, finishing up with a good look through Fink's department store. I was tired, and a little discouraged. Betty had bought a blouse, a silk scarf, and some very lacy, very expensive underwear. I'd bought a pair of stockings for work. So many beautiful things I'd seen, but I couldn't possibly afford them.

Betty, happily ignorant of the state of my finances, went on reminiscing about the days before she had her car. "We never went anywhere. It must have been so dull. I think we sat at the kitchen table and embroidered, didn't we? Without even a radio to listen to. I actually can't remember, can you Ollie?"

"We had sing songs," I said. "We read books. We went for walks or skated or sledded." I remembered the wonderful sled rides down Creston's Fourth Street hill and walks along the track to Aunt Charlotte and Uncle Andy's ranch and felt a wave of nostalgia for those slower, quieter times when we were satisfied with less. "We played word games, made toast over the fire, recited poetry." I remembered evenings of Robert Service poems with Uncle Bob.

"Gosh, it was awful, wasn't it?"

I wasn't at all sure that she was right.

But as the months went by, I became more involved with the faster-paced Cranbrook life and its excitements, and with my circle of friends there. I hardly ever went home to Creston on the weekends now. Of course it was always good to see Mum and the youngsters and Gran and Uncle Bob, but my brother, Dave, most of my old friends, and some of the Talbot kids had left Creston to find jobs in bigger places. There really was not much going on in Creston.

It was a backward, old-fashioned place, small enough that everyone knew what you were up to. Ladies still had to wear hats and gloves to walk uptown to the Mercantile or the post office, or they risked censure. Mum and Gran were appalled beyond reason the day I tried to go out with a kerchief tied over my head instead of a real hat. They felt it was a disgrace to the family, especially to the family of a respected milliner.

Ladies had to wear correct hats and gloves, and ladies did not smoke, at least not in public, and certainly not at Rosebank. I'd got into the habit of smoking with Gordon, and Mum, I discovered, used to enjoy the odd cigarette back in her Ish Kibbidle Club days. So after the kids were in bed and the streets quiet, she and I would sit out on the back steps and light up, risking discovery by night-prying eyes. That was about the only high living that went on during my Creston visits.

In Creston it was always necessary to be proper, or at least to give the appearance of being proper, even if everyone in town knew the real improper truth. Everyone knew, for instance, that Gramps was on a bender when he "was not himself" as Gran put it. Another pretence that irritated me was that no one was ever to mention the break-up of Mum's second marriage. Mum continued to be known as Mrs. Hooper and she acted as though the separation were a necessary, but temporary, absence, even though we hadn't seen hide nor hair of Rodney for years.

To me, it didn't matter if the neighbours knew that Gramps sometimes got drunk, that Rodney was never coming back, or that Mum and I were smoking on the back porch, but some of the hushing up that went on verged on the crime of aiding and abetting, in my view. There was a rancher who was known for mounting the ladders behind female pickers and thus getting into a good position to grope at them. Everybody knew this, but instead of confronting him, Creston women warned each other to keep an eye out for him and his lecherous habits. "It would be such a shame for his family if accusations were made publically," was the reason for the silence. The rancher's position as a respectable member of the community and an elder in his church was never challenged, and he went on groping any unwary female picker in his orchard.

Crestoners wanted no shame, no public embarrassment. We pretended that we were all model citizens in model families. We ignored any unseemly reality.

It should not therefore have come to me as a surprise that when Aunt Boo and Uncle Clary announced that they were coming to Creston for a visit, Mum and Gran pretended to be delighted, because a person is supposed to be delighted when family members come for a visit, especially when they take the trouble to travel halfway around the world to do so.

The news came on a Friday afternoon in July on a weekend that I happened to be spending in Creston for a change. Mum met me at the station in a state of high excitement, bursting with the good news. On the way down to Gran's to talk over the impending visit and make appropriate plans, we stopped at the bakery to pick up one of the Battenberg cakes Gran was partial to.

"Fancy them coming all this way. Oh my! It will be good to see them again," Mum said as we turned in to Rosebank.

"Isn't this wonderful?" Gran greeted us. "It has been years since I've seen Boo. And dear Clary. Does she say anything about Percival in the letter? Will they bring him too?"

Mum fished the letter out of her handbag. "Not a word about Percy. Though it's hard to imagine Boo would be apart from her dear boy for a whole month." She grinned. "She'll have to write him every day, or even telegraph, I expect."

"They're staying for a whole month!" I exclaimed.

"Yes, they'll be here for August. Won't it be lovely?" Mum set out cups and saucers on the kitchen table. "Boo always writes such good letters, but letters are never the same as a good face-to-face chin wag, especially with Boo. She can be so funny." Mum turned to Gran. "Remember the marvellous imitations she used to do? The suffragette and Lloyd George? With both voices? She could have gone on stage with that one it was so good. And the time she fell off the omnibus into the mud, and blamed the driver for it and had him down on his knees apologizing to her, and all the passengers applauded?"

"And the time she sent her twelve-year-old nephew away across the ocean?" I interrupted the reminiscences.

"Yes. I can't think why she did that. Inexcusable, really. But it did turn out for the best. Charles has done so well for himself." Indeed Charles appeared to have suffered no damage from the adventure of his childhood. He had stayed in Creston, finished school and was now managing the drugstore in town and courting a local girl. "Charles has always been a Creston fellow through and through," Mum declared.

Gran remembered what a help Boo had been to her in the early days of her widowhood and the Hammersmith boarding house. "I don't see how I could have managed without her. I shall be so happy to see her again."

I'd had enough of this hypocrisy. In my opinion the proper answer to Boo's announcement would be a telegram saying. "Do not come. Not welcome." I slammed the lid on to the enamel tea pot and cut savage slices of the pink and white cake. "You don't like Boo and Clary. You were so angry about the way they sent Charles away."

"I can't understand why you would think that." Gran brushed aside the reminder of that incident and changed the subject. "Boo is very fond of scenery. I am sure she will be delighted with the mountain views here."

"She says she is looking forward to seeing your garden." Mum pointed to the letter on the table. "And Clary hopes they will see a grizzly bear. I must tell him not to hope for that."

I could hardly believe this. They didn't seem to be pretending. They seemed to be genuinely pleased that Boo and Clary were coming. Did they really not remember what those two were like?

Soon they were busy with plans. Boo and Clary would stay at Rosebank with Gran. They would have the larger bedroom and Gran would move into the little room off the kitchen. Mum's house was too tiny, and Boo and Clary would not enjoy having the three Hooper children hanging about.

"I'll say!" I agreed with that, remembering our visit at Boo and Clary's in North Finchley and how we children stood for hours outside on the street because we were not welcome in the house. "I think they have a nerve expecting to be put up for a whole month. I don't see how you're going to manage, Gran, I really don't. Perhaps they could board at Mrs. Winter's?"

"I hope I have houseroom for my own daughter and her husband," Gran replied. "There is plenty of space. We shall manage very well."

I thought of the cost of extra food as well. Mum and Gran were always short of the essentials and I knew they'd want to put on the dog a bit for Boo and Clary. It was characteristic of both Mum and Gran not to worry about money. They would manage somehow. The bread and the fishes would extend themselves. To me, the way they kept their households going without any steady income was as much of a miracle as the Bible story. Mum was raising her children on almost nothing and Gran brought up the Talbot children on insurance money barely enough to pay for their needs. And now both women were delighted at the idea of welcoming two demanding people into their homes for a whole month's visit. I would have to keep a sensible eye on expenses for them.

"How very fortunate that your holidays fall in August so that you will be able to enjoy the visit with us, Olwen," Gran said.

"Very fortunate indeed," I muttered. I'd been hoping to spend at least part of my two-week vacation with my Cranbrook friends. Betty had come up with the idea of an automobile trip to Banff. All four of us would go: Betty and Jim, Gordon and I. We would take tents and camp along the way at the new parks that were being set up for tourists. But I might have known that the plan would fall through in the end, I thought to myself. We really weren't vacationing kind of people, Gordon and I. He'd never been on a holiday in his life, and except for the wonderful camping trip to Clear Lake, and the trips back and forth to England, neither had I. Tourist travel was for the likes of Betty and Jim, and, apparently, Boo and Clary.

Once again I would be doomed to spend my annual holidays in Creston. I couldn't leave Mum and Gran to the mercies of their unpleasant visitors. I would be the watchdog. I wouldn't let Clary order Gran around and I wouldn't let Boo make demands and complain that her nerves were shattered. I wouldn't let them be mean to the youngsters. I would watch the spending to see that Mum and Gran didn't go to extravagant lengths to please. I would help with the cooking, I'd try to keep the kids out of the way, and perhaps I'd even get some mornings' work picking in the orchards. Some holiday!

My friends were disappointed when I returned to Cranbrook and told them that the Banff trip was off for me. That meant it was off for them too. Gordon wouldn't go without me, and Betty's parents would never allow her and Jim to go off on a trip on their own. Cranbrook people were modern in their outlook, but not as modern as that.

"Ah, well, we'll make the best of it." Betty was never unhappy for long. "Mountains look the same pretty well anywhere, I guess." Soon she was making alternate plans. "We'll go up to the lake for a day. Maybe take a spin up to the Hot Springs." I envied Betty her freedom.

"Every cloud has a silver lining." She tossed me a careless consolation. "You'll have a good time with your family."

"I doubt it. Not with Boo and Clary in residence."

"Oh gosh! They aren't the ones who shipped your little cousin from England to Canada with a label around his neck, are they?"

"The very ones."

"Oh dear. Well, I hope it won't be too awful."

"What hopes!"

So at the beginning of August I went back to Creston. I wasn't happy about spending my holiday there, but when the train pulled up to the old hip-roofed station, the sight and scent of the place stirred my heart, as it always did. I loved the tang of evergreen forests that wafted down from the mountains and the dry, hot aroma of ripening grass and grain from the flats. Each peak outlined against the sky was like an old friend to me. Betty was quite wrong in saying that mountains are pretty well the same everywhere. The Kootenay mountains of Creston were *my* mountains, different from all others and dearer to me than the equally beautiful mountains around Cranbrook or Banff.

Creston had changed in the years since I'd begun to work in Cranbrook. Thanks to a new diking project, the flats along the river below the town would no longer flood each spring. The old flood plain was now prime agricultural land. There, where once in summer, wild grasses grew lush for anyone to cut and harvest, fields of wheat were now being cultivated. Where the Siwash had once set up their summer teepees and fished the river and grazed their horses, now ploughs and harrows, mowers and binders would clatter through the spring and summer months. The Siwash had drifted away like the smoke from their cooking fires. Only the mountains remained, to east and west, solid and friendly, the beautiful bastions guarding our valley.

There were changes in town too. The depression had made most of us poor, yet still we had luxuries and conveniences we wouldn't have thought of owning twenty years ago. A new dam on the Goat River provided the town with hydroelectric power. Most homes – although not Rosebank – now had electric lights and telephones, radios or gramophones, and even indoor toilets!

Uptown Creston had modernized itself. A new grain elevator stood by the tracks ready to receive the plentiful harvests that would come from the newly reclaimed fields. A new hospital could provide care for a dozen patients. Canyon Street was paved for car traffic. The splintery wooden sidewalks had been replaced. The telephone exchange had long since outgrown Aunt Olive's front room and now had a building of its own. We had a movie theatre where you could see a double bill for fifteen cents, and afterwards you could get an ice cream soda for ten cents at the new soda fountain.

On the benchlands around the town, the orchard trees in neat rows still blossomed and bore fruit plentifully. But somehow Creston had never become the premier fruit-growing region that Alphabetical, Gramps Little, and Mallandaine had envisaged. The Okanagan Valley had won that distinction. It was to that valley that settlers had flocked in larger numbers, bringing new business and prosperity, while Creston had remained just another small town with a few solvent businesses, a population that was getting by, and hopes for the future.

Gran, Mum, myself and the kids stood on the station platform lined up like an honour guard waiting for the arrival of the TransCanadian. Boo and Clary stepped off the train, smiling and waving like royalty. There were hugs and kisses all around, though mine were of a restrained nature. Then we all marched down the hill to Rosebank. I made sure that Clary did a fair share of the luggage toting. I was keeping a sharp eye on him.

Boo was enchanted by the mountain scenery, just as Gran had said she would be. It was actually hard to get her into the house for tea. She seemed to want to stand at the gate, exclaiming, "Beautiful! Magnificent!" over and over again, turning this way and that to take it all in.

Inside at last she drank down a great many cups of tea. "Delicious," she said. "The train journey was wonderful – I can't tell you – the scenery! The comfort! The meals in the dining car! Wonderful! But the CPR could not produce a decent cup of tea. A terrible brew they served! And yours is so good!" she passed her empty cup back for more.

"It's the pure mountain water," Gran said as she poured.

"I told her she should have ordered coffee on the train. That's what I did," Clary said. "The coffee was fine. Americans all drink coffee, don't know a thing about tea, I told her."

I bristled to attention. Here was Clary pontificating in his old authoritative manner.

Young Liz, who had no idea that she was contradicting a virtual dictator, indignantly pointed out that the CPR was Canadian, and that this was Canada, not America that Uncle Clary was talking about. I expected Clary to answer that with a scowl and a bad-tempered "Bah!"

Instead he asked in a perfectly pleasant way, "Ah, are there differences, then? In England, you see, we say America and we mean both Canada and the U.S.A." Soon we were all discussing distinctions in language, attitudes, food, commerce, cars. Gran got to air her view that British Columbia was a special case, almost a separate country on its own. The natural barriers of the mountains, she believed, protected us from nefarious influences from outside, both American and Canadian.

I couldn't remember conversations like this ever going on during our unpleasant visit in Finchley all those years ago. I seemed to remember mostly long cold silences there and a strong desire to get the meal over with and leave the table.

We were all still sitting around the table when Cousin Charles dropped in on his way home from work. Boo and Clary greeted him like a long-lost son. No one referred to the circumstances in which they had parted all those years ago. Charles was kind enough to enquire after cousin Percival. Cousin Percival was very well, Clary said. "He would have loved to join us on this journey but his office couldn't consider giving him a month's leave. He is very well thought of at his office, Barking and Sloane, Solicitors."

"Such a pity!" Boo added. "He would have loved the scenery here. All beautiful! The forests that go on for miles and miles. And the Prairies. Miles and miles of wheat. No hedge rows or fences. Just wheat!"

"And dust," my friend Gordon might have informed her. "Thin wheat and lots of dust."

"And most magnificent of all, the mountains," Boo continued. She seemed to have taken up talking in gushing superlatives. I didn't remember that habit from earlier times either.

I kept up a careful watch for signs of the old arrogance and cold-hearted indifference to others that I did remember, but I saw none that day, nor in the days that followed.

Boo and Clary loved Creston. They declared they were very comfortable in their room at Rosebank. They made no complaint about the outdoor biffy.

They loved walking through the town and watching the trains come in. They discovered the soda fountain and its ice cream sodas, and after that they'd round up the three kids and sometimes me and Mum too every afternoon and take us out for sodas. Gran wouldn't come. She believed that ice-cold drinks caused jaundice and warned us against them.

Mornings Clary worked as a fruit picker or accompanied Uncle Bob on his walks through town and listened to the long, screeched story of the caaaaaamping trip to Cleeeeeeear Lake.

One evening Charles took the guests to a baseball game and Clary never missed an in-town game after that. He sat in the stands and called out loud encouragement like a local: "Bring him on home, boys. Bring him home." Occasionally his old authoritarianism took hold of him and he'd shout, "Not to third, you idiot!" or "Hold on to the ball, butterfingers!"

As for Boo, her admiration for the landscape was insatiable. I would sometimes come upon her standing in front of Rosebank, simply gazing at the mountains or down into the valley, muttering, "Splendid! Magnificent!" She was an artist in spirit, if not in fact, she informed us. She took rolls and rolls of film. Charles had them developed at the drugstore but when I brought the photos down to her one morning and she spread them out on Gran's table, she was disappointed. "Without colour the beauty is not apparent. Nor is there any sense of the shimmering light and shadow. Percival will never be able to see in these the beauty I've been writing to him about." She went out again to look at the real thing and gather material for the daily letter to Percy.

I took advantage of the temporary absence of the two guests to gossip about them with Mum and Gran in the kitchen. "I can't believe two people could change so much," I said. "Has age mellowed them? Or is it because they're on holiday here? They're so different."

"Boo is as she always was," Gran said quietly. "I could never understand why you formed such a poor opinion of her. Of course, you were very young when you knew her. As for Clary, he has, I believe a forceful character. That is always an asset in a man and of particular benefit to a man married to Boo, who can, at times, be a little indecisive – I could even go so far as to say irresponsible."

"Like when she sent Charles away."

"Indeed."

Mum said, "You didn't see them at their best, Olwen. Clary and Boo were going through a hard time when we were there in twenty-one. Clary had wanted to enlist in the war, you see, but the government wouldn't allow it because he was needed in his engineering work for the railways. His brother did enlist and was wounded terribly at Mons and spent years in a hospital for hopeless cases before he, blessedly, died in twenty-five. Clary used to visit him two or three times a week and he'd come home from each visit either raging or weeping, Boo told me. It wasn't easy for her either. And then she herself was in shock from Charlotte's death. We were all sad, but Boo had always been especially fond of Charlotte. I should never have left Charles in their care at that time. I thought he might cheer the household up, but of course he couldn't, poor boy, only made things worse. It's a blessing that in the end everything worked as well as it did."

"Things generally do work out for the best, I find." Gran took a dish of scalloped potatoes out of the oven, and I hurried to set the table for dinner.

On the last weekend of my two-week holiday, Dave drove up from Trail where he was now working at a bank. On the Saturday he took Clary and the youngsters up to Kootenay Lake for a day of fishing.

We womenfolk would make use of the quiet day to do down preserves from the fruit Clary had picked. We worked all morning in the stifling kitchen with a good hot jam-making fire crackling in the kitchen range. We peeled and chopped and pitted, boiled and stirred and skimmed "like the witches of Endor" as Mum said until the last sealer was filled, the fire in the range allowed to burn itself out, the canning pots washed, the table wiped down and the beautiful sealers, glowing with their fruit, set to cool on the sink shelf. Then we retired to the porch and sat on the stairs to cool ourselves.

"Dinner," I said after a time. "I'm getting peckish."

"I cannot and I will not cook another morsel today," Gran declared. "With the men and children away, there is no need to exert ourselves.

I suggest a sandwich luncheon." Another of the old-fashioned ideas that prevailed in Creston was that women didn't need to eat proper meals; it wasn't worth bothering cooking for us. Only men and children deserved three proper meals a day.

"Jam sandwiches, I suggest," Mum said, and Boo shrieked her terrible laugh and said she intended never to eat jam again.

"There's a small bit of yesterday's pot roast left, and tomatoes from the garden. That should do us nicely," Gran said. I was just heaving myself to my feet to set about fixing this bit of a scratch meal, when a familiar Buick with a dented left fender pulled up in front of the porch. The driver tooted the horn like a trumpet fanfare, and out climbed Betty, Jim and Gordon.

"Surprise! We've come to drive you back to Cranbrook!" Betty shouted while I and the other women of my family hastily pulled off our jam-spattered aprons and stepped down to meet the visitors. "Thought you might like a bit of a motor trip to finish off your holiday, since the great Banff caper was nixed.

"What a drive!" Betty bounced up the path. "Three flats! Lucky to have two stalwart men along to fix them. Such a pretty town Creston is. We've driven all around it looking for you. And here you are." Betty gave me a hug. "Grand to see you, Ollie. You're looking swell." Then she looked towards Gran, Mum and Boo lined up behind me.

What will my friends be thinking of this family? I worried. Here we are, Gran's house smelling like a jam factory, and the three of us sweating like work horses and probably smelling like them too, my hair all straggly – I was planning to wash it this afternoon – and it's dinner time and what on earth will we offer them to eat? I worried all the time I was going through the introductions. If Betty should ask to use the little girl's room and I had to lead her out to the biffy in the garden, I would die of shame. Why did they have to arrive at dinner time anyway? Had they no sense of tactful timing? Could we get away without offering them anything to eat? Cold tea, perhaps. Gran almost always had a sealer of cold tea in the cellar.

And then, for that matter, what will Mum and Gran be thinking of the ebullient Betty, wearing trousers, and with two men in tow, and talking as usual. If she lights up a cigarette Gran will faint dead away.

Whatever Gran was thinking, she was playing the gracious Duchess. "Do come in. I believe it is a little cooler in the drawing room." The "drawing room" of course was hotter and smellier than the porch. "I am so pleased to meet you. Olwen has spoken of you often. You will have luncheon with us, won't you?"

"Wouldn't say no to that. I'm famished," Jim said.

"Motoring is indeed taxing on the strength." Gran spoke as if she knew.

"'Specially when it's Betty driving," Jim said. Gordon laughed, and Betty pretended to be vexed.

I couldn't laugh. Luncheon! Trust Gran! Betty would be thinking of jellied chicken or ham, perhaps; potato salad, sherbets or ices, and we had nothing but yesterday's pot roast to offer.

After a few minutes of conversation about the journey, Mum and Boo slipped away to the kitchen. While Gran held forth on the delights of Creston, I followed. "What on earth are we going to feed them?" I asked in despair.

Mum was nonchalant. "Don't worry about the food," she said. "We'll manage."

"Leave it to us, my dear." Boo shooed me towards the door.

"But there's only that bit of cold roast we were going to finish off for sandwiches," I worried.

"Stop fretting," Mum said. "We shall do very well off a sausage," and she and Boo went off into peals of laughter. That old family joke again. I could never understand why Mum and her sisters got such a kick out of it.

It concerned an occasion in their girlhood when Mum, Boo and Charlotte were at dinner at an elderly aunt's and she served them one sausage, cut into three. When they'd finished the frugal meal, the aunt said, "There now, girls, you've done very well off your sausage. Very well indeed."

Whenever she served a skimpy meal, or a particularly lavish one, Mum would bring out the old punch line and I remembered how it never failed to render her and Aunt Charlotte helpless with giggles. And now Aunt Boo as well.

"Go back to your visitors," Mum gasped. "We'll do our best for you."

And of course they did. They sliced the meat thinly and surrounded it with pickles so that it didn't look so pitifully skimpy. There was plenty of bread and butter and a great platter of tomatoes and for dessert, inevitably, plum preserves.

"Delicious," Betty and Jim said.

"A feast," Gordon said.

"Thank you," Mum said. And then she couldn't resist; she had to say it. "We have done very well off a sausage." And she and Boo went off into hoots of laughter.

"It's a family joke," I explained to my mystified friends.

After lunch, Mum was clever enough to suggest that we walk over to her house so that I could finish packing my suitcase, and so we escaped to a house that had a bathroom at least, not to mention a grand piano.

If we were to drive all the way to Cranbrook, it was time to be off. Mum had conjured up a picnic supper and we loaded it into the car along with jars of preserves for Betty and the Somers. We stopped in at Rosebank to say good-bye. My farewell to Boo was much warmer than my welcome had been. "And do give my love to Clary and tell him I'm sorry I missed saying good-bye to him myself." I wasn't at all worried about the rest of their visit. They were perfect guests. Everything was working out well, just as Mum and Gran said it would. And then we four piled into the car and we were off, with Betty honking farewell, and Gran, Mum and Aunt Boo waving good-bye.

Gordon leaned toward me and took my hand. "You're not sore at us for crashing in on you and your family, I hope. It was my idea actually."

"Not that he had any trouble persuading us," Jim added. "Betty's always up for a drive."

"Why would Olly mind us coming to drive her back to Cranbrook in speed and comfort and style?" Betty asked. "This is better than a dirty old train any day of the week, I'd say."

"We meant it as a consolation prize for having to miss the Banff trip, and for having to spend your whole holiday with your family," Jim said, "though actually I thought your aunt with the crazy name wasn't so bad – a little too ecstatic about scenery, maybe – and your Mum and Gran are very nice."

"Boo is not so bad after all, I discovered," I said. In truth, I hadn't minded spending the holiday at home at all. I'd enjoyed it. Everything had worked out well in the end.

"But I'm awfully glad you came," I said. I was happy to be with my friends again, going back to Cranbrook and my job. I was happy Boo and Clary's visit was going well. I was happy to be sitting beside Gordon with my hand still in his.

We stopped at a clearing beside a mountain stream to eat our picnic supper. Betty and Jim went off to explore upstream. That was when Gordon proposed. And I said, "Yes."

Chapter 16

Leaving the Empire

In Cranbrook, B.C., we had connections with the Prince of Wales. For one thing, he loved the Rockies and the Canadian West. He'd said so. And he'd bought himself a ranch, which happened to be just across the Alberta line, but still very close to us. He'd travelled on our Crow's Nest Pass Railway and admired the scenery.

We even had personal connections. My friend Ruby Somers, my landlady's daughter, had travelled all the way to Revelstoke to stand on the station platform to see the Prince when his train stopped there on its way to Vancouver, and Edward had come out and waved. "He looked straight at me, he did," Ruby claimed. "Handsome? My word! Photos don't do him justice. You have to see him for yourself."

Even more exciting than merely seeing the Prince was having the opportunity to talk to him. And there again we knew someone, or at least knew of someone, who had had that honour. It was the older brother of Ruby's friend, Frank. This brother was a waiter on the CPR and he had once served afternoon tea to the Prince of Wales on the royal train.

Everyone in Cranbrook knew the story. Frank was often called on to tell it. "My brother George was very nervous about the job, see. Course he's used to waiting on big shots, working in the dining car, you know, but royalty, well that's something special. So he was pretty darn scared. Pleased to be chosen, mind you, but nervous. They tell him he's supposed to call the Prince Your Royal Highness. 'Would you care for another cup of tea, Your Royal Highness?' he's supposed to ask.

"But when the moment comes he's so nervous he can't get it out right. 'Would you care for more tea, your Highness?' he starts, and then he sees his mistake and goes back, 'Your Yoyal,' is what he gets out this time, and then he really gets the heebie jeebies.

"The Prince smiles and, nice as you please, he says, 'It's all right. Just call me sir. And yes, I'd like another cup of that delicious tea.'

"'Yes, sir,' George says, and pours the tea. Doesn't spill a drop. That he can do right.

"He wasn't stuck up at all, George says. Just a swell fellow."

Whenever Betty and I heard the story, we would sing,

"I danced with a man,who danced with a girl,

Who danced with the Prince of Wales," just to tease Ruby. She was so stuck on the royal family that I sometimes suspected her attachment to Frank was based largely on his brother's having spoken to the Prince.

Ruby carried it to an extreme, but the fact was that most of us in the Dominions adored our royalty, and especially the Prince of Wales. Probably just about every community in the Empire treasured its own particular anecdote or connection to the popular Prince. He had toured Canada and the U.S. in 1919, and in the next years he visited Australia and New Zealand and India. In 1927 he was back in Canada for the Diamond Jubilee of our Dominion. His travels were recorded in detail by the press, and we read about them with avid interest. Everywhere he went, he had a magic gift for endearing himself to his people. He was our golden Prince, and when in January, 1936 he succeeded to the throne, we knew he would be a glorious king. Edward VIII must have been the most popular British monarch ever.

Until the autumn of 1936, that is.

That was when the rumours started.

Our King had apparently become close friends with a Mrs. Wallis Warfield Simpson, a commoner, an American, and a divorcee. And if the American papers had it right, he intended to marry her!

Loyal subjects were shocked. Bad enough that she was not a princess, not even a duke's daughter, bad enough that she was not British, not even a British subject, bad enough that she was divorced once already, but worst of all, she was still married to Mr. Simpson. The King could therefore not possibly marry her.

Yes, the pictures in the magazines were evidence that the King was going around with her. That seemed to be clear enough, and no doubt they were good friends. But could they really be intending to marry?

At home in Creston at Thanksgiving, I discussed the question with Mum and Gran.

Gran scoffed at the very idea of our King's marrying Mrs. Simpson. "It's gossip from those American magazines everyone is reading," she said. "Edward would never demean himself to marry that woman."

Mention had been made of something called a morganatic marriage. We looked up the meaning of that and didn't think much of it. Mum said she'd read of it in connection with some penny-ha'penny European monarchs, but it would not apply to the British royal family.

Abdication was another solution being offered, but that course of action would be far worse. Look what happened to the Czar of Russia after he abdicated! Such things could never happen, not in Britain, not to our King.

"Stuff and nonsense is all it is," Gran claimed. "Those magazines will print anything to create a sensation."

"He caaaahn't be thinking of marrying that woman," Mum said. "Queen Mary would never allow it."

Back in Cranbrook, as the autumn progressed, there was more difference of opinion on the subject.

My landlady, Mrs. Somers, shared my view. "Even if he is in love with her, he'll see his duty clear, and give her up for the sake of the Empire."

My friends Betty Ferguson and her fiancé, Jim, professed to be shocked by such hardness of heart. "I don't see why he should give her up," Betty said. "Not if they're in love. Why should they have to forfeit their chance of happiness just because of some stuffy old Victorian prejudice against divorcees?"

Ruby and Frank, for whom the King could do no wrong, didn't know what to think.

And my fiancé, Gordon, didn't care. He groaned in boredom and tried to change the subject whenever I or one of the others got going on the subject of the King's marriage. Everyone else in Cranbrook, in Canada, in the whole of the British Empire was concerned. We talked about it endlessly, but not Gordon.

"I don't give a darn whether the nincompoop marries her or not," he said in irritation one evening as we walked up town to meet our friends at the Star Theatre.

"You can't call the King a nincompoop," I hissed, and looked around to see if any one might have overheard. Luckily, Baker Street was almost deserted as the autumn evenings were drawing in, and the air was cold. "Mrs. McBride would have you thrown out of church for a remark like that."

Gordon leaned close to whisper in my ear, "Yes, but I trust you not to tell her." Then he continued in normal tones, "I wish the man would hurry up and decide one way or another so that the country can get back to caring about what really matters. We should be concerning ourselves with unemployment, the drought on the prairies, fascism – not fretting about the love life of two very silly people."

"He's not silly; maybe she is." We closed the argument there, seeing Betty and Jim, Ruby and Frank waiting for us in front of the cashier's box at the Star.

Anyway, Gordon and I had had the argument before, and there was no making a monarchist out of him, I feared. He didn't seem to see the point of it. "Might be all right for the British," he would concede, "but not for us in Canada." He would stand for "God Save the King" in deference to society's view, but he would never sing the words. "It's a disgrace of a national anthem," he claimed. "It doesn't say a word about our nation. It's all about the English king and I can't, in all conscience, pray for preferential treatment for him."

Gordon was not to be spared further discussion of the great controversy that evening, for the News of the World showed Edward and Mrs. Simpson disembarking from the yacht *Nahlin* some place on the Mediterranean.

This was much more interesting than the main feature, and we set to discussing it as soon as we'd all squeezed into a booth at the Zenith Cafe and asked Fran to bring us coffee and pie.

"Oh pshaw. Here we go again," Gordon sighed.

"Eat up your pie and pay no attention to us." Betty slid a plate across the table to Gordon.

"Now then, girls, what do you think they were up to on that big fancy white yacht?" She raised her eyebrows suggestively.

"They looked more like movie stars than royalty, didn't they?" I mused.

"What does he see in her anyways?" Ruby wanted to know. "She's way too skinny to be attractive."

"Definitely. And did you notice the shoes he was wearing?" I asked

"Yeah. Like ballet shoes," Ruby said.

"Not at all the kind of shoes a king should wear," I agreed.

"Exactly what kind of shoes should a king wear?" Betty asked indignantly. "Army boots? On a yacht?"

"And his shirt open," Ruby continued. "I tell you, Queen Mary sees that newsreel, she'll be mad as blazes. It's that Mrs. Simpson that's to blame. You never saw him like that before he met up with her. When I seen him the once at Revelstoke? He was wearing a proper suit then."

"He likes informality," Betty argued. "He's not stuffy like old King George was, eh? Do you know, they say King George wore his army uniform to bed, including the boots and all his medals."

I ignored Betty's facetiousness. "Informal is fine. But going around in public with an open shirt is taking it too far."

"I blame Mrs. Simpson, I do," Ruby said. "She has no idea of what's fitting for royalty and what isn't."

"Lord, I wish he'd send that floozie packing," Frank agreed. "And the sooner the better."

"He will," I said. "Don't worry. He will, and any time soon."

"Don't be so sure. Two bits says he'll marry her." Betty held up a quarter.

"Never," Ruby and I chorused.

"No gambling, if you please," Gordon said in his preacher's voice. But he couldn't get us off the subject.

"A divorced American Queen will do us good," Betty said, being provocative. "She'll shake up the Empire a bit. Maybe it will be one of those – what do you call them? – marriages. Sounds like a kind of horse?" she searched for the word she wanted.

"Morganatic?" I supplied.

"Yeah. Maybe it will be one of those. But they'll marry for sure. Love will find a way."

"No," I insisted. "He'll do the right thing. He'll renounce her."

But he didn't.

He abdicated.

We read it in the paper, but we still couldn't quite believe it. What was this Instrument he was supposed to have signed?

"I, Edward the Eighth, of Great Britain, Ireland and the British Dominions beyond the Seas, King, Emperor of India, do hereby declare My irrevocable determination to renounce the Throne for Myself and for My descendants."

The news broke on December tenth. The King would broadcast a message to his people the next day, they said. We were on tenterhooks, waiting. At the bank, on the streets downtown, in the shops, everyone wondered what the King would say. Was it true? Had he really, truly abdicated?

At Mrs. Somers's boarding house, we gathered round the radio in the kitchen, anxious not to miss a word.

"At long last I am able to say a few words of my own," the King began.

My heart leapt. He was going to tell us it was all a hideous mistake. It had come about because those news reporters didn't know what they were talking about.

But he said it was true. He'd abdicated. He said he'd made the decision himself.

Bitter and angry disappointment surged through me.

He talked about duty. "...you must believe me when I tell you that I have found it impossible to carry on the heavy duties and responsibilities and to discharge my duties as King as I would wish to do without the help and support of the woman I love."

Duty was a hollow word coming from him, I thought. All my life I'd heard of duty to King and Country and Empire. Men had left their loves, their families, their jobs, and gone to die for King and Country and Empire. My father. Dorothy Bacon's Bill. Young Archie Murdoch. Thousands and thousands of others. They gave their lives because of duty. And their families bore the pain of their sacrifice proudly. And this man, our King, wouldn't even give up marriage to a loose-living woman for us and for his Empire?

The shock and disillusionment were terrible.

In his closing words our ex-king tried to rally us to the old passion. "And now we have a new King. I wish him, and you, his people, happiness and prosperity with all my heart. God bless you all. God save the King!"

Ruby burst into tears. "How could he?" she sobbed.

"I'm ashamed of him," Mrs. Somers said when she could speak. "He's shirked his duty, the scrimshanker."

"Oh don't say that!" Ruby wailed. "He spoke so good. I guess Mrs. Simpson put him up to it. Oh what will we do now?"

I tried to imagine what Mum and Gran would have to say about the news. Nothing, I guessed. Would Gran, who mistrusted radios and wouldn't have one in her house, have gone to Mum's to listen to the broadcast? Even if they had listened together, they'd be too ashamed to discuss it, both of them. In the best tradition of the British army, they'd close ranks and ignore the fallen. George VI had stepped into the King's place. Edward VIII was to be obliterated from our minds. The Empire would march on. Ours not to reason why.

"We have passed through the most anxious and astounding day in the history of our empire," the newspaper reported the next day. "Nothing will assuage the universal disappointment that the King was unable to respond to the entreaties not only of Mr. Baldwin (the British Prime Minister), but of all his subjects."

Betty was indignant. "I think it's a shame that the papers aren't sticking up for him. They used to print such nice things about him. Now all they can do is find fault. It's a disgrace that he was forced to abdicate for love. And now he's being hounded out of his own country like a thief in the night. It's just horrid. The poor dear man. I feel so sorry for him."

"So do I. So do we all," I agreed. "But he should never have let himself get into the situation in the first place."

"It's his family that created the situation," was Jim's opinion. "Queen Mary, she's made of solid steel. She wouldn't bend one inch to accommodate anyone."

"It's the Simpson woman," Ruby said. "She's the one to blame."

"He would have been such a good king, if only they'd let him," Betty said.

"Well, you've got another king now. The institution of monarchy will apparently survive." Gordon really couldn't understand what all the fuss was about.

"But it's not the same," we said.

"Do you know what I read in a magazine a while ago?" Ruby asked us. "I think it was *The Post*, but I'm not sure. I didn't say nothing at the time 'cause I didn't believe it, but now I do. It said Edward claims he's five foot seven, but really he's only five four."

"A short little man," I said. "Huh. Maybe that's why he couldn't find a princess to marry. They all towered half a head or more over him, and being a King and Emperor himself he wouldn't tolerate that."

"Funny, he didn't look so short that time I seen him at Revelstoke. I always thought he was a tall man. Tall and handsome," Ruby said.

"Well, he still is handsome," Betty said. "Don't get nasty about the poor guy now. I hope he and Mrs. Simpson will be very happy together."

"They don't deserve to be," Ruby sniffed.

Whatever our reactions, the abdication came as a profound shock to all of us. Whether we felt his act was due to an appalling dereliction of duty, or to a hard-hearted imposition of an outdated code of morality upon a good man and woman, it was an act we had believed could never happen. Yet it did, and because of it, our world changed. As we listened to the fateful words on the radio we could almost feel ourselves slipping forward into a new era.

So many changes! Twenty some years ago, when I had come to British Columbia as a girl, there had been no radios. Now every home had one, and our King could speak to us in our own kitchens.

Back in 1913 Gramps Little's automobile was such a novelty we'd all run out to the street to stare in wonder as it passed. Now the roads were full of cars and even I might learn to drive one someday, but not yet. Airplanes we had thought were strange machines of war, and now the rich rode in them to reach destinations faster than a train could take them, and even ordinary folks could send a letter by airmail across the country or even across the sea.

Everything was changing and no one knew any longer what was right and what was wrong.

Not so long ago Bennett had said he'd get rid of unemployment or perish in the attempt. As soon as he became Prime Minister he said unemployment was not a problem. He said all the country needed was a sound dollar. He said no one needed relief. Poverty, he said, was the greatest asset a young person could have in life.

But through the years of the depression we'd seen many hard-working, honest men, who surely deserved to prosper, lose their jobs. They and their families lived in poverty, while dishonest boot-leggers had made fortunes selling booze to Americans – respectable Americans, too – who were openly breaking the law of their country.

Everything was changing.

In 1935, with an election coming up, Bennett had changed his tune and said the country needed reform and relief programs to get people on their feet again. He lost the election anyway, and we got our old prime minister, Mackenzie King, back, and he said we couldn't afford the relief programs so they were gradually dropped.

Back during the Great War they'd said this was the war that would end all wars. Then they decided the world needed a League of Nations to keep the peace. Now they were saying the League of Nations was no use at all and there was war in Abyssinia and in Spain.

Everything was changing. Our prime minister had lied to us, and our King had betrayed us. Who could you trust?

I'd decided to put my trust in Gordon and in his simple pioneer values. In the spring he and I married and moved east and began our new life together.

I've never regretted the choice I made and my life with Gordon. But still I have only to think of the day of the abdication, and a wave of sorrow comes over me as I remember how Ruby and I sat until late that night in the kitchen and drank tea and cried.

I cried then, not just for a weak-willed king, but for lost certain-ties. I cried for my father's death, and all the deaths and suffering of the war in which he died and the wars that would come. I cried because I was leaving my family, my friends, my beautiful mountains and I knew that even if I came back, they would never be the same. I cried because I was leaving my working girl's independence to start a new life with a man who set no store by kings, a man who believed in duty, yes, but duty to God, to family, to the work one had chosen or the land one tilled. A man who had no truck with an Empire across the sea, or with fine houses and fancy hats, titles, and proper accents and grand pianos. I cried because the King was leaving his Empire, and now, for better or worse, I was leaving mine.

Chapter 17

The Hero on the Wall

I didn't go back to Creston for many years. There was never the opportunity or the money for the trip. In 1944 Mum came to visit me back east, bringing Rodney, the youngest, with her. They stayed all winter. I was beginning to wonder if this was going to turn into a visit like ours to Creston that had started in 1912 and went on for years. But in the spring, the thought of apple blossoms and green mountains drew Mum and Rodney back to the Kootenays. A part of me would have liked to go with them, but my life was in Ontario now with my husband and children.

It wasn't until the summer of 1952 that I finally had a whole month free of responsibilities and money enough on hand to undertake a visit to my old home town.

You don't realize that your home country has its own unique scent until you come back to it after a long absence, and there it is, enveloping you in its old familiar breath. Creston's breath was the smell of pure mountain air and woods and cultivated fields, cold rivers and fresh lumber and ripening fruit, and it hummed faintly with the drone of bees at work in the orchards. It flooded me with the physical sense of home the moment I stepped off the train. In my years away I had come to love the Ontario countryside, its small towns of red brick houses with peaked roofs, its untidily fenced fields of green pasture and grain, the weathered cedar barns, the sombre swamplands and the bright autumn woods. They were beautiful. But this was home. I stood on the station platform and breathed it in. I felt like a girl again.

And then there they were, hurrying along the platform to meet me, Mum in a pale grey dress with matching jacket and a stylish hat in darker grey straw with a purple band, Gran in magenta, dazzling with several glittering brooches and a broad-brimmed hat in electric blue. But she was leaning on a cane. It came to me in a sad rush that she and Mum were old, and I was no longer a girl either. But that didn't matter now; I was home.

We went straight to Mum's new place and got the tea going and set to talking. We talked through dinner and supper and all through the evening. I'd been too long away from talking. Gordon's family, taciturn Scotch Presbyterians, would sit together through a Saturday evening in almost total silence and consider at the end that they'd had a very good visit. Here we were talkers: we talked of the old times and new changes in Creston. I told them all about my Ontario family, even though they knew all the news from my letters, and they told me all the news of my Creston family, even though they'd already told me in the stream of letters that had flowed between us over the years.

My brother David and the three younger children, most of the Talbots and my old school friends had all gone to Vancouver to find work. It was what seemed to happen in small towns.

Mum, who had always liked change, had taken to spending the winter in Vancouver and returning to Creston for the summer. Gran had had to give up her beloved Rosebank. She couldn't manage the wood stove and the garden and the walk up to town any longer. She'd taken up residence in Mrs. Bolton's boarding house for elderly ladies, which she said was quite satisfactory. She was doing very well there, though of course she missed her roses.

And she missed Uncle Bob. He too had become frail with age and it was thought best that he should live in a home for the handicapped. As none was available in Creston, he'd been taken off to Vancouver, acquiescent, as always, to the arrangements made by others for his welfare. "But I shall never forget the sadness in his look as he called out his long 'Goooood byeeeee! God bleeeeesss!' when we saw him onto the train." Gran shook her head and took another sip of tea. "Poor Bob. He died among strangers in Vancouver a few months later."

Gramps Little too was dead, and Colonel Mallandaine, and Alphabetical. Gran was one of the few pioneers left.

We talked all that month long, Mum and Gran and I. We talked of family and gardening and orchards and family and cookery and fashions and family and books and music, and family, family, family, past and present.

Yet in all those family stories, there was one conspicuous silence. I heard again the stories of Grandfather Young and his terrible temper, of eccentric Uncle Walter and his barefoot daughters named after the Greek muses, the sad story of Uncle Bob's brother, blind from birth, like Bob, but sent to languish in an institution, while Bob was educated at the Brantford School for the Blind. I heard about Uncle Roland who had invented new kinds of bombs in the Great War. There were even one or two stories about my father's family: the wicked Uncle Will, and the opera singer, and the connection with the famous poet, Hedd Wynn. But there were never any stories of my father himself. I couldn't remember Mum talking to us about him, ever. There must have been letters from him, but she didn't share them with the family. I remembered helping Mum pack up parcels for the Creston soldiers during the war, but I didn't remember our packing any parcels for my father.

The only time I'd heard from him myself was during the war, at Christmas 1917. I got a Christmas card from him then, a regimental card with a picture of the Welch Fusiliers in furious combat. "Merry Christmas" was the printed message. "*Nadolig llawen.*" Underneath he'd written, "Daddy," nothing else.

I never heard from him again. I knew almost nothing about him.

I was five when I saw him for the last time, and had only the vaguest remembrance of him; the scenes I recalled seemed more like memories of memories. I remembered a man in a scratchy black jacket holding me on his knee and singing. I think that was my father. But I'm not sure. Mostly it's the black jacket I remember and the smell of tobacco.

A little clearer is a memory of entering a dark office. My father and I are hand-in-hand, laughing with the pleasure of anticipating a joke we are about to play. A man stands at a high counter, dipping a straight pen into a bottle of ink, and asks, "Name of child?"

"Eifion," my father says and spells it for the clerk, while smiling down at me, his fellow conspirator. We are registering the birth of my brother David as Eifion Evans, so that he will have a real Welsh name, like mine.

My mother was not amused when she heard what we had done. She had decided on the name David, which was quite Welsh enough. She, for one, would call the boy David whatever name was on his birth certificate.

Any other memories of my father faded as completely as our laughter that day of our Welsh joke.

I had two photographs of my father, both given to us by his family during our brief, unhappy visit to them after the war. One is of a woman in black, seated, holding, stiffly, an infant in her arms. The woman is my grandmother, Mary Evans. We aren't sure that the infant actually is my father, Thomas Richard, her first child, but most probably it is. Mary looks thin, tired, worn out. Her large dark eyes appear to be on the verge of tears. If that is indeed my father in her arms, then she, poor woman, is only at the beginning of her weary years of travail. She was to bear nine living children and die at the age of thirty-one, giving birth to the still-born tenth child.

The other photograph was taken on the day of her funeral. It shows grandfather Hugh Evans surrounded by his nine surviving children, all of them dressed in their best funeral black. The death, the funeral service and its poetic reminders of the transience of life must have urged upon my grandfather the desirability of recording the image of the family that remained. Besides, when else would all the children be so clean, dressed up and presentable?

My father, the eldest, stands in the back row. Like the other children he looks solemn and frightened either by the photography studio or by the death that has torn apart their world. At the same time, he appears eager. He leans forward, staring directly at the camera. He seems to be looking towards the unknown future, anxious to get started in a world of his own making. While the other boys wear flat Eton collars, he is dressed in a man's suit and collar. A watch chain stretches importantly across his narrow waistcoat. He is already a working man.

After that photo was taken, the family dispersed. The younger children were sent to different relatives in Wales, America, and Australia. My father went back to London, where he had found employment as a junior clerk in the customs office.

There he worked and studied with energy and ambition. After his work days at the customs office, he took evening classes and wrote poetry.

As his circumstances improved, he moved into the respectable boarding house in Hammersmith run by Mrs. Mildred Young. And there he fell in love with her second-youngest daughter, the beautiful Sarah, my mother. In March, 1907 they married. She was nineteen; he was twenty-five. If there was a wedding photo taken, I've never seen it.

As a child growing up in Creston I had learned not to talk about my father. In later years his role in the family history was eclipsed by Mum's flamboyant second husband.

Yet he was not entirely forgotten. In all the many houses we lived in, a corner of the living room was always organized as a sort of T.R. Evans memorial. There were his two Welsh bardic chairs of oak: one solid and simple and one ornate with rampant lions and twining grape leaves, both uncomfortable and much too historic to be sat on. Behind these throne-like chairs hung the wall display, consisting of his ceremonial sword, a framed photo of him in uniform, and, also framed, the letter of condolence upon his death, signed by

George V himself. These objects made a sort of family shrine, like the sacred heart or the statue of the Virgin in a Catholic household. "He was a Welsh poet." "He died for King and Country." "He made the Supreme Sacrifice." This was what was said about my father whenever a visitor remarked on the display.

Familiar objects are seldom really seen. I never really looked at the face in the sepia photograph. I dusted those chairs for many years and never gave them a thought. They were just there, part of the landscape of home.

When I married, Mum gave me the ornate chair and the framed photograph with the King's letter and I dutifully set up the T.R. Evans corner in my living room down east.

Now, on this family visit, I was an adult with children of my own, and I wanted to learn more about my forgotten father. I determined to pry into the silence that surrounded him. Even if what I learned proved to be one of those shameful secrets that Creston people were so good at keeping quiet about, I wanted to know what it was.

There came at last an evening when Mum and I were alone. We sat on her front verandah watching the purpling of the mountains in the distance. I began my questioning. "What was he like, my father?"

"A brave man. A hero." She trotted out the old, familiar litany. "He died for King and Country."

"What about before the Great War, before he became a hero?"

"He was a poet. He won bardic chairs."

Because the chairs were so large and impressive, we'd always assumed he'd won them at the great National Eisteddfod. I'd managed some time before to find a list of the winners of the chair since the first national Eisteddfod was held in 1880, but my father's name was not on it.

I learned then that there are dozens of 'chair' eisteddfods in towns and cities of Wales every year. These are contests in which prize money and a chair are awarded for the best poem in the classical Welsh form, the *awdl*. The chair symbolizes the welcome given to ancient bards in the great halls of the Welsh kings, and is a sign of the esteem that Welsh society accords its poets.

Mum had no copy of the chair-winning poems, nor did she know where and when the chairs had been won, only that it was after we'd left. The chairs had been stored at Aunt Boo's house until we collected them after the war. Aunt Boo had removed the brass plates that had been on them, giving the date and place of the Eisteddfod because she thought "they made the chairs look as if they'd been stolen from a public hall". Now, it seemed, we'd never know where and when they'd been won, nor the works that won them.

The only evidence of my father's literary career Mum had was a copy of an English magazine called *The Bookman* with a notice of a Welsh play he'd written, and underneath a picture of him still looking young and eager and ambitious. The date on the magazine was 1913. She'd shown it to me before.

"So did you go to the play?"

"Of course not. We were in Canada then."

"Well, did you read it?"

"No. It was in Welsh."

"What was it about?"

"I don't know. But it says in the article it was well received."

And that was all I could find out about my father as a Welsh writer.

The writings having led to a dead end, I asked my mother again, "What kind of a person was my father? What was he really like?"

"I told you. He was brave. He won the DSO." A dedicated member of the Canadian Legion, my mother never, her whole life long, lost her belief in the glory of his hero's death, no matter what the historians said, or what some cowards or shirkers had written in their memoirs. Her faith in the rightness of the British cause and the infamy of the Hun never faltered

I interrupted her patriotic paean. "I mean, what was he like as a person?"

"Oh." She paused to think, and perhaps to censor her memories. "He was a great talker. Talk. Talk. Talk. I'd have his tea ready at six, and he wouldn't get home 'til the last train got in after ten o'clock. 'Where have you been all this time?' I'd ask him.

" 'Talking with some chaps,' he'd say. And he'd start in telling me all the things they'd talked about – politics and the theatre and poetry, 'til my head would be spinning, and I'd be dropping with tiredness."

"Were you happy together?"

"Of course we were. We were married."

"Yes. But." My mother's second marriage, the one all too clear in my memory, was a marriage of love, but also one of strife and monumental rages that eventually turned the love into a passionate hate.

Were there similar elements in the first, forgotten marriage, I wondered.

My mother had come to Canada to visit her mother, bringing my brother and me with her. In later years, during her second marriage, a visit to her mother was always the reason she gave for her temporary separations from her husband.

Of course, there was good reason for Mum to make a trip to Creston. She had always been close to her mother, and must have missed her in the years after Gran left England. She would want her mother to see David and me before we grew up. And from London to British Columbia was half way around the world, not a journey to be undertaken for a two- or three-week visit. But we stayed in Creston until 1920, 'til after my father was dead.

True, the war intervened and travelling was more difficult and dangerous. But people did make the journey. Gran herself went back to England for a visit in 1916.

Why, I wondered, did my mother not travel back with her? I couldn't believe she would be afraid for her own safety. Perhaps it was us, her children, she was concerned for. Perhaps my father had urged her to remain where we were safe. Or had my father talked himself out of her affection? Did she spin out her sojourn in Canada deliberately? Did he encourage her to do so?

"Can't you tell me anything more about him," I pleaded.

Mum sighed. "It was so long ago. I was very young.

"He was an ambitious man and he worked hard for us. At the office all day. Out most evenings at his university classes, or with his literary and theatre friends. I hardly saw him most days.

"He was never mean about money; I'll say that for him. I remember once when you were little, only about three, I took you to the shop for new shoes, and the silly salesman showed us a pair of beautiful patent leather boots, much too expensive for us.

"As soon as you saw them you were bound and determined you'd have them. Kicked and screamed when we tried to fit some other shoes on your feet. I had to take you home in disgrace with no new shoes at all.

"When your father heard about it, he gave me his dinner money for the week. "Buy her the pretty shoes," he told me.

"You loved those shoes. And your father went without dinners for a week so that you could have them.

"Then, when I wanted to go to Canada to see Gran, he came up with the money for our passage. I don't know what he did without to pay. We came to Canada. Then the war came. We wouldn't have seen him much even if we'd been in England. He was at camp, or out on the front. He sent us money every month." She paused. "Most months," she corrected herself.

That was all I could learn about my father from Mum.

So I tried Gran. I chose an afternoon when Mum was busy at the Canadian Legion and Gran and I were having a cup of tea in her room at Mrs. Bolton's. She sat in the rocker by the window. She liked life at Mrs. Bolton's. She enjoyed having a warm room, a comfortable rocker with a view over the garden, and endless cups of tea. I sat with my feet up on the bed. "Tell me about my father," I asked, once we were comfortable.

"What would you like to know?" she asked in turn, giving me some hope.

"Well, for one thing, was he intending to follow us to Creston? Would he have come if war hadn't broken out?"

"No." Gran was certain. "Whatever gave you the idea he would do that? He never had any intention of coming to Canada. He was very much involved with the Welsh community in London, you see. He had ambitions as far as they were concerned, writing for their magazines and such. Perhaps he had political aspirations even."

I'd got the idea from the way we used to talk about his coming that first winter. He was supposed to come in the spring. And then in the fall. And then we didn't talk about it. He was going to come and then he wasn't. No one ever explained why. Now, according to Gran, he had never intended to come at all.

"I know he was a poet and a soldier, but what else do you know about him?" I pressed Gran for more information. "What do you remember about him?"

"He was not a handsome man," Gran began, "but he had a beautiful voice and manner, so that when he spoke, one was quite charmed by him. He turned my quiet boarding house upside down with his play readings and poetry readings and musical evenings. He had us all taking parts, the girls and I and the other gentlemen. I was Lady Macbeth one evening. That was my best role, I believe. Another time your mother was a wonderful Puck in Midsummer Night's Dream. And then there were poetry evenings. Tennyson and Swinburne, we had. Sometimes Tom read his own poems. The girls and I were even learning a little Welsh. Oh, we had quite the literary salon!" Gran smiled at the memories but had no more to say about them. "It was so long ago," she excused herself. "I've forgotten most of that time. It didn't last very long. Your mother and Tom married and set up their own household."

"And then you left for Canada?"

"Yes."

"Why did you come, Gran, you and Aunt Charlotte?"

"I thought it best," Gran said, and offered no other reason. Well, she was right. If she hadn't come, then neither would Aunt Charlotte and Mum and David and I. She had led us all to Creston. It was for the best.

Some years later, in the sixties, I was able to fulfil a dream I'd been cherishing and saving for since my visit to Creston. I took a trip to England and Wales. I visited my Aunt Ruth in her little cottage in the Midlands and listened to her memories of her days as an *au pair* in our young family. She spoke of my father as if he had been some kind of musical saint. She sang me songs he'd sung, but couldn't tell me much about him as a person. "A lovely man," she called him, and that was all.

I visited the village of Llanaelhaearn where various members of the large Evans family were still living in the dark crowded cottage on the main street. They proudly showed me his name on the war memorial, but few of them could remember him. They had no photos. They knew nothing about the bardic chairs.

Finally I visited Uncle Took who still lived in his cottage in Havering near our old Hero's Home. Took was able to tell me more about my father, but only in the context of the war.

"Tommy and I were in it right from the start. Different outfits, though. Tommy wanted to be with the Welch Fusiliers. I was with the Essex regiment, start to finish.

"Say what you like about the Great War, the British infantry put up a good fight, we did. Oh yes, there were blunders – bound to be when you've got a fighting force of that magnitude to deal with – but on the whole I'd say we British were as fine a body of fighting men as the world has ever seen.

"Back then we believed in values like courage, patriotism, pride, keeping a stiff upper lip, the sort of thing everyone makes jokes about now. But we believed in those principles and we fought by them. Those were the values that kept us going. The Hun had to be crushed, and by Jove we did it. We all pitched in. No matter how filthy the conditions were, or how dangerous or distasteful the job was, we got it done. I've never seen in peacetime anything like the spirit of cameraderie, the loyalty, the adventure of that Great War.

"Oh yes, the casualties were terrible, quite terrible. That was the price we had to pay. We were all prepared to pay it.

"Tommy, for instance, could easily have wangled a safe staff posting. Or even something in Whitehall. No one would have blamed a married man with two young children for taking such a job, especially once he'd already done his stint at the Front. But Tommy wouldn't take the safe posting, not he. He stayed on the Line, in active service.

"He was a good soldier.

"I was the last of the family to see poor Tommy alive. It was in September, 1918. We were preparing for the show on the St. Quentin canal. All kinds of units were in on that; the training for it went on for weeks. My battalion was just coming in for training and Tommy's going out. The adjutant came to tell me there was some sort of snafu about our billets; another regiment was already occupying them.

"I set out for the commanding officer's billet, ready to chew his head off for the mix-up. From outside the farmhouse, I heard a familiar voice, talking, talking in that Welsh sing-song. 'Tommy Evans!' I shouted as I burst into the kitchen, 'What the hell are you doing here?'

"Tommy leapt up from the table and bounded over to slap me on the back. 'Took, of all people! You old son! This calls for celebration.' He called to a woman standing by the stove, *'Vin rouge, s'il vous plait.'*

"I wanted to sit down and drink and enjoy the visit, but I had the billets problem on my mind.

"'Muck in with us. Plenty of room. See to it, will you, Mr. Jones?' Tom called to a young lieutenant who saluted smartly and ran off at the double.

"'Now sit down, Took, old chap. Meet your hostess. Madame Mercier.' Madame had just brought in a bottle of wine and glasses. She set them down on the table before us and smiled and bobbed.

"*'Merci beaucoup. Tres bon. Tres bon.'* Tom gave her a warm smile. *'Souper. Soon.'*

"The woman went back to the stove.

"'Now, what news, Took?' We settled in to talk and wine. Presently madame served us an omelette with fried potatoes and more wine. Tom and I caught up on family news and discussed the progress of the war. Tom was sure it would end by Christmas. We drank to victory and to our families and to our regiments and to madame, who sat on Tom's knee to receive the toast. It was a fine evening we had.

"Tom's regiment fell in about one in the morning to march back up towards their assembly point. I was vaguely aware of him gathering up his things in the room we shared, of orders being shouted in the courtyard, of the tramp of hob-nailed boots on cobblestones, snatches of song. I drifted back into sleep.

"He was killed shortly after the great battle for the St. Quentin canal. At least he had the joy of that success. His outfit covered themselves with glory. He'd have been so pleased.

"He copped it in some counter-attack. I didn't hear about it 'til the war was over. Couldn't believe it. Tommy Evans dead. And the war over.

Some time after the war, Uncle Took went back to France to tour the old battlefields, and to visit my father's grave. He had a picture of the grave to give me, and I added it my pitifully small collection of memorabilia: the photos and the Christmas card.

Took lived to be 102, a firm believer in the British Empire to the end. Until well on into his nineties he never missed an opportunity to don his uniform and medals for a church parade or Armistice Day ceremonies. He would snap to attention for "God Save the Queen" and stand so ramrod straight, he seemed to be in peril of toppling over backwards.

Was my father just as avid a supporter of the empire? Was he too imbued with the heady, idealistic patriotism of the times, offering, like

Rupert Brooke, thanks to God "who has matched us to His hour?" Was he driven by a sense of duty? Or did he go for the adventure of it? What did he feel as, after a leave, he crossed from England to France for another tour of duty in the trenches where the danger and confusion, the mud and cold and misery, the horrible, futile suffering have been so graphically described by men who experienced it?

I returned from Britain with pictures of a war memorial and of a grave and still not knowing much more than before about my father.

Then towards Christmas in 1974 a parcel arrived for me from Auntie Oliver. Auntie Oliver was the wife of my father's brother, Wyatt. Mum, I knew, had disliked Oliver. An "outrageous woman," she called her. Oliver had been a militant suffragette. She dressed like a man, called herself Oliver and finally went off with Wyatt to Australia, and a good thing that was too, in Mum's opinion. But every year at Christmas there came a letter and a card from the outrageous Oliver, giving news of all the Evanses in Australia.

Oliver, an old woman by now, was dying, her letter said. "It's the big C, and the doctor gives me six months. Never mind. I've had a good innings. One thing before I go though, Olwen. I want you to know that your father was the one and only love of my life. After he was killed, I married Wyatt, but it was always Tom I loved.

"I'm sending you the letters he wrote to me from the war and a few of his unpublished lyrics that I managed to get hold of. I've kept them all my life. Now I'd like you to have them."

Here then, after all these years, was the answer to the questions Mum would never answer. My father had not followed us to Canada because he had been in love with another woman! The outrageous Aunt Oliver! No wonder my mother had always disliked her.

I tore open the bundle of letters. By the time I'd read only one or two of them, I was beginning to doubt the great love affair Oliver had written of. These were not love letters. They were letters full of light, friendly chatter. "Hope this finds you as it leaves me, in the pink."

"I'm sure you'll enjoy reading Wells' latest novel." "Thank you for the very nice gloves." These were pleasant letters that could have been written to anyone: an old aunt, a hostess, a friend. There appeared to be no sense of deep attachment to "My Dear Oliver", though I gathered that Oliver might well have been in love with my father. I remembered Gran's words. "We all loved your father. He carried us along with his enthusiasms." But, on this evidence I had to suspect that my father's affection for Oliver was not as strong as hers for him.

The other curious thing about the letters was that they could have been written almost any time; the war was mentioned the way an office job might be referred to. It was just an occupation, sometimes annoying. "The weather is very wet." "My office hut has burnt to the ground." "I am suffering through a wretched cold." There was nothing about suffering through a wretched war, nothing about death or fear of death, nothing about grief or horror or hopelessness, nothing even of the misery of cold, muddy trenches. Perhaps this was the correct way for officers to write about the war. My father, Took had said, had been a good soldier.

I turned to the poems. They were all in Welsh, of course, written in a tiny, neat script on pages now yellow with age. My father had been a clerk before the advent of typewriters, when a fine hand was a requisite for an office job. It touched me though that he hadn't been able to resist adding in last-minute alterations with a blunt lead pencil even though it spoiled the fine copy.

Were these war poems? love poems? With a Welsh dictionary to hand, I tried to read them. Welsh poetry is difficult. As far as I could make out they seemed to be nature pieces about the beauties of the sea, of a mountain stream, of a green valley. One word I did recognize and found recurring several times through the pages was *hiraeth*, an evocative Welsh word which means something like 'longing for something, but at the same time knowing you could never have it'.

I still wonder what it was he longed for, this unknown father of mine, before he was killed, and became a name on a grave in France, a few vague memories in my heart, a bundle of poems, a packet of cherished letters, and a stranger to me. A hero on the wall.

Afterword

Olwen, when she was a young child, imagined England as the most wonderful place on earth. She had come to this belief by listening to her Mum and her Gran reminisce about their native country where, to hear them talk, you'd think everything was just about perfect. When the family moved back to England she discovered that it wasn't so, that really she much preferred British Columbia.

In my turn, I, Olwen's daughter, grew up in Ontario with the conviction that the Kootenay mountains of British Columbia were the Mecca of the west, the Garden of Eden on earth, and Creston was their centre. Certainly it was beyond dispute that the hills of British Columbia were higher than any in Ontario, and the valleys deeper, but it appeared also that gardens were greener there and fruit sweeter, the snow crisper, the sun warmer, the sky bluer. People were friendlier and more colourful. Happy days lasted longer and sorrows were less distressing. All this I gathered from my mother's stories.

I was an adult before I finally got to see Creston with my own eyes. The Creston I saw was and was not the same place as Olwen grew up in. There were the mountains to the east and to the west and the broad flat plain of the Kootenay River between them. The old station was gone and the CPR trains no longer stopped in the centre of town, though the grain elevators of the thirties and forties still stood waiting for them. There were more roads and wider, and a traffic light too, and motels instead of hotels. The buildings of downtown Canyon Street had changed owners and purposes and show windows but still stood, most of them. Orchards were flourishing on the benchlands and now vineyards as well. Gran's Rosebank still stood on Fourth Street, but her roses were gone.

Gran was gone too. She died in 1959 just before her hundredth birthday. The rest of the family – Sarah, Olwen, David, the Hooper kids, the Talbots – were scattered in faraway places.

The Creston I saw was a beautiful mountain town, but it surprised me that I could see no trace of a heavenly aura surrounding it. That's an aura, I've since learned, that lies in the eye of the beholder, and attaches itself only to the landscape of one's childhood. It comes from the conviction that this place is exactly the way a place is supposed to be; it's mother earth's own lap. Whether that landscape is mountain or seaside, busy city street, northern woods, prairie or farmland it imprints itself on one's emergent soul and sets a standard that stays with one for life of what a home place should look like and what makes it beautiful.

To discover then that Creston was after all not quite the heaven that Olwen's stories made of it was not a disillusioning insight for me. It was, rather, a reassuring proof that she had spent a happy childhood and youth there.

At the age of ninety Olwen fell victim to the old lady's nemesis: she fell and broke her hip. She spent some time then in a rehab centre building up her strength to walk again, but even after a good recuperation, it was clear that she would need household help and the services of caregivers if she was going to remain in her own home in Peterborough, which she dearly wanted to do. My sister and I agreed that we would each spend a month with her at her home to help her adjust to her new condition and household arrangements.

I approached my month with some trepidation. I am not the Florence Nightingale type. Administering a whole month of tender loving care might do me in, I feared, and perhaps Mum as well. What could I do to make a month of talking and tea drinking and slow, slow walks around the block more appealing for both of us? That's when the idea about her stories of her life in Creston came to me. She'd often told us those stories, and from time to time we'd urged her to write them down, but Olwen was a talker, not a writer. During our month together, I suggested now, she should tell me her stories, and I would write them down.

It turned out to be a wonderful month for both of us. She told her stories. I listened and took notes and prodded her memory with questions and read back my notes to her. This book is the result of that happy month of storytelling and writing.

Like Gran, Mum died just short of her one-hundredth birthday. I was with her the day she died. She was beyond speech by then, but at one point she looked out the window to a sunlit Ontario May morning and she smiled as though she was seeing out there something amazingly, joyfully beautiful. At the time I thought it was the sunshine and the play of light on the lace curtains that pleased her. But later I got to wondering if it could have been the pearly gates of a Presbyterian heaven she saw out there waiting for her. Or could it have been a last fond vision of the Creston valley of her childhood, and Rosebank and Mum and Gran?